Greg Bennett

TRINITY'S WAKE

A Robert Tulliver Story

ISBN-13: 9781073062270

The front cover of this book features a photograph of a nuclear explosion one millisecond after detonation.

Taken from the Tumbler Snapper series of tests at the Nevada Proving Grounds in 1952, using a high-speed Rapid Action Electronic 'Rapatronic' camera, it shows a ball of fire 65 feet wide. The maximum yield in this series was 31 kilotons of TNT.

The Hiroshima bomb measured at 15 kilotons.

Russia's 'Tsar Bomba' test in 1961 hit 50,000 kilotons.

The yield of the W76 warhead, as used in Trident missiles, is 100 kilotons.

The yield of the upcoming "combat-friendly" or "usable" W76s will be 6 kilotons.

For all hibakusha – past, present & future

&

For my Dad

- PROLOGUE -

The End of Killing

Hard left off the Berliner Straße onto Bundesallee; revving high to frighten a scrawny Dobermann Pinscher off the road, I jammed down hard on the pedal. The Zündapp KS750 – its sidecar currently a mobile coffin for an unfortunate Wehrmacht soldier – bolted hungrily ahead beneath me, its air-cooled, twin cylinders pumping me up to sixty.

There was a let-up in the bombardment. For a moment, it was all about the growl of the motorbike. I tried not to think about my lolling-headed companion – I'd needed the bike and the negotiation hadn't gone well. I prayed he would be my penultimate kill. Just one more, then I could try to remember how living was supposed to work. It was the first of May 1945; news had reached me that morning that Adolf Hitler was dead.

I didn't believe it for a moment.

There was a smattering of Wehrmacht ahead; the howitzer of a Panzer IV pivoting my way. I veered off down Güntzelstraße – eyes on the road, not wanting to allow the devastation into my mind. I was done with devastation.

The rain of explosives intensified. I listened to the children, curled up in corners and under beds, hands clamped over their ears; the dregs of their innocence dissipating. Terrified of an enemy painted to be a lower form of human. This was leadership now: the message that these *other* human beings were out to get you.

I heard them behind the walls, whispering like ghosts, praying, grasping for the embrace of a father now lost; the pipe tobacco of a grandfather; the cooking smells of a grandmother; the wisplike smoke of a mother's birthday cake candles just blown-out. One child somewhere back there was thinking of Christmas – a memory so distant it seemed he must have dreamed it, of hurrying downstairs to find... It distressed me, the feeling of *loss* I snatched from that boy –

of clawing for a time when a magical being visited his home and just *gave.* A time of gifts, before the taking began.

I put my foot down: a human bullet cutting into the city, seeking its target – just one more soldier, his story lost in the dust, smoke and flame. Any Allied troops were days away: it had been agreed Stalin would take Berlin. The Soviets were sweeping in around the city – closing a curtain behind me.

Its high, classical buildings were rubble. I felt a pang – the memory of dinner with my friend Alexander Beer at a restaurant nearby, after completion of his synagogue here. Alex was an architect, a German and a Jew and a distinguished example of all three. When they torched his synagogue during the pogrom in 1938, he'd been heartbroken. The 'Kristallnacht', they'd called that night, because of all the shattered glass.

I'd known Berlin as an elegant city, steeped in culture and heritage, populated by sophisticated, liberal-minded people. How had I failed to recognise the festering seed? Perhaps I suffered from the same delusional complacency that had numbed the good-hearted amongst the Germans.

Somehow, Hitler had taken a tiny minority of the population who had hitherto gone about their lives in freedom and prosperity – and siphoned vitriol onto them. He'd played his people like a maestro, digging into their psyche to whip up a maelstrom of jealousy and resentment, taken their love of their nation and turned it into a burning, acidic superiority which devalued everything that was other.

Alexander had died at Theresienstadt, the concentration camp in Czechoslovakia – a boarding point for Auschwitz. There was a deportation from there of sixteen hundred Polish children, who were gassed in groups. I hoped to God he did not go to his grave having witnessed anything like that.

We hit a pothole and my dead friend almost bounced out of his sidecar. *Damn you, why did you have to walk in at that moment?*

Things had been going fine: from parachuting in during the RAF Mosquito bombings, through the forests of the Döberitzer Heide to swim the Havel, I'd kept my head down. All my encounters had been one-to-one and a single mind was always an easy trick.

There was no telling how many of Hitler's Gifted were at large in the city, however – and they would not be so easily fooled. I'd needed that uniform. It had never been my intention to kill: a distraction put me on the back foot; I'd lost control of the situation, been forced to lash out. In his last moment, I'd seen his thoughts – seen his loved ones…

A faded poster sharpened my resolve: an emaciated man, hand contorted into a paralysed claw, legs twisted uselessly beneath him; an orderly behind him; it declared that in his lifetime, the 'person' would cost 'the People's community' sixty thousand marks. Reminding all citizens that "this is your money too", it urged them to read 'A New People', the monthly magazine of the Nazis' 'Office for Enlightenment on Population Policy and Racial Welfare'.

'Enlightenment.' Ugly use of a beautiful word.

I was soon upon Motzstraße. I'd spent time in this neighbourhood in the company of literary giants: Christopher Isherwood and Jean Ross had lodged just around the corner, where he had been inspired to recreate her as his heroine Sally Bowles; W. H. Auden and Paul Bowles had walked here, revelling in heady Bohemian open-mindedness…

As if from nowhere, the Nazis had oozed out of the woodwork to pulverise the homosexual community: thousands died in the camps, a threat to the purity of the 'master race'. Homosexuality would outwit Nazism. Motzstraße would applaud difference again, but the *bloody fools*: they'd smashed into Europe in a wave of seething disgust for everything that affronted them, blind to the fact that alternative faiths and questioned sexuality are part of us – you can't erase the humanity out of humanity.

The Nazis came to power in 1933 with only two million members – out of a population of nearly eighty million. Even at their peak in 1945, only ten percent of the populace were members. Where had the good, ordinary Germans *been*?

All along my route, I'd glimpsed 'traitors' hanging from the trees and lampposts – those who had tried to avoid Goebbels' final call to arms, or who'd looted to feed their starving families. They hung like macabre decorations, over the steadily streaming scramble westward.

Having lost friends, I felt vindicated by the fear of the refugees. But their haunted eyes disturbed me: now their invincible hero was gone, everything they'd allowed themselves to believe was unravelling. The glorious future they'd envisaged was being rewritten to be replaced by a history in which they were monsters. They shared a stare and it was directed within, to truths crumbling before a reviving memory of all the times they'd looked the other way.

In some of those faces, I saw a conscience flickering back to life. Those were the worst.

They'd long convinced themselves that the consequence of their inaction, the boogeyman, was far away. Russia had borne the greatest cost of the war, having lost thirteen percent of their population – nearly ten times British and American losses in Europe. Now Soviet wrath was being visited upon the city with a ferocity ten thousand times anything the Berliners had experienced during the blitz.

Across the city, in a final loving act, parents were overseeing their children's deaths, husbands their wives'. The taking of cyanide was openly encouraged by the authorities, capsules distributed by the Hitler Youth. Fathers drowned their flailing offspring in their bathtubs. Out in Babelsberg, the head of the German Red Cross, an enthusiastic experimenter on concentration camp inmates, was settling to dine with his family – the main course was a hand grenade.

Shooting across Martin-Luther-Straße, I remembered fondly crossing it in the company of Isherwood – his expression as I explained that I'd met Martin Luther once when he was alive. And numerous times since…

The sewage system was failing and all sorts of substances that did not burn well were spewing an unholy, acrid stench into the air. Every street was choked with debris, reduced to narrow alleys between collapsed walls and burnt-out vehicles. I slowed to navigate barb wire barricades, craters full of toxic water, fresh anti-tank trenches. Black smoke poured from unchallenged blazes. Embers and ash clawed the back of my throat – and coated the city in a grey layer.

A woman ran past pushing a pram, a blanket over her head, no features discernible behind her gas mask. It felt like Purgatory – a world suspended half way between the living and the dead.

I was well aware that the Russians were converging upon my position.

Their field artillery had been concentrating upon the bridges of the Spree and railway stations to the north. Tempelhof Airport had fallen. Their troops had crossed the Moltke Bridge and were taking the Reichstag; they were pushing through Mitte from Alexanderplatz. To my right, they were streets away, pouring in from Kreuzberg. Up ahead, at Potsdamer Platz, they were basically in my way.

Accelerating, I emerged onto the Landwehrkanal. Across the water, the Bendlerblock – HQ of the German Ministry of Defence and the Wehrmacht – seemed undamaged. They'd dumped poor, tragic Rosa Luxemburg in the canal here back in 1919 – if she'd lived, she would have been sixty-four now. History might have been very different.

The roads were stuffed with soldiers, but the dregs rather than a proud breed of Aryan superman: Hitler Youth, the girls of the Bund Deutscher Mädel, the Nazi 'Dad's Army' the *Volkstrum*, armed with whatever was to hand. This 'people's storm' was a sorry sight.

Many of those bearing arms towards the Russian onslaught were barely teenagers. I didn't feel so sorry for the old men. Through gritted teeth, I imagined them idly preaching armchair nationalism, mouthpieces for the malignant wisdom of their daily newspapers – encouraging the young to lay down their lives for the Fatherland, safe in the knowledge that any blood would be spilt far from their own doosteps.

Stopping to get my bearings, I spied the undulating façade of the modernist Shell-Haus – subsidiary of Shell last I was here, now the German naval high command. Beyond, towards Potsdamer Platz, a loud explosion was followed by a flurry of figures in retreat before a wall of Soviet soldiers.

Russians – and I was in a Wehrmacht uniform.

I spun the motorbike off north. The Bendlerblock had been much expanded. A high-ranking group had come together here a year earlier to conspire to lose the war: their leader, Klaus von Stauffenberg, Bavarian count and army chief of staff, had set out to assassinate Hitler at his Eastern Front HQ, 'Wolf's Lair'. Behind him had been a network of those waiting to wrest back control of their country.

Von Stauffenberg left his conference to take a call, leaving a bomb in his briefcase. The explosion killed four, slightly injuring the Führer – but von Stauffenberg believed he had been successful and initiated the coup. Only upon arrival in Berlin did he realise his error – by which time, the conspirators were exposed. He had been executed in a courtyard somewhere to my left. By the time the Gestapo had finished reacting to the plot, nearly five thousand were dead – including Field Marshall Rommel.

This was one of many attempts by Germans to reclaim their country: during the Third Reich, over seventy thousand were killed for various – tragically isolated – acts of resistance. I intended to finish their job for them.

Sharp right, with the roar of battle pounding in my head – the psychic residue of souls being violently ripped form this Earth tearing into me. The Tiergarten was a shadow of former glories. Through ravaged tree tops, a constant volley issued from the huge anti-aircraft guns atop the monolithic, virtually impregnable flak towers near the Zoo. I wondered how the animals were faring. Had the giraffes been eaten yet? Were lions prowling through the U-bahn?

Racing along Tiergartenstraße, my attention snapped to the right. I screeched to a halt outside an innocuous, three-storey building, set back behind a low iron fence. It oozed malice.

These were the offices of Hitler's 'merciful death', his programme of involuntary euthanasia for those who failed to achieve the Reich's benchmark of proper humanity. Officially the 'Charitable Foundation for Cure and Institutional Care', bureaucrats and doctors rubber-stamped papers here, making judgement calls by quota. To be categorised as mentally infirm, have a congenital defect, or be 'racially unhygienic' was fatal – the Nazi judging the happiest of 'imbeciles' to possess a quality of life simply not worth preserving.

It always begins with a list. In this case, it had begun with the creation of a register of sickly children and the requirement of midwives to report disabled newborn: these had then been removed from their parents for special care – and returned to them in an urn.

The assessors at 4 Tiergartenstraße swept through the sanatoriums into the nursing homes, to dementia sufferers. Any institution that resisted would be subject to inspection. Their chosen were ushered onto 'Charitable Ambulance' buses, for transfer to a new clinic – where 'pneumonia' came in a syringe. They'd be dispatched via injections, starvation and later, carbon monoxide gassing. Sometimes they just shot them. In all, seventy thousand beds were 'freed up'.

Aktion T4 ended in 1941, once public outcry forced the Nazis to stand down. Sadly, the forces of protest subsided once the moral watchdogs learnt to fear for their lives. Swallowing my disgust, I went to set off again…

A gunshot. The Zündapp went out from underneath me and I flailed through the air. Landing on my shoulder beneath trees just off the kerb, I tried to roll. The Karabiner 98 rifle strapped to my back wrecked any chance of grace – instead, I crash-landed in an undignified mess and a lot of pain.

There was a second small explosion, inches from my head – splintering the branches of the nearby tree. Rifle fire, thank God – a machine gun would have cost me – but a third shot immediately after, followed quickly by a fourth and a fifth told me I was in a shooting gallery.

With the tree shattering around me, I used the momentum of my landing to scamper into undergrowth – unholstering my Walther P38 and emerging the other side of the bushes spraying bullets. A brief glimpse: four Russian soldiers advancing eagerly, emboldened by their advantage, flicking little fiery wasps at me from their Mosin-Nagant 91/30s…

Bolt action rifles. Five rounds loaded via a stripper clip. Two of the men were pausing to reload. I targeted the two who had their rifles raised.

Reaching out with my mind, I saw in the instant it took them to tighten their trigger fingers that I was dealing with non-Gifted. No psychic signatures: these were ordinary men, pumping with adrenaline – still quite dangerous. I aimed for the thigh area. They fell. Neither would be limping for the rest of their lives and they'd both be able to father children.

The third soldier hesitated, startled by the sudden loss of advantage, fumbled while reloading. I got him in the shoulder. The fourth was made of sterner stuff: he advanced, firing fast. I felt him wing me in my left arm.

Five rounds left in my revolver: I decided to save them. Still on the move, I closed my eyes just for an instant – although there was thirty feet between us, I imagined delivering a right hook to the man's jaw. His head snapped to the side and he blacked out.

I probed quickly for valuable intelligence: they were a breakthrough from Chuikov's Eighth Guards Army, looking to hook up with the Soviet Third Shock Army and seal the Tiergarten. The Third had taken the Reichstag and the new priority was the park. It was happening very quickly – they were a tsunami flooding the streets.

Unless I beat them to the bunker, Hitler would just slip amongst them. It would be no effort for him to confound every mind he encountered – he'd had a lot of practise. I checked my wound, but it was only a graze; I'd been shot before – quite a lot.

The Russian soldiers would soon be dangerous again.

Any moment, there'd be more of them.

Keeping down, I found I was peering across a street that in my long lifetime had known several name changes: it was currently known as 'Hermann-Göring-Straße'. I was old enough to remember two small cities either side of the Spree, when this street had still been home to remains of the medieval western wall. I'd seen the Brandenburg Gate installed at its northern end and seen it occupied by Napoleon. Across this street, at the old Palais Schulenburg, I'd met with Bismarck at his request to hear dire warnings of a 'great European War'…

I'd dutifully relayed Bismarck's concerns to my masters in London. His talk of escalation due to "some damn foolish thing in the Balkans" had seemed tenuous and alarmist and was not taken seriously. There was a direct chain of consequences from ignoring those warnings to this moment.

The old palace was pockmarked by shrapnel and many of its windows had been blown out, though its roof was intact. You could still make out hints of former grandeur. Next to it stood the new Reich Chancellery Albert Speer had built for Hitler – bombastic, imperialistic, intimidating. Where the palace was all flowing contours and rococo ornamentation, the home of the Third Reich was hard edges and Roman classicism. Running at a right angle from the palace, it lined the Ministergärten – a forbidding wave of marble.

The air erupted. The German soldiers across the road, behind sandbags and barbed wire, saw me coming and provided supporting fire. There was a loud explosion nearby – I was spun, landing with a grimace upon my wound. I launched myself to my feet again, leapt for a gap between the metal barbs and – with bullets whizzing by inches from my ears – vaulted the barricade, landing beside their officer.

His shoulder straps and collar patches told me he was an SS-Unterscharführer – a junior squad commander – but it was the medal that caught my eye: he wore the Knight's Cross of the Iron Cross, the greatest military honour in Nazi Germany. Intriguingly, he spoke with a French accent.

A glimpse into his mind: his name was Eugène Vaulot; a Parisian, he'd joined French pro-Nazi collaborator militia at eighteen and fought against the Russians on the Eastern Front. In 1944, he'd joined thousands of other volunteers to form the Waffen Grenadier Division the SS 'Charlemagne' – the French brigade in the Waffen SS – and been sent to repel the advance of the Red Army through Poland. Only three hundred and fifty had made it back to Berlin.

Eugène had seen too many friends die to dare to question. His resolve was strong. The Charlemagne now bolstered the 'Nordland' division, made up of troops from Norway, Denmark and Hungary. Along with Hitler Youth and Volkssturm, they'd bloodied the Russians. Using the anti-tank 'Panzerfausts', Eugène had personally taken out eight Soviet tanks this past week. Now twenty-one, he'd been wearing his Iron Cross for two days.

Eugène Vaulot would be killed the next day.

I looked around their faces: so much fervent conviction. They really believed that somewhere out there the greater German army was grinding the Red Army into the earth. "They say he is dead," I ventured, seemingly frightened.

Unterscharführer Vaulot was seeing a man slightly younger than he was. He reached out to grasp my shoulder reassuringly, saying, "Never. Remember: the hour before sunrise is always darkest."

I wondered how many times a day they recycled Goebbels' propaganda to one another.

Keeping low, I stumbled across a stark landscape of savaged trees, a contorted mimicry of the formerly glamourous Ministergärten. Dusk was falling and the shadows starting to reach for me as I entered the building. Stopping just inside the doorway, I straightened my shoulders and lifted my chin. An elderly lady curled up in the shadows blinked, questioning her own eyes: one instant, I'd been a stooped, injured Wehrmacht soldier; the next, I was Gestapo.

I listened for him. Despite there being thousands in the Reich Chancellery at that moment, normal people register faintly on the psychic spectrum. Their distress was distracting, but I waited as my mind began to tune them out – sorting through the psychic signatures in the building.

It didn't surprise me to find that there were several dozen psychics behind these walls – after all, they were the nucleus of an exercise in bending the will of a nation. Many of my kind had clearly been drawn to Hitler's endeavour. Many of my kind regarded the ordinary folk with contempt.

I reached quietly out.

The Gifted *glow*, emanating coloured auras according to the nature of their Gift. Hitler's aura was incandescent – I knew it well. I'd met him three times before: twice during the Great War and then again in 1932, just before the Reichstag fire. On each occasion that glow had been more intense, as he'd been building in power. Thirteen years on, he must be even more powerful – surely there was no way to disguise it…

There seemed to be no such presence in the vicinity. But the existence of bunkers beneath the Reich Chancellery was well known to the Society – the concrete between us could be masking him.

An explosion blew in the last of the windows, provoking a collective scream. I set off, along corridors lined with the despairing and defeated. In corners and hastily constructed alcoves, there was Babylonian excess going on. For these people, it was the End of Days.

With the garden behind me, I entered – through a doorway twice my height, doors hanging from their hinges – a grand room of high ceilings, deep brown mahogany and marbled granite walls. His huge desk was still there, remarkably well preserved. People were keeping away from the large rectangular windows, which looked right out onto Voßstraße.

Emerging onto the Mittelbau Marble Gallery, I paused – my breath taken away. It must have stretched nearly five hundred feet. I knew that Speer had boasted it was twice the length of the Hall of Mirrors at Versailles. The symbolism had been deliberate – it had been before those mirrors that the treaty which brought Germany to its knees had been signed. His marble gallery had sought for associations of epic grandeur and mighty empires spanning the centuries: Versailles' 'Sun

King', Louis XIV, had seen the longest reign of any European monarch. Alas, Hitler's reign had been rather shorter.

There were many terrified people crammed into this space, among them men who had known great authority in recent years. Parting for me – even now, everybody feared the Gestapo – they all believed the Führer was still alive. I headed away from the street – our intelligence talking of a long corridor beneath the Ministergärten.

Following increasing numbers, I found a staircase and was soon hit by the smell: sweat and urine, with nowhere to go but hang in the air. People were packed in so tightly it was a squeeze to get through. Dust and plaster were falling from the ceiling and the lights constantly flickered. I glanced into a makeshift sick bay, saw exhausted doctors and nurses trying to save lives.

Amongst these, a man called Helmut Kunz struck a chord with me. I started to read him: he was a dentist by trade – and agitated about having just administered some anaesthetic. He had no psychic signature.

The rooms heaved with the injured, children and pregnant women, core military, secretaries and aides. The mood was of deep deflation. I stumbled across SS-Gruppenführer Hans Baur – beside himself with grief. Kneeling, I gently eased him into a daze then pried open his memory. With responsibility for the squadron that ferried the cabinet and key generals about, he'd been Hitler's official pilot for twelve years. The Führer had once given him a Mercedes Benz as a gift and even been his Best Man…

Despite Baur's attempts to convince him to escape, the Führer had shot himself at 3:30pm the day before. Before he'd died, he'd given Baur his prized eighteenth-century portrait of Frederick the Great, by the Swiss artist Graff. Hans Baur definitely thought Adolf Hitler was dead.

It didn't take long to find the underground corridor. An unshaven sentry, his turnout decidedly slovenly, attempted a half-hearted identification check. In the corridor, the overcrowding eased, but the growing stench of lapsed hygiene mixed with sewage failures and diesel fumes to brew up a potent cocktail. Two hundred and sixty feet long, it was starkly lit with naked light bulbs, which made those passing the other way seem eerily spectral. With every step, I could feel the hornet's nest in my gut being kicked into angry life.

The guards at the end were easy; but there could be no 'blending in' this far down. To the occupants of this gloomy dungeon, I chose to look like SS-Gruppenführer Hans Baur.

Somebody was quietly sobbing.

The shelling was deadened in the Vorbunker, but the constant thudding made the six feet of concrete feel meagre. It was deserted in comparison. Through a corridor with toilets and shower cubicles on the left and a generator room to my right, the next section doubled as a canteen, with a kitchen and wine store, in which servants were working very quietly. I glimpsed quarters – men sleeping on bunks. Then came a conference area or waiting room, with the entrance to the Führerbunker at the far end.

Hitler had probably sensed my arrival by now. Could he be in the Vorbunker with me at that very moment? One of the servants, or a sleeping soldier… In this waiting room, the left-hand door had been left ajar and the room beyond was darkened; the sobbing was coming from the right – it sounded female.

Goosebumps: a warning sign. I listened at the door for signs of life, then nudged it open. The horror hit me hard, forcing me to recoil back across the corridor, to collide loudly with a chair. The sobbing abruptly halted.

I turned to find a twenty-five-year-old woman gazing at me through puffy eyes, her cheeks stained with tears. Her name was Gertrude Junge, but she was known as 'Traudl'; until yesterday, she'd been Hitler's private secretary.

"She did it," Traudl said, incredulously – seeing only Hans Baur, a man she'd worked with for years. "She actually did it." Then her eyes flicked beyond me. "And *he* helped her."

Following her glare, I found Doctor Ludwig Stumpfegger – a thirty-four-year-old SS-Obersturmbannführer and surgeon to Hitler – swaying in the doorway, a bottle of red wine in his hand. His furtive, darting eyes betrayed terrible guilt.

"We're all going to die, Traudl," he retorted, arms flung out too wide as he tried to illustrate his point. "It was a mercy."

"Mercy?" she snapped, eyes blazing with accusation. "Tell me their names."

He grimaced, as if slapped. "The boy was Helmut," he began, uncertainly. "Then there was… Hilde!" He said this name with great triumph, as if winning a game. But after this he struggled, trying to count to six on his fingers.

"You bastard," she snarled. "I hope you rot in Hell." And she ran off on into the Führerbunker in tears.

Stumpfegger peered blankly after her. "Well, yes," he muttered, "that's a given. And it won't be long now." Turning to go, he paused and cocked his head, then clicked his fingers. "Helga. The one who struggled was called Helga."

The doctor seemed to finally take me in. After a moment, he declared, "Who the hell names all their children with the same initial, anyway?" Taking another slug of wine, he left.

In shock, I pulled the door shut on the six Goebbels children. The youngest, Heide, had been four, while Helga the eldest had been twelve. Magda Goebbels had summoned the dentist, Helmut Kunz, to inject them each with morphine to sedate them – passing this off to her babies as medicine.

When she'd broached the subject with Kunz, days ago, the prospect had appalled him. Upon learning that the Führer had taken his life, however – and that the Goebbels intended to follow suit – Kunz had administered the sedative 'as a mercy'. When it came to be crushing cyanide into her sleeping children's mouths, Magda had balked – and Kunz had refused. So Stumpfegger had become involved.

It seemed that twelve-year-old Helga hadn't quite succumbed to the morphine and that the end for her had been anything but merciful.

In the waiting room, with the light bulbs flickering, I stared at the floor – anger bubbling. I slowly descended a small flight of stairs, turning a corner to descend another small flight. At the steel bulkhead door, I gave the guards little of my time. Then I was in the Führerbunker – twenty-eight feet below ground – and I could virtually taste him.

"Getting warmer..." Hitler's mocking tone in my head was unmistakable – he was looking forward to good sport.

The layout was similar: segments, with rooms on either side. In front of me was a loungelike waiting room for the powerful, lavishly decorated; but it felt dank. Across to the left were toilets leading to a bathroom, with linking doors onto what had been the Hitlers' quarters. To my right was a generator room – a figure at work on the ventilation system in there: Johannes Hentschel, who'd been grappling with the mechanics of the Reich Chancelleries for eleven years. A talented, effective engineer, but not a psychic.

"Colder..."

Damn you.

"That's not very courteous – in my house..."

It was grim down here, cramped and oppressive – like a bank vault stocked with the walking dead. Its occupants wandered in slow motion, mumbling. Beyond the generator room on the right was the telephone switchboard room. Distraught, Traudl Junge was being comforted by twenty-eight-year-old Polish-born telephone operator, Rochus Misch – a member of Hitler's bodyguard for six years. These two had shared an affection for the Goebbels children. Just the day before, Traudl had been playing with them when Hitler's Walther PPK had gone off in his study.

The children often played around Misch's work station: barely an hour ago, he'd seen them head up to bed in their nightgowns, the girls with ribbons in their hair, little Heide teasing him with a rhyme. Misch was haunted by the older girl Helga's parting expression – he was thinking about the care with which their mother brushed their hair for bedtime and lavished them with adoring kisses... He'd suspected what was about to happen and was consumed with regret; but he was young, out of his depth among giant personalities.

It was those giant personalities that concerned me.

You could have allowed the children to leave.

"That is not how the Goebbels want it."

You could have ordered their survival.

"I adored those children."

I got a brief glimpse of pyramids. He was thinking about the pharaohs of ancient Egypt, who often took their loved ones with them when they died...

Misch had been among the first to lay eyes upon the bodies of the Führer and new wife – both on the sofa, he slumped slightly forward, she with her legs drawn up. Eva Braun had chosen cyanide. Misch had been fourth in after Hitler's personal adjutant, Otto Günsche, his valet, Heinz Linge, and Martin Bormann.

The room had smelled of gunsmoke and almonds.

In the lounge, soldiers and officials were hovering listlessly, some getting drunk, others trying to maintain a semblance of order. Günsche and Linge, the adjutant and the valet, were both playing the memory over and over in their heads. They remembered clearly the hole in the Führer's temple, the splash of blood on the wall beyond. Linge had been partaking of the bunker schnapps ever since.

Lately, it had been his responsibility, along with Doctor Werner Haase, to administer the Führer's 'medicine' prescribed by now-absent personal physician, Theodor Morell – varying quantities of strychnine, bromide, caffeine, morphine, testosterone, amphetamines, cocaine and heroin. He had been one of the small party of men who had borne Hitler's body up the back staircase to the garden. Günsche had carried the Führer's wife. They'd been joined by Erich Kempka, who – as Hitler's chauffeur – provided the gasoline the Führer had insisted upon for a thorough cremation.

Among the other witnesses to the cremation had been Goebbels, Krebs, Burgdorf, Rattenhuber, Bormann...

I knew how he'd done it. Hitler had confused a small group into thinking he was dead. To be able to project this illusion, he would have needed to be present or nearby from the discovery of his 'body' to its cremation. All he'd need to do was maintain his disguise until he was well away.

One of the men down here had been killed and his body burnt in the Führer's place. But which one? Goebbels and Bormann were famous. The others – well, I was going to have to get to know some new faces – and fast...

The embers of German government were being rekindled in these rooms. Word had gone out to Admiral Dönitz in the far north, that – in accordance with the Führer's will – he had been named President and Supreme Commander of the Armed Forces. Goebbels was to be Chancellor. A number of General Helmuth Weidling's men had joined him from their headquarters at the Bendlerblock: their focus now on negotiating surrender. But neither Weidling nor his chiefs-of-staff had been present for Hitler's suicide.

In the conference room, I received a curt nod of recognition from thirty-four-year-old General Wilhelm Mohnke. While Wiedling had been defence commandant of the city, Mohnke had overseen defence of the Reich Chancellery. He was now concerning himself with a planned mass break-out at nightfall. I had an hour at most.

Some had not been above ground to witness the cremation: I discounted Misch and Traudl for this reason. It wouldn't be a woman anyway – if any remains were ever found, they would have to be male.

In the lounge, I came across Fritz Tornow, Hitler's dog handler – at twenty, the youngest person present. He was visibly distressed. Two days earlier, Hitler – obsessing over the news of Mussolini's humiliating capture and execution – had become convinced that his proposed method of suicide, cyanide poisoning, might fail him. He'd ordered a capsule test on his pet German Shepherd, Blondi.

Tornow had had to hold Blondi's jaws apart while the pill was crumbled into his mouth. The dog's demise had been pitiful. It hadn't stopped there for poor Fritz: following the suicides, he'd also had to shoot Blondi's five puppies, Eva Braun's two Scottish Terriers and the secretary Gerda Christian's dogs – as well as his own dachshund.

Hitler's affection for dogs had been well known – he'd become distraught after Blondi's death. I had another brief impression of that pharaoh, his wife and pets walled up beside him as he entered the afterlife.

Linge. Günsche. Goebbels, Krebs, Burgdorf, Rattenhuber, Bormann. Kempka… The head of a fleet of forty vehicles and their chauffeurs, plus a team of mechanics, Kempka's role in providing the gasoline placed him at the scene of their cremation – but he had not been present when the bodies were discovered in Hitler's study. He seemed unlikely.

Wehrmacht General Hans Krebs had been away from the chancellery, meeting with the Soviet General Chuikov under a white flag – easily corroborated in the minds of his aides. An army veteran, the forty-seven-year-old was a broken man, his aura one of the faintest present. Slowly, I prowled the bunker – reaching out, testing the ground with each mind – running into Gestapo chief and SS-Gruppenführer Heinrich Müller, who greeted me as a friend.

"Hans, are you feeling better?"

"Much better, thank you," I replied, blandly.

I was watching General Wilhelm Burgdorf: at fifty, one of the oldest. He was drunk. Hours earlier, he'd followed ministerialdirektor Hans Fritzsche out of the bunker, confronting him in his office on Wilhelmplatz. Having guessed the civilian minister was about to surrender, he'd drawn his pistol, but Fritzsche had escaped.

What about SS-Gruppenführer Johann Rattenhuber? A faithful bodyguard for over ten years, he'd served in the Bavarian Infantry in the Great War. When Hitler had declared his suicidal intentions to his old friend, Rattenhuber had tried to talk him into an escape attempt. Although present at the cremation, Rattenhuber had not been present when the bodies were found. Other minds confirmed this.

Linge. Günsche. Goebbels, Bormann... Müller was speculating about escape, expressing doubt that it was possible to break through the Soviet encirclement. He said, "We know the Russian methods exactly. I haven't the faintest intention of being taken prisoner."

Thinking that talk of 'methods' was rich coming from the Gestapo, I met his gaze. I even *lived* in a Secret Society – and still we didn't have an organisation that spied on our own. It was highly obvious that the people who are drawn to such roles are exactly the sort you shouldn't be empowering.

Beyond those beady, humourless eyes were snatches of proud achievements: the arrest of thirty thousand Jews during the 'Kristallnacht' pogrom; the undermining and destruction of left-wing opposition groups; being instrumental in 'Operation Himmler', which provided Hitler with the pretext he'd sought to invade Poland – requiring the provision of fresh corpses, to be passed off as the victims of belligerent Poles. Müller had enthusiastically overseen the deportation of eighty thousand Polish Jews to their deaths. He'd been a party to the activities of the mass-extermination *Einsatzgruppen* death squads, to the blocking of Jewish emigration, to the use of the gas chambers and the roll-out of 'the Final Solution'.

I was gazing into the eyes of a monster. But reaching into the memories of those present, I found that none placed Müller near the bunker at the time of Hitler's death... Shuddering at the company I was keeping, I made my excuses and ducked into the nearest room. There I found Magda Goebbels, playing patience.

"Warm again..."

With Eva Braun discreetly out of the limelight, Magda had been as close as the public got to a 'First Lady' of the Reich. A handsome woman, with presence and glamour, she'd always liked money: her first husband had been a rich industrialist and her son by that marriage was heir to a sizeable chunk of BMW. Following her divorce, she'd been courted by a nephew of American President Herbert Hoover.

The great heroine of Nazism, who had just murdered her own children, turned over her next card and blinked. Seeing me, her features softened – and she switched her charm on. "Come sit with me, Hans. Let us talk of the days of glory."

Her head was filled with Wagnerian romanticism, mist-filled forests and mountainsides, where in reality now there were only craters and desolation. She'd first spoken of ending her children over a month previously, despite opportunities to get them out of Berlin. This was the end she'd craved.

I did not engage. Instead, I turned to go.

Her husband, the new Chancellor of Germany, stood in the doorway, peering at me with black, shark-like eyes that had overseen countless death warrants.

There was no doubt he emitted a strange, mesmerising energy. To women, there was a sexuality in his intensity; to men, he represented a role model of charisma and potency, a being simmering with ferocity of purpose. He was a powerful psychic: Hitler might have told him everything – about the Society, about the Dreamstate, about the Astral Universe we live in. About the Blood. He might have known the Society would be sending agents…

"You don't seem quite yourself this evening, Hans," he said, almost casually, as he took a seat beside his wife; but I thought there was a flicker of suspicion.

"The Gruppenführer does not want to chat about the old days," Magda pouted.

The doorway was now occupied by a hulk of a man: Hauptsturmführer Günther Schwägermann, Goebbels' personal adjutant. Schwägermann was twenty-nine and physically the strongest man in the bunker; he was a low-level psychic too – ordinarily no match for me, but with the Goebbels in the room… Beyond

Schwägermann, Gestapo chief Müller was peering this way, with a degree of interest best characterised as 'nasty'.

The psychics in the bunker were starting to switch on to me.

"Getting hotter…"

"I'm sorry, Chancellor," I began, accentuating my nervousness – after all, I was a humble pilot in the company of the greatest living German. "It is difficult for me – you know the Führer and I were very close."

This was the right thing to say.

"Of course." Reaching to hold Magda's hand, he continued, "He was our Best Man too – in so many ways." He beckoned. "Come, take a final drink with us."

As Goebbels poured me a brandy, Magda began to sob quietly – tugging gently at the golden party pin she was wearing. Having spent the last few years pinned to the Führer's lapel, it had been his parting gift to her.

"Be strong, dear, we've known this moment was coming. All here can hold our heads high: we stood by him, when others weaker scurried away like rats." He was talking about Ribbentrop, Himmler, Göring – none of whom had been seen since Hitler's birthday party on the twentieth. Himmler had incensed the Führer by making unauthorised peace overtures to the West.

Once again, I had a vision of the bunker as a pharaoh's tomb, with all of Berlin the pyramid above: his wife, his riches, his pets and now his servants, all entombed here…

Except you've no intention of dying today, have you, Adolf?

"Oh, Adolf Hitler is dead sure enough – have you not seen his funeral pyre? He is taking all of Germany with him!"

"We are the last," Goebbels was saying, "the ones who truly loved him. He was a God amongst us. All is lost, except to follow him one last time."

The Goebbels rose. As he crossed to the coat rack, I noted his limp, remembering a congenital deformity – oh the irony, that the great advocator of Aryan perfection and genetic superiority had to wear a metal brace and a special shoe! Helping his wife into her coat, he paused to consider me.

"I believe you plan to live, Hans – good. I will tell you what I told my stepson in my final letter to him: there will be much clamour now; do not be overwhelmed. The day will come when all their lies will fold up upon themselves and our truth will shine bright in triumph..."

I was struck by how rational and composed he seemed.

"There are three types of citizen: sheep, wolves, wolfherds. The sheep wish only to belong and be humble; we must numb them with trivial distractions. The wolves seek power and validation; they rejoice in hierarchy and keeping the sheep in line. The wolfherds are born to rule: we own the State. We are natural aristocrats. While the masses are kept 'entertained', we change the world to suit our ends..."

Pausing, he scrutinising me, frowning slightly – confused that he could not read Hans Baur's mind as easily as usual. I remembered to breathe. "But sir, how is it achieved?"

He seemed pleased to share his brilliant wisdom one last time. Pulling on his gloves, he continued, "The people always need enemies, Hans: if there are none, create one. The more amplified the threat, the more gratefully submissive they will be. Give them the thrill of horror they crave and they will allow you to spend public money on anything you choose.

"One uses nostalgia and mythology: the 'good old days' are a fine sedative; invoking God always works well. Keep them looking backwards at when 'things were better'. The last thing you want is for them to start thinking forwards. Discourage 'vision' – it rarely reinforces the status quo.

"Find ways to allow them the *illusion* of change. Throw Christians to the lions by blaming those with no voice – convincing the people that these are looking to steal their privileged position in the gutter. They must never be allowed to blame *upwards*, for they outnumber us – the State should supervise the formation of public opinion. Never stoop to reason: be crude and repetitive and appeal to emotions, not the intellect. A lie told a thousand times becomes the truth."

His face smiled, but his eyes did not. He reached to my shoulder, enjoying the warmth he was pretending to feel.

"*Live*, Hans – you are about to see a renaissance. My propaganda is music to confound the people, lull them into constant slumber or rouse them into useful iconoclasm. With film and radio, it is entering a new level of complexity – and new technologies will enrich my art in the century to come. Watch as I become a 'set text' for world leaders..."

He actually winked as he left, arm-in-arm with his delirious wife. Schwägermann followed – checking his revolver. They exited via the back staircase up to the Ministergärten. I listened using senses heightened beyond ordinary hearing: there was a gunshot, barely audible above the rumble of shelling – that was Magda. A moment later came a second.

Schwägermann checked the bodies for signs of life. He instructed a soldier to unload his gun into them. Another soldier stepped forward to douse them with petrol...

A slow, mocking chuckle came into my head.

"Growing colder..."

The break-out was springing into action. I scanned each mind, urgently, doubting my reasoning – as clearly he could mask his power, he could be anybody. Hitler's private secretary Martin Boorman, was registering significantly on the psychic spectrum. I felt for my revolver –

And then it hit me – he *needed* the witnesses! Somebody's body had been burnt in his place. The real Hitler was impersonating them. Once he had escaped, he'd drop that disguise – and that person would slip out of history, their disappearance forever unexplained... Which is why it *couldn't be* one of the core witnesses – those who had discovered his suicide and witnessed the destruction of his remains – he needed them to spread the story of his death.

My mind whirled. Around me, the occupants of the bunker were assembling into groups. Under orders from Mohnke, several SS were pouring gasoline over Hitler's study in preparation to incinerate the Führerbunker. Joining the migration to the Vorbunker, I started identifying the groups: Mohnke was leaving with Traudl and the other secretaries, as well as the cook Constanze Manziarly, the doctor Schenck and the diplomat Walther Hewel...

It had to be someone who was not a key part of the story of Hitler's death – someone peripheral, but who had not left the bunker in the past few days.

Schenck had been out of the bunker, working in the hospital. If Hitler was pretending to be General Mohnke, he was putting a lot of effort into the part – Mohnke was busily ordering an assembly of commanders to brief them. Hitler's friend Hewel, however, was very quiet – I noted Traudl had found his behaviour to be out of character since yesterday…

Schwägermann was the last to leave the Führerbunker – swinging the airtight bulkhead door shut on the fire. We were out of the Vorbunker now: some turned left towards the old Reich Chancellery, while the rest proceeded along the long corridor towards Speer's new Chancellery. The sounds of battle overhead intensified. The world was reeling.

Martin Bormann was proposing to leave with Doctor Stumpfegger and Hitler Youth leader Artur Axmann; he had in mind to invite Hans Baur to join him. As I currently looked like Baur, I chose the long, crowded corridor, full of flickering shadows, to drop that disguise. Now I just looked like myself in a mid-rank Wehrmacht uniform.

Axmann had not been in the bunker at the time of Hitler's death, but Stumpfegger seemed unaccounted for… We emerged in the cellars of the new chancellery. In the sea of frightened faces, I was in danger of losing him. The word was that everybody would make a break for it at eleven.

Two hours at most. Process of elimination. Stumpfegger had been drinking for hours and was out of his tree. I found him with Baur, drunkenly insisting to the confused pilot that he'd just seen him in the Vorbunker. After a while, he staggered away to find a dark corner to urinate in. I didn't have the time to mess about, so I stepped up behind him mid-stream and – placing my hand on the back of his head – tranquilised him on the spot. Stumpfegger slumped messily to the cellar floor. In all the noise, nobody even noticed.

Seconds rooting about in the man's mind was enough: he was carrying a lot of self-contempt and remorse – as well as the Goebbels children, there had been medical experiments at Ravensbrück concentration camp. I almost felt sorry for him, as he'd not signed up for any of that. But Ludwig Stumpfegger didn't have to carry his guilt around for much longer: he'd be killed not far north of the Tiergarten, just after he'd managed to cross the Spree – probably the last man to see Bormann alive, as their bodies were discovered near one another. Twenty-seven years later.

I found Walther Hewell in the old Reich Chancellery, staring numbly at the floor, waiting while Mohnke briefed the Wehrmacht commanders regarding Hitler's death: suicide was not being mentioned, only glory and self-sacrifice.

Hewell did not see it that way: he felt abandoned. He'd followed Hitler for twenty years – even serving as his valet during Hitler's prison sentence. His friend had written 'Mein Kampf' in that period and Hewell had found it intensely inspirational. With the flickering glow of burning Berlin on the carpet at his feet, Walther Hewell thought back to the early days of the Nazi Party – when, excited to make Germany great again, he'd been amongst its first three hundred members. They'd struggled through several poor election showings. Then the recession had come – and that had been all they'd needed...

He didn't look up as I stood over him, reading him like an open book: Hewell had no Gift. Were it not for his association with Hitler, he would have lived the life of a moderately successful businessman. As he contemplated the cyanide in his left pocket and the Walther 7.65 handgun in his right – a gift from Hitler – he wondered whether that might not have been a fuller life.

Becoming frantic, I began to explore other possibilities. It didn't seem as if Hitler would be amongst Weidling's men heading under a white flag to negotiate, since they would all likely be imprisoned.

Krebs and Burgdorf were ripping into any alcohol they could lay their hands on, revolvers ready on the table before them. The medical team that included Werner Haase and Helmut Kunz meant to stay with their patients until the bitter end – and the mechanic Hentschel stayed with them to service their generator. The young dog handler, Fritz Tornow, simply didn't see the point in running.

An hour before midnight, feeling defeated, I joined the exodus. In small groups, we slipped out of a cellar window and darted across the firelit Wilhelmplatz, into the pile of rubble that was once the elegant Kaiserhof U-bahn station.

Mohnke's group was first. I tagged along, watching Hewel disappear along the tracks towards the U-bahn tunnel with one of the secretaries. Traudl Junge did better than most, falling in and out of captivity until she made it to Bavaria to join her family some time mid-1946. She claimed that she did not find out about the Holocaust until after the war.

Down the station steps they poured at intervals: Bormann and Stumpfegger with the pilot Hans Baur, who would be wounded that night then imprisoned for ten years, thereafter living a long life to ninety-five; the valet Linge and Hitler's adjutant Günsche, followed closely by Goebbels' man, Schwägermann; the chauffeur Kempka soon afterwards.

They would cross each other's paths in the hours that followed, become separated, glimpse one another again. Linge and Günsche, captured by morning, spent the next decade in prison. Schwägermann slipped past the Soviets and spent less than two years in American custody. Kempka was passed off by a sympathetic Yugoslav as her husband; by June, he'd made it to the Bavarian Alps, to be captured by the Americans. By late 1947, he was free.

I stayed frozen in my little pool of darkness and did not move a muscle, scrutinising each of the hundreds of faces for something I'd missed, as they dissolved into the night. Once or twice, I heard his teasing voice in my head; but I suspected that he'd lost track of me and was testing the water.

With the exodus dissipating to a trickle – not long after Rochus Misch had passed by, into the train tunnels – a lone figure slipped out of the cellar window and *went the other way*.

It was Gestapo chief SS-Gruppenführer Heinrich Müller.

He darted across the road, into the Wertheim Department Store. An instant later, I launched myself along Voßstraße – running at full pelt. Part of the building was aflame. I threw myself in anyway, listening for a signature – suspecting now that Hitler could mute his aura, but not mask it entirely.

Müller was up ahead, two rooms away.

The Wertheim Department Store had been one of the largest in Europe. Being Jewish, the Wertheims had fled the country in 1939. Even putting all his shares in his 'Aryan' wife's name and divorcing her had not saved Georg Wertheim's fortune – he had been forced to sell at 'discounted' prices to Aryans.

Hadn't that on one level been what the Holocaust had been all about – a shift of wealth? One massive 'hostile takeover'.

A German 'Harrods', it was said to have over eighty lifts. As I passed beneath its shattered, once-magnificent glass atrium, amongst tall pillars and high arches, it felt like a cathedral to capitalism. In the darkened nooks and crannies of the store, beneath staircases and behind counters, where once they had come to worship with notes now worth less than paper, the middle-class of Germany were cowering for their lives.

Müller was peering onto Leipziger Platz, face bathed in flickering warmth – the Russians were pouring into the square and he was within sight of becoming one of them.

I said, "Am I getting hot again yet?"

He started, his hand hovering near the Gestapo chief's revolver, eyes on the barrel of my Walther P38. "Why get in my way? I am properly one of you now."

So, he'd taken the Blood – now he could lie low for decades, barely ageing. One day, he could reemerge into a different age, where they had long forgotten…

He nodded. "Like the twelfth century Holy Roman Emperor, Barbarossa. A descendant of two great German families, legend has it he sleeps still beneath the Bavarian mountains. Waiting to restore our beautiful nation to greatness…"

He'd be probing my mind now, looking for a way in – suggesting I turn the gun upon myself…

"Get out of my head," I warned, threatening, "my trigger finger only needs to twitch."

"Then do it," he challenged, eyes blazing.

I found that I couldn't – despite sending the message to my finger to squeeze. He dropped all pretence. Müller became the Führer.

"Müller?"

"Ashes."

"Along with the wife you 'cherished'?"

He twitched. "I gave recognition to her loyalty. History will record there was only one Mrs Hitler."

"That's big of you," I muttered, dryly.

He blinked. "Is the gun getting heavy?"

It felt like I was trying to lift a coffee table one-handed.

"Nothing I can't handle." I looked to disrupt his focus. "You're looking *old*, Adolf – in fact, I'd say 'ravaged'. Conscience finally catching up with you?"

He had aged markedly since I'd seen him last. His face was like a skull, its pasty, bloated skin drawn taut across the bone, with bloodshot, lidless eyes staring from hollowed sockets. His body was contorted into a pained stoop; he seemed to drag it along with him. His hand was trembling.

"The Blood will repair me," he countered, with a sneer. "Which is more than can be said for you – even the Blood cannot undo a bullet to the brain."

I thought of the Goebbels, Krebs, Burgdorf, Hewell – how good it would be to join them in eternal peace. Life was so stressful and humans such *loathsome – ungrateful creatures*, for whom nothing could be done. Why suffer in a *hopeless cause*? Hope... Hope, what was it worth? *We are undone as a species.*

The gun was turning.

"I see the German people let you down in the end."

The twitch again. I got some control back.

"Those traitors?" he hissed, quivering with rage. "Weak-willed and spineless. I offered them immortality, but they lacked the moral fibre." Stabbing his finger out at the red night sky, he continued, "They chose this! Let them burn."

"Yet they thought you loved them," I cooed, trying to prod the exposed nerve.

His voice changed softened – cocking his head, he said, "Trying to push my buttons?"

I felt winded. The floor went from beneath my feet. I landed in the middle of a display of mannequins, their features melted grotesquely from recent fires – leering at me.

The gun was still in my hand. I recovered quickly enough to stay his advance.

"It is not just the German people who failed me," he continued quietly, in a sort of growl. "I thought *you* would see reason – that you would recognise our kinship."

He was talking of the British.

"We are nothing like you."

He actually laughed. "Tulliver, you have been mixing with the great of your country for centuries – yet you have still not worked it out? It is not Nazism that will be seen as the great threat to democracy in our century – the *Soviets* are our common enemy, with their barbaric notion of the 'power of the people'. We are cousins, genetically and ideologically."

I shook my head, hatred catching at the back of my throat. "What sort of 'master race' gets its kicks out of watching children shiver naked in the mud on their way to a humiliating death?"

This didn't bother him at all. And now I was the one making myself vulnerable with my anger. "For your leaders," he replied nonchalantly, "my 'final solution' will be a handy scapegoat. They won't have to engage with the truth."

"Which is?"

"I disrupted the flow of business. That was my only crime."

His hand swiped through the air – and I went flying, hurled several feet to crash into a glass counter, which buckled and shattered beneath the impact. Shards burst into my back. I spasmed with the pain.

"You *liberals*, with your podgy complacency and your smug idealism, you have never suffered."

He was in a bad way – his hands shook, and the next blow missed, bringing down a display case behind me. But I'd lost the gun; and I was flailing about, semi-conscious, my clothes soaked with blood.

"If I made one error, it was my lack of stealth," he muttered, slowly advancing upon me. "I should have bided my time over Poland."

He stopped just feet away, triumphant. "Remember when we retook the Rhineland in '36? I had only thirty thousand troops. The French could have decimated me, but they and the Belgians slept, the Americans saw a business opportunity – and you declared that we had a right to the land.

"I knew then that we were lovers."

A gentle, dreamy smile played upon his lips, but it faded as another thought occurred to him, unguarded. I saw Pearl Harbor. He wondered whether his great strategic blunder had been supporting Japan against the United States.

I felt my head clear a little.

"Had there been no perception of an alliance against them, the heads of American industry would happily have continued to favour me…" He appeared almost to have forgotten we were enemies, his manner imploring, as if we were having a debate. "You have a recession, there is a reaction from the people – and it leads to opportunities. America was ripe for a war – and look at them now. They'll be the new world empire, dwarfing our own…"

I saw the gun. It was underneath a table just beyond him.

"Germany was ripe too: the people felt humiliated – we could not afford to pay our war reparations, as we struggled to feed ourselves – and all the while, the banks enthusiastically lent to all sides." He dropped his voice to a whisper, nearly drowned out by the destruction outside. "Recessions… Ever noticed how they come along at regular intervals – almost as if planned? The puppeteers are safe far from here: when the fires die, they will be richer than ever."

Staring, I asked, "And what of the sixty million who died?"

With a shrug, he countered, "The money outlives us all. It moves itself about to protect its interests, triggering uncertainty and misery with its selfish inconstancy, funding the wars that result – and all along, it *grows…*"

Despite his deterioration, he was still mesmerising. He exuded euphoria."For ten beautiful years, the people really *lived* – they reclaimed their sovereignty. I *empowered* them! I alone guided them to take back control…

"It was just a case of convincing them they were a part of a great endeavour," he explained. "But greatness is expensive: the state will need to worship at the altar of austerity for a while. And there will need to be cuts, sacrifices made – some *rationalisation…* Now these cripples and spastics, they're a drain on the state. And these Jews and gypsies and homosexuals, all these foreigners, they steal what's rightly ours. We're going to need to trim the fat, if we want to make our nation great again."

He breathed out a long, elated sigh. "You should have seen it in their eyes: fervent joy, like they'd never known."

"Was that like the look in Blondi's eyes," I asked, "as the cyanide crushed her brain? Or more the look in her puppies' eyes, as they took a bullet?"

He faltered, frowning. His eyes widened.

The Walther P38 slid along the floor and leapt into my hand. I shot him – once, twice, then struggling to my feet, a third time. Each time, he jolted and staggered back – face frozen in astonishment. Lurching, I fired a fourth time – he fell, crashing to the floor over near the window. And lay still.

I sagged, exhausted, reached out for a support. Listened to the gunfire in Leipziger Platz. Some of the returning fire cut through the windows, shattering glass and strafing the high ceiling.

He wouldn't be dead. I was myself already starting to heal: within hours, the Blood would reclaim my back, squeezing out the smaller shards; tomorrow, the larger shards would fall out; the next day, it would begin working on my scars... *Even the Blood cannot undo a bullet to the brain.*

One bullet left. As I approached him, he made a gurgling sound and coughed blood. It turned into a low, darkly ironic chuckle. "The great shepherd of Germans felled by his love for a German Shepherd..."

I levelled the pistol at him.

"I'm nothing," he said, growling. "I'm just a chapter. A minor skirmish in a great battle..."

"I already know there is an organisation called 'The Invisible Nation'," I replied calmly, advancing. "I imagine they see you as some sort of General."

He nodded. "The elimination of rich Jewry represented a pleasing acquisition of capital. The war has been highly profitable."

Adolf Hitler eyed the Walther P38. Looking for something to offer, he said, "There is a project. They call it 'the Hum'."

"Go on."

"It's the global anaesthetic. They've found the frequency our minds work on..."

Our world turned red. A blast of heat blew me across the room, spinning me at the heart of a tornado of debris and shrapnel, burning my clothes and skin. I helplessly reached out, managed to pull the trigger on that last bullet.

I'm sure I hit him. But by then he was the faintest dark blur, flared into oblivion in a world of flame.

- CHAPTER ONE -

The British Bulldog

We'd just had our first general election in ten years. Although it would take weeks for the result to be declared, the rumour was that Attlee's Labour Party had scooped a landslide over the Conservatives. It seemed hard to swallow, given the job that Churchill had done for Britain. Apparently, the public – the euphoria of VE Day still ringing in their ears – had signalled their intent to purge the last six years and make a fresh start. Washing themselves clean of the entire filthy mess and everything associated with it meant throwing 'the British Bulldog' out with the bath water.

In just six years, the human race had turned on itself and eradicated three percent of its population. Over sixty million people. We had descended into madness and savaged our brothers and sisters.

To me, it had felt more defensible than the Great War: Hitler had been a threat to all our freedoms and it had seemed clear-cut that I was fighting for a good cause. Whereas during the 1914-18 war I had largely avoided fighting and focused on damage limitation, this time I had often found myself in the thick of battle.

War compromised all men: I had blood on my hands and had seen too much. Things that turn my stomach even now. Following that encounter in the bunker in Berlin two and a half months previously, I felt sullied to the core. I wanted to rise again, cleansed. So, I too had voted Winnie out.

I was in a buoyant mood as I answered the Prime Minister's summons that day in July: the seventeenth. Little did I know, little did the British people know, that some stains can never be washed out. Due to events of the day before in New Mexico, a countdown had started – and only a handful of men knew about it.

One of those was Winston Churchill.

The summons was to Potsdam, where the Prime Minister was attending a conference at the residence of the German Crown Prince, along with Joseph Stalin and Harry S. Truman. Clement Attlee was also there as Prime Minister in waiting. I had been attending to personal affairs near Belgrade but had an aeroplane at my disposal, so was able to make it there just after nightfall. Upon arrival, I went straight to attend him at his temporary residence, the Villa Urbig near Babelsberg.

The villa was an elegant two-storey building in salmon-pink stucco, with tall French windows and a smattering of loft windows. It had belonged to the founders of the Deutsche Bank. I found Churchill on his own, sipping whisky on the veranda at the back, gazing down a long lawn bursting with hydrangeas – his eyes set on the glistening depths of the darkened lake beyond.

Though Winston was undoubtedly the boss, I was actually his mentor within the Society – having recruited him following the Battle of Spion Kop during the Second Boer War, when he had been a mere lieutenant and a journalist. I'd watched with pride as he had risen through the ranks. Because of the Blood, I had barely aged in the past forty-five years; but the war had taken its toll on the seventy-year-old since we'd last met.

I sensed immediately that he knew he had lost the election.

"Why don't you stop lurking?" he called from his chair.

That voice! Bullish, indefatigable, reassuring – I'd heard it so often these past few years, defiantly issued from the wireless. Stepping from the shadows, I grinned – it was our first meeting since he had won the war. Brushing away my congratulations, he poured me a whisky.

"It's good to see you. But the war is far from over."

I nodded. "Japan."

He handed me a note. It read, '*Babies satisfactorily born.*'

His eyes were burning. Winston had a famously unconventional relationship with sleep, choosing to nap for five hours at night from about three in the morning and then again for another two hours in the late afternoon. It worked well for him. He seemed sharp as a bell, even as it was approaching midnight.

"Are you familiar with the Manhattan Project?" he asked. When I shook my head, he tried, "You certainly know James Chadwick."

Chadwick, I knew. One of our finest minds, who'd won the Nobel Prize for Physics following his discovery of the neutron, he'd just this year been knighted. He was a member of the Society, naturally – and like all members, like myself and Churchill, a powerful psychic.

"He has been in the States," the Prime Minister said. "Continuing his research in tandem with the Americans. Several of our best men are out there. Remember Rudolf Peierls, Otto Frisch? They've been researching into the explosive power of uranium."

My heart skipped a beat.

"You're talking about an atomic bomb."

He held my gaze. "Yesterday, out in New Mexico, we had the first ever detonation of a nuclear device. Went by the codename 'Trinity'. The word is it was massive. There's talk of a yield of twenty kilotons of TNT."

"I don't really understand the science."

"You don't need to. All you need to know is that it's going to end the war."

I saw the logic – the strength of the explosion would be such a show of power that the enemy would immediately fold. But the Japanese were stubborn, fiercely set on honour; in the field of battle, their definition of defeat was famously to take as many of the enemy with them as possible…

For some reason, my stomach lurched.

"You intend to terrorise them into submission."

"It is the only way," he countered, catching my tone. "We are talking about the Japanese: surrender is not in their dictionary. They are 'one hundred million hearts beating as one' in a holy mission from their God-Emperor. They think in a way no westerner could ever grasp. Did you know that at Okinawa there were reports of civilians leaping from cliffs to their deaths – including mothers *with their children in their arms* – rather than face capture? As a nation, they are convinced that we are barbarians and that to succumb to us is a fate worse than death."

Setting the whisky down, I rose to my feet and peered into the night, following the rationale out loud: "No matter how much you hit the military, they'll keep on coming. They'll resist in the most ferocious manner possible…"

"The samurai is in my opinion the most formidable human fighting machine in history," he continued. "And he inhabits – no, his spirit *possesses* – every single Japanese soldier. We're up against centuries of feudal law and brainwashing about 'the way of the warrior'. How does one combat the kamikaze mentality? Its very definition is 'divine wind'...

"They will stand and fight to the bitterest end."

Looking at my feet now, I asked, "You've crunched the numbers, I assume?"

He knew what I was driving at – could this really be preferable to a land invasion?

"It was called 'Operation Downfall' and until today it was set for October. From Okinawa, we were to strike at Kyushu, then in a separate strike we would hit Honshu and from there take Tokyo. And here is the crucial point, Robert – here are your numbers..."

He held his hand in mid-air, pointedly, demanding my complete attention.

"Before you come at me over this, consider this: the Combined Chiefs of Staff met two years ago to estimate what level of resistance we might expect to encounter in a land invasion of Japan; the British contingent was led by Mountbatten. From the outset, they anticipated being opposed by – and I quote – a 'fanatically hostile population'. And I stress that this was two years even before Okinawa.

"Our casualty estimates vary wildly, but I predict around half a million American and a quarter million British. If the locals continue to hurl themselves off cliffs at the current rate, civilian casualties would be well into the millions – Okinawa was home to around three hundred thousand, of whom it is estimated at least a tenth, and perhaps as many as a third, died during the battle."

I wanted to say that it wasn't our battle, that Japan was far, far away and couldn't it just be left alone; we had peace in Europe, could we not leave the Pacific to its own devices? But I knew that he'd talk about our allies and how Japan was virtually on the American doorstep and how there was a score to settle after Pearl Harbor. Like so many Brits, I'd protest that the blinking Yanks had been three years late to the party, but Winnie would overrule me – saying that had the sleeping giant not awakened, we would all now be learning how to goosestep and eat sauerkraut.

"So, we massacre civilians?" I asked bitterly.

He downed his whisky.

"Trinity and her brood are Heaven-sent, my friend. A gift from God. The moment I read that note, I actually felt a weight lift and the spectre of a protracted, horrendous nightmare dissipate. I read that note and saw a vision fair and bright – the end of the war in one or two violent shocks."

Seeing my expression, the man I'd personally recruited into the Society smiled wryly and asked, "Are we having a 'Frankenstein's Monster' moment? Yes, this is what you created. And you created it because Great Britain needed it. I was here at the right moment to make the right decisions – so you didn't have to."

I couldn't help myself. "Aren't you just rushing to clear the decks before you have to move out of Number Ten?"

"Attlee is of a similar mind, I think you'll find."

"And Truman?" I was desperately looking for somebody to turn to who had enough authority to veto.

"It was Truman who approached me, with his intentions to strike should the test go well. It's his call really – though ironically, I've known about it longer than he has. The project may be American, but we have supported it all the way. It was Roosevelt's baby, God rest his soul."

Harry S. Truman had only found out upon entering office in April that the Allies were close to creating a new, massively destructive weapon. He had been Vice President for just three months before Roosevelt's poor health had stolen him from the world. In three months, Truman had gone from Senator for Missouri to the man who could mete out death and destruction upon a nation. It seemed to me he could hardly be even remotely qualified to make this sort of call.

I silently shook my head in disbelief at the place we had come to. In my youth, war had been about swords, muskets and armadas… I did not like the twentieth century.

"Stalin, then?"

This was a futile hope. Joseph Stalin had already well established his reputation for human rights abuses – and that was with his own people!

"He doesn't know yet. We're going to tell him here."

I wondered how the Russians would react to the news. Undoubtedly, they already had their own atomic weapons programme in place, but I feared this would simply goad them into a greater distrust of the West.

Churchill nodded in agreement. "A slippery customer, that one. You know the Japanese believe they can count on Russian neutrality?"

There was a pact, which Japan and Russia had signed back in 1941. In our twisted 'world war' up until now, Russia had been at war with Germany but not with Japan. The treaty would have meant considerable peace of mind to Stalin and Emperor Hirohito, as neither had needed to be concerned about a fight breaking out on their back doorsteps.

"Well, at the Yalta Conference back in February," Churchill continued. "Stalin agreed that following the surrender of German, the Soviet Union will *declare war* on Japan. How's that for slippery?"

He eyed me with a wily glint in his eye.

"Which brings me to my next point: this has been for some time the most important race in the history of the war, albeit a race that for most people has gone unnoticed. It was Einstein himself who sounded the alarm to Roosevelt that Hitler was developing an A-bomb and thank God he did, because it gave our own programme the shot in the arm it needed." He chuckled to himself, adding, "There's a pleasing irony in Adolf driving all those talented Jews our way."

It struck me that Winston had undone his own argument.

"But ultimately, we didn't *need* to use it on the Germans," I pointed out.

He grumbled at me. "The Germans had a programme, the Russians certainly have one – the Japanese have one too. If we hold back, it will be our civilians who pay. We need to establish our authority, Robert."

"Over the USSR?"

He eyed me with distant irritation, saying, "Those left-wing leanings – you've always been too soft on the Soviets."

Did I have 'left-wing leanings'? The twentieth century had left me utterly bewildered. I only knew that I loved the human race and my country – in that order, not the other way around.

"The Russians have paid the highest price in the war," I countered.

"We couldn't have won without them," he conceded. "But you should always remember that Stalin would happily have sat it out and watched Hitler carve us up."

That was true – up until Hitler's 'Operation Barbarossa' in June 1941, Russia and Germany had enjoyed a pact of mutual non-aggression.

I sighed. This seemed to me to be the tip of a particularly nasty iceberg – and that we were all on the Titanic.

"Have you considered the long-term implications?"

Churchill was lighting one of his trademark cigars. He puffed on it and blew out a smoke ring.

"Indeed," he answered, wryly. "Think of all those millions of children and grandchildren who will have happy memories of elderly fathers and grandfathers; of all the potential that will now pour into our culture and economy, instead of draining into the soil of some jungle on the other side of the world; of the poems that will now be written, the paintings painted, the inventions invented, the romances romanced. Because our boys didn't die on Japanese beaches."

He rose and came to stand beside me. We took in the crisp midnight air and listened to the sounds of the lake for a while. I could not speak. When he finally broke the silence, his tone was softer and more solemn.

"I do not mean to sound flippant, Robert. Our enemy entered this war with their eyes open. God knows, I dearly wish I could have closed mine tight shut these past six years. But the things I see when they *are* closed…"

I knew he was talking of the other war – the one all psychic sleepers were waging. Our secret universe, hidden from the eyes of ordinary mortals, reflected every horror in the physical world like a malevolent mirror and was currently a very dark, unwelcoming place.

"Why did you summon me here, if you'd already decided?"

"For a fresh, honest perspective, from someone I knew would challenge me."

I had thought that perhaps he had finally decided it was time to take the Blood and retire from service to this world – with the end of the war and his defeat in the election, it seemed a good time. The vial was in my pocket.

"Don't think that hasn't occurred to me," he said, reading my mind. "But I've at least another twenty years in me yet – and I rather fancy a second term in office."

Impulsively, I reached out and grasped him by the arm.

"Evacuate Okinawa," I urged. "And drop your bomb there. Fire a shot across their bow, rather than going straight for the jugular. They're *civilians*, man – think of the children…"

His expression hardened. Though we were old friends, there was a warning in his gaze that said I should know better – after the grief we'd endured – than to remind him of all the little ones who must have suffered as a result of his decisions.

"Robert," he growled, "we must compel their surrender forthwith, by any means necessary. We shall bring them low, shock them, shatter their resolve by undermining any illusions they are clinging to. If it is mass suicide they want, we'll serve it up to them in the shape of one hundred pounds of enriched uranium."

The subject was clearly closed – but the conversation was far from over.

"There is another reason for my bringing you here." He had changed tack and now seemed concerned, even a little rueful. "Two of the Society's best are on a mission out there and have been ignoring my orders for them to return."

"Which two?"

"The Mayfairs."

I rolled my eyes. "Oh, bloody hell, Winnie…"

There were few who could have gotten away with snapping at the British Prime Minister like that, but he could be quite childlike and self-effacing with close friends – especially when he was at fault.

"You know what Cassie Mayfair is like," he offered with a grimace. "She had her peacemaker's head on again – and to be honest, if anybody could charm the Emperor…"

"She's gone to negotiate with *Hirohito*?"

I'd brought Cassandra and Jack Mayfair and their children into our fold myself, back in 1832. Jack had been a docker in Liverpool, while the rest of the family had worked at a cotton mill. They were the only all-psychic family I had ever encountered: while Jack and the older girl were powerfully Gifted fighters and the youngest had extraordinary powers of projection, Cassandra's ability was empathy.

She could walk into a room and within seconds take the measure of the tensions and relationships of all present; she could sense your secrets and pick them open before she'd even said hello. She knew what frightened you, what pain you were in, how screwed up you were – even before you could say hello back. Best of all, by the time you'd shaken hands with her, she'd have worked out how to make you feel better.

Cassandra Mayfair had played a part in defusing every major British conflict of the last century. Her modus operandi was to 'alleviate, pacify, reconcile'. It made sense: if Cassie was to be anywhere on the planet right now, it would be Tokyo.

Jack, on the other hand, was a cross between a hothead and a Rottweiler, who'd punch you in the face as soon as look at you; but he worshipped the ground she walked on. Somehow, they made a perfect team.

"It was her idea, of course," the Prime Minister continued, "and I'd hoped that somehow we could avoid more bloodshed. The reports from Okinawa have led me to conclude that we cannot."

He glanced indoors and checked his watch.

"I've paperwork to attend to." Turning to go, he added with a wink, "Lovely chat."

"Wait," I started. "That's it?"

He shrugged. "Get them back, Robert. That is all."

"How long have I got?"

He hesitated, seemed to decide that he'd given away enough state secrets already this evening – and that one more wouldn't make much difference.

"They're going to need to be well clear of Japan by August. And absolutely nowhere near Hiroshima..."

- CHAPTER TWO -

In A Thousand Years Was Her Beauty Built

Driving back through the ravaged, desiccated skeleton of Berlin, I wondered how many knew – whether it was thousands yet, or still just hundreds, and how many of them had found themselves wrestling with the right and wrong of it. I wondered how many new conspirators there were today – checking my watch, I found it was now a few hours into Wednesday. He'd told me just an hour ago…

Was I the first on this date in history to learn they were going to drop a bomb on the children of Hiroshima? As exclusive clubs went, I could have done without being a member. Had any of the others also thought about breaking rank, trying to warn the Japanese of the oncoming horror?

By now, Churchill and the other Allied leaders – not to mention the leaders of the Axis powers – had all become acclimatised to making decisions that signed the death warrants of thousands. I did not doubt that they were sick to their stomachs of it; but it must have grown easier. At times, sat in their offices a long way from the bloodshed, they must inevitably have become disconnected from the reality of it.

What disturbed me most was that I could see the justification: why *not* sacrifice a few thousand more pawns on the chess board if it really could bring about a decisive end?

Having distinguished himself, *Major* Robert Tulliver was deemed important enough to merit his own driver. I was free to gaze out the window onto the passing husk of the German capital, street after darkened, eerily unpopulated street. What was left of the populace God alone knew: while at the centres of occupation we had generators to provide electric light, the once-triumphant metropolis seemed a deserted wasteland. There was the odd fire or flickering candles at shattered windows, but the Berliners had been reduced to little more than vermin scurrying through the rubble.

The numbers were simply too huge to grasp. Once the dust had settled, over eighty thousand Soviet troops and more than two hundred thousand Germans – military and civilian – lay dead.

I was jolted from my reveries by a glimpse of a young boy, caught fleetingly in our headlights. Dirty and malnourished, he peered at us with a feral glare before darting into the moonlit shadows.

"Stop here," I ordered. "You may head home for the night."

Climbing out of the car, I waited for the glow of his headlights to fade then called out in German, "I know you are here."

The boy peered out from behind a burnt-out Opel Blitz truck. His frightened mind was easy to read: he was an orphan and his name was Jürgen. He was very hungry.

"There are soup kitchens, Jürgen," I said. "I will take you."

Producing my secret weapon – a military-ration Hershey bar – I wooed him out. He could have been no more than fourteen. Just six years ago, as a carefree eight-year-old, these streets would have been his playground.

And now we were about to pour fire upon another playground…

"I need to get to the Unter den Linden," I continued. "Could you guide me there?"

The boy nodded and, given the 'candy boost' that was soon fuelling him, it was a workout keeping pace. My driver could have taken me there in half the time, but I wanted to ensure that young Jürgen was cared for.

The Unter den Linden was one of the most famous, historic boulevards in Berlin, running from the Brandenburg Gate to the Stadtschloss Palace at the Lustgarten; about a third of the way along it heading west stood the Prussian State Library. I had no idea how its precious collections had fared during the bombing, but I knew one thing: beneath its Neo Baroque columns and pediments lay the Waiting Room for the German Hub of the Society – and my easiest access point into our secret universe of dreams.

As there was still concern about possible guerrilla resistance, the boulevard was teeming with uniforms. Jürgen was uneasy around the foreign soldiers. I dreaded to think whether he might have witnessed any reprisals.

As we walked, I realised that I had encountered the boy before, dreaming of Christmas presents in the ruins of his home. His had been the feeling of *loss* I snatched as I'd passed through. It had been he who had been desperately reaching to believe in a time of gifts, before the taking began. I became determined then to look in on Jürgen from time to time, for the rest of his life.

Because of its thick granite walls, the *Staatsbibliothek* had withstood the worst of the bombs, though closer inspection revealed that it was pockmarked with blast damage and bullet holes. The main entrance was chained shut, but we found an unlocked employee's entrance. Inside, there was evidence of a huge explosion: the bomb looking to have dropped in through the dome over the main, circular reading room. Debris was strewn everywhere, not one pane of glass remained intact and the doors hung from their hinges. You could peer down into several levels of basement.

Concerned about the structural integrity of the building, I hesitated.

"And so, it is over."

I started, surprised to have missed the presence of another in the room. In the shadows, amongst the buckled book cases, I spied a familiar face – and joyfully bounded across to shake his hand.

"Kästner! You are alive, man! Happy news at last."

"Despite my best efforts, I think," Erich Kästner replied with a weary smile. "How is peacetime finding you?"

"I wish that it *was* finding me," I countered, bitterly. "But what about you? I heard they burnt your books."

He nodded. "They were 'contrary to the German spirit', apparently. They burnt very well, in the company of some splendid fellows: Thomas Mann, Heinrich Heine, Karl Marx, Erich Maria Remarque. I was very proud of them."

At forty-six years of age, Kästner's ardent pacifism, satirical bent and supposed 'Bolshevist' leanings had attracted the personal attention of Goebbels and Hitler. Although he had publicly opposed the rise of the Nazis – and despite interrogation by the Gestapo – he had remained in Berlin for most of the war.

We had met in our dreams several times, but this was the first time I'd encountered him physically.

"How did you manage to survive?"

"Attending the funeral of my own works showed a degree of willing," Erich replied, dryly. "I played ball with the Nazis during the war, keeping my head down and participating in the odd snippet of propaganda for the Reich. It was probably my being a children's writer, and thus deemed a bit simple, that saved my life – talking of children, who do we have here?"

His eyes had dropped to Jürgen, who was hovering behind me. I explained how I had acquired my young ward.

"I see," Erich continued. He beamed at the boy. "Have you read 'Emil und die Detektive', young man?"

The poor, bedraggled boy nodded, mutely and wide-eyed.

"Well I wrote that."

He approached the boy, eyes twinkling. "If you stay with me, at least until we can find you a comfortable home, I promise to tell you some very good stories! If you head into the next room, you will spy near the door my bag, in which you will find a cheese and ham sandwich and an apple – I rather think they were meant for you."

As Jürgen dashed off after this feast, Erich explained how he and his fellow filmmakers – anticipating the imminent carnage – had managed to smuggle themselves out of Berlin, using the cover story of filming on location. They had been in the relative safety of the countryside when the Soviets fell upon the capital.

We surveyed the ruins of the library for a moment.

"It looks bad, I know," he said, "but we have their senior administrator Hugo Krüss to thank – he ensured that much of the collection was removed last year and squirreled away to safety in various monasteries and mines. Alas, Krüss poisoned himself on the day of the Soviet invasion – he loved this place so much, he came to die here."

I felt desperately sorry for Krüss. It must have seemed to him that the apocalypse had begun and the world was coming to an end – when in fact it was about to be reborn. But through his actions, all those works had been saved; hope had risen again out of the ashes of tragedy.

If an orphan can begin to heal through chocolate and stories, if an author can survive the killer gaze of twisted minds to make it his life's work to lift young ones, if a librarian can defy blind destruction to rescue a wealth of wisdom, there would always be hope.

My own mentor, Thomas More, had once said to me, "You will always find a candle of light glimmering in the darkness, no matter how deep the night may seem."

Erich and I shook our heads at the absurdity of it all.

"In 1821," he began, "over a hundred years before they danced on these streets hurling his work into the flames, Heine wrote 'where they burn books, they will ultimately burn people as well'. I think the state of a nation's libraries will always reflect the state of mind of its people."

He gestured to the desolation before us. "A perfect metaphor, don't you think?"

I nodded – and wondered whether the libraries back home stood empty.

Taking a breath, I declared, "I have to travel into Halcyon."

He stared at me. "You are a brave man."

It was the only way, I had decided. To *physically* travel to Japan – surely one of the most dangerous journeys in the world at that time – would be madness. The travel time alone was prohibitive and there were countless people along the way who would want to kill me.

I would have to reach the Mayfairs with my mind.

"I'm sure you have thought this through. The collective subconscious is not a pretty place to be right now – and to enter it from Berlin…"

"I have no choice," I interrupted grimly.

Erich Kästner blinked. "Follow me."

Pausing to encourage Jürgen to curl up on a nearby mattress and to lay a small blanket over him, we took stairs down a level then along a subterranean corridor leading away from the desiccated reading room. As the moonlight ceased to penetrate, we found the corridor was lined with candles. The further down we went, the less damaged the corridors were: by the third storey down, things felt normal – and familiar.

In London, our Waiting Room was beneath a Gentleman's Club off Pall Mall. Down there, the walls were paneled wood; here they were polished marble and granite. The approach felt similar but sounded different, our footfalls being sharper and less muffled.

He wordlessly opened a door for me, his eyes advising me against this. Within was a familiar arrangement: a vast, darkened dormitory-style room populated with numerous beds, like a luxurious refugee centre…

Back home, there was a constant turnover of sleepers, a busy traffic of psychics dropping in to sneak a few hours of astral travel into their day before returning to the 'normal' world. There were always a number of long-term sleepers too, people who lived long stretches of their lives in our subconscious universe.

From her desk over in the corner, the solitary waking soul in the room, a nurse in her sixties looked up – surprised to have company. Her bunks were mostly deserted. I counted just seven lonely sleepers.

"They are the lost," Erich said. "Their minds have never returned to their bodies."

"How long have they been here?"

The nurse joined us now, introducing herself as Gertrud. Like Erich, she thought me mad to want to enter the dreamstate – explaining that when she slept these days, she always made a point of taking sedatives to deaden her senses.

"When word spread that their physical bodies might be endangered by the Soviet invasion, most of our sleepers returned to their bodies and fled. Many said they would have left Halcyon anyway – it is no longer a nice place to be."

Having astral travelled quite recently, I always endeavoured to avoid the congested areas of the dream world – knowing all too well how the shared subconscious can be distressed in times of war.

"Has any effort been made to bring these people back?"

She shrugged. "They are hiding, or they are lost."

Perhaps they had eschewed physical existence entirely: it was not unknown. Some never returned to their still-breathing bodies. A vast, psychic library of everything ever learnt or imagined – it was all too possible to become disorientated in there…

But Gertrud lowered her voice, as if she feared that we were being listened in on. "The returned have talked in terms of Halcyon itself *screaming…*"

Erich frowned. "As if in pain?"

She nodded, fearfully. "Some have told stories of it turning on them in anger at the crimes being committed. Engulfing them…" Gertrud peered pointedly at the lost sleepers and added, "Perhaps these are not so much the lost, but the *taken*."

I took a breath. It would be a long time before the collective memory of the horror could begin to fade. We fell silent, each thinking of the daily revelations about the fate of the Jews of Europe…

I steeled myself. I had friends to save.

There was however a practical concern: the presence of so few sleepers, in a weakened state, might mean it would be hard for me to generate the kind of psychic energy required. I was looking for an intense level of immersion, deeper perhaps than I had ever before achieved – and I'd hoped that a Waiting Room full of sleepers would amplify my powers.

Taking off my jacket, I lay down on the nearest available bed and glanced to Gertrud. "Keep an eye on me, won't you?"

She reached down to my shoulder, reassuringly.

"Good luck," Erich said, his worried frown giving way to a warm smile.

"Look after Jürgen."

"I promise."

I looked inside, searching for that ball of energy, fizzing and crackling just outside my conscious existence. Still drowsily clinging to the normal world, I slurred, "Will you go home?"

Erich Kästner comes from Dresden, I thought, remembering a happy conversation in Halcyon some years ago. He was visiting the British Hub, keen to share our love of our country; I remembered showing him our little fishing village and taking him out to sea. It had been a beautiful day and Erich had said, "You must visit me in Dresden. I was born in the most beautiful city in the world."

I felt my eyes slide up under my eyelids. The dreamstate was coming. *Goodbye, Erich, we will meet again in happier times…*

His voice was very far away. It sounded sad.

"Munich for me now, I think. Dresden is gone, my friend. 'In a thousand years was her beauty built, in one night was it utterly destroyed.'"

I know. And I wish I didn't.

But five and a half thousand miles away, there was another city like her…

I was drifting now. Drifting in the night sky, only it wasn't night. It was a galaxy of tiny lights and each light was an idea.

Reaching within, I propelled my spirit far across the globe.

- CHAPTER THREE -

Tokyo Ghosts

It's like swimming. The energy generated by other minds focused on psychic activity can boost you, help you plunge deeper in. You swim down, down and slowly a great, luminous coral reef of knowledge and learning takes shape in the depths. All around you others are immersing themselves in escape of the humdrum, to cultivate their minds and soak up the vast wealth of experience left by the human footprint, where everything that was ever imagined takes flight.

But I describe the Halcyon of modern times.

In 1945, the luminescence had been reduced to only a bleak glow and the psychic waters were clogged with the flotsam and jetsam of self-slaughter. There were many souls adrift here, floating by like corpses; I could pick up some resonance from them – the telepathic equivalent of occasional, bewildered blinking, signifying that the lights were on but nobody was at home. I couldn't know whether these were the lost of the Waiting Room, or sleepers from the dank cellars of Berlin. They seemed numb with shock. Wisplike apparitions, I would have taken them for ghosts, but these were the disconnected spirits of the living haunting Halcyon.

I'd visited the German Hub in peacetime. Back then it had been an Alpine landscape, rich with edelweiss and distant cowbells; its meadows had been heaving with young lovers whispering Goethe in one another's ears and the air had soared with Wagnerian harmonies.

Now there was only a black void, rippled with cracks of fire.

I passed it by, putting Germany behind me with a shudder.

Then the wailing began. From somewhere in the mists came a banshee cry of bottomless torment – first one then another, then more and more until it was a cacophany of ferocious anguish. So many grieving souls... I tried to block them out, but they nearly overwhelmed me.

Fleeing, I lost my way for what seemed like days. The calls for help and solace seemed to emanate from the mist itself and I expected to collide at any moment with some lost, deranged soul, or to be snatched at and clung to by someone just outside my field of vision.

The children were the hardest to bear.

Japan. I needed to concentrate and envisage my destination, reach out to my friends. I held Jack and Cassie in my mind's eye and called out to them. *Hear me – please – for God's sake.*

After a time the lament began to fade, though it rang around my head long afterwards. The mists parted and I found myself flying high above the ground, so high that I could see the curve of the Earth and the sky above was turning a deeper blue. With relief, I realised that I had left the epicentre of the war behind and was passing over sparsely populated countryside largely free of the scars of the fighting. Far over to my right I briefly glimpsed shimmering blue, but the landscape that way soon dissolved into oases and desert.

"I hear you."

Who was that? It was neither of the Mayfairs. Instead, it sounded like a girl – but the language she thought in was not European. For a child to pick up my calls, she had to be extremely powerful.

"Why are you looking for Cassandra?"

There was a suspicious, protective tone to her thoughts.

She and Jack are my friends. I have an urgent message for her. Can you help me?

"What is your name?"

My name is Robert. Robert Tulliver. What is yours?

I called out to her several more times, but she had gone.

If that splash of blue had been the Caspian Sea, I was now heading east over Kazakhstan or even Mongolia. Relishing the sense of release from the darkness over Europe, I contemplated dropping down, immersing myself in the lives of those who barely knew a war had taken place. The war had probably reached even here, though – I knew Stalin had crushed the intellectual elite of Kazakhstan and the country was effectively Soviet. There were labour camps now and the Kazakhs had contributed divisions to Stalin's army.

"She will see you."

It was the girl again. I was certain this time she was Japanese. While I had still not managed to make contact with minds well known to me, this girl had intercepted the telepathic signals of a complete stranger from hundreds of miles away. What power!

Your gift is extraordinary.

"I have been told this."

Is it how you found Cassie?

"I hear all psychics long before they are aware of me. Cassandra and Jack were very obvious."

I bet they were. I wondered how two caucasian westerners had managed to smuggle themselves into Tokyo, let alone make contact with the Emperor.

"You are not concentrating effectively: my people have many Gifted and they are always vigilant for subversive elements. We must be mindful not to undo any of Cassandra's hard work."

Not only had I just been scolded by a child – who much to my chagrin had a point – it sounded like Cassie might be making progress! My heart leapt. Could this be something I could take back to Potsdam?

I promise I will stay properly focused from now on.

"The Chinese are watchful also, Robert. Let us be silent for a while."

That was Peking below. With a population of one and a half million people, it was currently the capital of the Japanese-installed, puppet 'Provisional Government of the Republic of China'. In contrast, the greater part of the Republic of China was still in the control of the Chinese Nationalist Party, the 'Kuomintang', under its leader Chiang Kai-shek – and was a key Allied power.

The Chinese and Japanese had been at war since 1937 and butting heads for some years before. My head ached at the statistics: between five and twenty million dead, depending on who you believed.

Once we were out at sea and heading towards Korea, I chanced breaking the silence.

Do you have a name?

"My name is Sachiko. It means 'child of bliss' and can also be taken to mean 'happiness'. My friends call me Sachi."

Nice to meet you, Sachi.

"You are premature."

I apologise. Sachiko, it is.

Korea had been annexed by Japan in 1910. There had been an anti-Japanese independence movement ever since, with protestors often harshly dealt with. There was a 'Provisional Government of the Republic of Korea', based in exile in Shanghai: they had their own military, the Korean Liberation Army, which – although barely a thousand strong – had participated in Allied missions.

Soon, we were soaring over the Sea of Japan and out of habit I began gathering intelligence on the enemy – I'd spent much of the past six years in etheric travel, roaming the Earth with my mind on behalf of my country. The Society had been extensively engaged in espionage activities: uncomfortable territory ethically and morally for us, as traditionally we'd sought to exclude ourselves from the wars of normal men.

Hitler had been a different case.

I spied for an estimation of Japan's naval strength. It's not easy to see huge chunks of steel using the Gift: the mind looks for life, for telepathic signals, so it's easier to seek out people – much easier for sea than land, obviously, there being fewer souls on the sea.

These waters were quieter than I'd expected.

"You will find no big ships, Robert."

They are all in the Pacific?

"They are mostly at the bottom *of the Pacific. Those that are left have withdrawn to the naval base at Kure."*

By 'big ships', I assumed Sachi was referring to the capital ships of Japan's navy, the lead warships in the fleet, markedly larger than others – battleships and aircraft carriers, as opposed to destroyers. If what she said was true, the Japanese navy was on crutches – surely this could only strengthen the case against any further bombing of their civilian population?

Where is Kure? I will need to go there.

"It is near my family home, in the Hiroshima prefecture."

A shiver of dread rushed through me.

We dropped from the sky, swooping low across Japan. Half again the size of the United Kingdom, we shared an 'island nation' identity: for them Honshu was the mainland, with Hokkaido lying to the north and the smaller Kyushu and Shikoku to the south. A country of meadows, forests and mountains, Honshu was not dissimilar in size to England, Scotland and Wales combined, while Hokkaido was comparable to Ireland. Japan's total landmass included all the islands in its archipelago, however, which numbered nearly two and a half thousand.

When the Allies had taken Okinawa, it must have hurt the Japanese as an invasion of the Isle of Wight would hit home to the British; or like the loss the Americans would feel if Hawaii was occupied.

Sachi brought us in towards Tokyo via Mount Fuji. Gazing out across the Pacific, indifferent to the oncoming storm, the volcano hadn't erupted since 1707 – but I could well understand why it was deemed holy. Dotted with shrines, it seemed like one of nature's humbling sentinels: a warning to know our place. Barely hours ago, I had learnt that mankind had created similar destructive power in a laboratory and turned it into a weapon against himself.

In the shadow of Mount Fuji, a reminder of our transience, it was a bitter pill that we had eschewed all humility in a quest to be the new gods of this planet...

"Getting a bit mawdlin in your old age, Robert?"

There was no mistaking the Scouse irreverence.

It could only be Jack Mayfair, whose sanity I had saved – along with his family – one hundred and thirteen years earlier. It was hard to believe that over a century had passed since I'd first come across a very different man – tormented by a Gift he did not understand and practically wild with grief as his children lay dying from cholera.

That you, Jack? What did you do with Sachiko?

"She's not one for chatting."

I'd noticed.

"I'll be your guide for the approach into Tokyo. Welcome to Mayfair Airways."

These were 'mind miles' and we were there in minutes. Coming in low from the south-west, over spectacular mountain ridges and along verdant green valleys, I was soon passing over sparsely populated areas with thatched farmhouses, then more densely packed low-roofed merchants' *machiya* townhouses – wooden with red or grey baked slate roofs. Occasionally, I glimpsed intricate and colourful pagoda-style temples and this was a thrill, because the architecture would always be exotic to me.

This wasn't my first foray into Japan. I'd been here physically centuries earlier and had a samurai encounter of my own. Nostalgia fireworks were going off in my mind.

Tokyo's cramped network of cobbled streets and alleys, sprung from centuries of sprawling growth, were heaving with life. At the outset of the war, the population of the Japanese capital was nearing seven million, as opposed to London – the second largest city in the world, after New York – with its population of over eight and a half million. By the end of 1945, it would be reduced by over five million.

Swooping in with the coast to my right, I could see the new metropolis spraying inland from Tokyo Bay, through dense forest and cloud-catching mountains – but it was the sight to the east, in the direction of the docks, that stalled me. It looked like God had poured a bucket of acid across the city.

There was no way to tell whether I was looking at industrial or residential areas; all that was left was a grid of streets dotted with the occasional skeleton of gutted masonry, standing like a headstone over stretches of razed earth. The destruction was so dizzyingly obscene I struggled to get my head around it. As much as a quarter of the city had been seared away.

"Isn't she pretty, Tokyo?"

It looks recent.

"March. The ninth if you want to celebrate an anniversary. You've got to love the B-29 Superfortress – she's sooo *super!"*

Once the Americans had captured the Pacific, particularly the Northern Mariana Islands in late 1944, they had been positioned to launch their bombers upon the city. On the ninth of March, they'd dropped one and a half tons of incendiary bombs on Tokyo – each one unleashing enough white heat to melt a brick wall, onto a populace living within flimsy wood.

"She's a thing of beauty, the incendiary bomb. Pure, you know? Uncomplicated. She doesn't quail at right or wrong, she just gives birth to thirty-eight bouncing babies in the sky over your house and one of those punches a discreet little hole through your roof; then after a polite pause for introductions, her baby vomits napalm all over your carpet."

You're not sounding your usual merry self, Jack.

"Oh, I'm a warmonger, Robert – you know that. I don't suffer fools and the stuff Hitler and his cronies got up to, well, that's a whole nasty orgy of malice. I've no time for cry-baby pacifists who mewl on about people's rights. Put the gun in my hand, that's what I say."

I was being drawn away from the firebombed remains of the docks area, back over the heart of the city and then a little further north – down, down towards a temple…

"I think it's safe to say the Yanks have had the last word about Pearl Harbor, though."

In his unique acerbic way, Jack was right. To this day, historians cannot decide how many Japanese civilians died in the bombings of the ninth of March, but the estimates starts at ninety thousand. In contrast, the death count at Pearl Harbor had been two and a half thousand – of which less than a hundred had been civilians.

"If ever there was evidence that the Japanese don't have an air force any more, there it is."

How do you mean?

"It took the Germans most of a year to kill half the number of British civilians that we managed to kill in one night *here. We might celebrate the Battle of Britain as the RAF's great last stand against the Blitz, but the Japanese will never get to have any such party."*

I found him standing beneath a Japanese willow tree, dressed in the saffron robes of a monk, casually dragging on a Lucky Strike. The disguise wouldn't have fooled anyone who looked closely, but Jack Mayfair had long ago perfected telepathic techniques to befuddle the close look…

"What's up?" he asked with a smirk. "Don't I carry it off?"

Will you be wearing it home?

"Could get used to it. It's very cooling on the old knackers."

With it being the height of summer, I could sense the heat and humidity – not least from the beads of sweat on Jack's forehead. Of course, I couldn't *feel* the heat…

"Thinking of converting," he was saying. "All this talk of enlightenment and harmony with nature – not squishing flies and whatnot – is very endearing. They do so much chanting and weaving, it's a wonder they ever find the time for butchering their neighbours."

He finished his cigarette and unceremoniously flicked the butt away. Gestured towards the temple.

"We lucked out with our monks. Religion is a big part of the problem here."

You're talking about the 'holy' war?

"Who do you think whips up all the fanatics? Kamikaze pilots don't nosedive destroyers because they adore cherry blossom; hundreds of mothers don't cradle their children to the bottom of Suicide Cliff because they're a bit scared. These people have not one shred of doubt that their Emperor is divine, a God on Earth – and that his word is the absolute truth. If he says a glorious death leads to eternal honour and joyous reunion with your ancestors, and that their fate in the hands of the Allies would be unbearable, that's the way it is."

He briefly brought me up to speed: they'd smuggled themselves in from China, using Society connections to speed their journey, which even then had taken over a month. This had involved great diplomacy, as loyalties were just as polarised in the world of the Gifted; but psychics have empathy and intuition and the Mayfairs' peace mission had fallen on favour.

Reaching Tokyo, they had sought an open-minded reception amongst the monks, Shinto and Buddhist – both religions sympathetic to the potential of the mind to enter a spiritual state and achieve higher being. But despite having a list of the Gifted among the priests of Tokyo, they had ended up on the streets: most of the shrines and temples had been bombed and many of their contacts were dead.

Two weeks ago, they had established contact with a Japanese member of the Society, the chief priest – or *gūji* – at the Kanda Shrine, not far from the Imperial Palace. Since then, Cassie had spent her time exploring local connections to achieve an audience with the Emperor – while Jack had haunted the area like a ghost, listening in to conversations at teahouses and markets, or stalking the periphery of the palace to eavesdrop on the thoughts of Hirohito's advisors.

I'd swear he could actually see me, but to Jack at that moment I was just a disembodied voice in his head. Even if he had been in trance, I would have appeared to him as a blaze of auras.

"Come for a walk with me," he said aloud. "I'm afraid it's not pretty."

The Kanda Shrine consisted of several small buildings clustered around a large shrine building and lined with peaceful gardens, dressed with maples and acers and larger bonsai trees, all elegantly pruned. All the buildings were rectangular and in the *irimoya* style of the hip and gable roof, sloping down to verandas on all four sides, their tiles rising and falling in undulating peaks and crests. Decorated with lanterns, they were striking vermillion lined with gold. There were numerous kami statues here as well as the familiar guardian lions. Although twelve hundred years old, it had seen extensive restoration following the devastating earthquake of 1923, but you would not know there was more concrete here than in most Shinto shrines – with its pillars and sliding doors, it seemed like a wooden structure.

"I like going inside the monks' heads – the Japanese have nailed tranquil contemplation. Which is why what is happening to this gorgeous nation is so disturbing."

What do you mean?

"These people have put their reason to sleep."

I followed him out of the gate. The shop frontages here were laced with lanterns and the Japanese *tategaki* style of vertical writing in logographic symbols, so impenetrable to the eyes of a westerner.

"Check out the average passerby."

He was keeping his head down. It must have been a constant, incredible danger to be Caucasian in the Japanese capital at the height of war. Jack could easily blend in amongst the ordinary populace, but Japan had psychics too…

I listened in to passing thoughts: my mind drifting from a shopkeeper to a geisha girl, onto a rickshaw runner and a crippled beggar. They seemed a humble, peaceable people, little concerned with the war.

"They're a bunch of darlings. Note, however: very little dissent..."

We'd seen this before, many times: people the world over prefer to plod on with little awareness of 'affairs of state'. They reason there's little they can do to affect such matters, it's above their station, the guys at the top must know what they're doing, and so on. In the name of an 'easy life', they actively cultivate blissful ignorance. Because to engage with such highfalutin issues as the morality of their country's foreign policy might lead them to catch a glimpse of something in the mirror that will disturb their bliss.

"They are content to follow like lambs wherever their Emperor leads. Apparently, he is literally a descendant of the goddess Amaterasu. His is a divine ancestry 'unbroken for ages eternal' – or something."

We stopped at a school, two ghosts at a window – one a shadow, the other barely there at all. It was an elementary school. The children must have been about eight.

"Aw bless," he chuckled, darkly. "They're singing."

To my ears, the song was enchanting.

"It's the second national anthem, *Umi Yukaba.* More popular at the moment than the more traditional *Kimgayo.* The words are very stirring; they go, 'Across the seas, there are corpses in the water. Across the seas, there are corpses in the grass. We shall die at the side of our emperor. We shall not turn back.'"

He left the lyrics hanging in the air. We listened on – and I wondered whether an atomic bomb might *save* these children. Dropped far away, but close enough to establish that the war could not be won, it would ensure they would not fight, that they might never have to kill.

"Many of these schools have a small temple building about the size of a garden shed called a *Hō-an-den,*" he whispered, "in which are housed photographs of the Emperor. The children are encouraged to worship regularly at this mini-shrine. It is held in such devout veneration that when said photies were accidentally burnt in a fire, the principal responsible for their care took his own life in atonement."

He turned and grinned, adding, "A photo gets burned and you top yourself. How do you like them apples on the state-sponsored, fanatical overreaction front?"

Jack turned his back on the school, stalking away.

"There's a document they keep in there, which the kids are required to know off by heart and gets read aloud at assembly; it's called the *Imperial Rescript.* It says that in a national emergency they should 'Offer yourselves courageously to the state'...

"Then it goes on to say that it's their duty to guard the Imperial prosperity, which is *coeval* with heaven and earth. Now that's a good word, 'coeval' – had to look it up. Means 'having the same origins of'. So, they're brainwashing those kids daily to believe that they have a personal responsibility to safeguard, with their *lives,* Hirohito and the greatness of Japan for all time..."

He ducked down an alleyway to lean against a wall. It took him a while to calm down.

"I've been in their heads for weeks. Don't get me wrong, these are beautiful people, which is why they're breaking my heart."

He looked furtively both ways along the alleyway. At the far end, a Japanese peasant woman in a kimono was struggling towards us carrying her wares for the market.

"One of their teachers has in her possession a ticking time bomb – an Allied leaflet air-dropped a few weeks ago. It names the Jap cities that may be destroyed by American bombs; says they're targets because of military installations or factories producing military supplies. It warns that 'bombs have no eyes' and that the Yanks don't wish to injure innocent people, so they should evacuate. It urges them to demand better leaders!"

He grimaced then laughed, bitterly.

"If she's found in possession of that leaflet, she's had it. The authorities respond harshly to any hint of defeatism. But the Yanks are away with the fairies – there's no chance for any civilian who tries to 'demand better leaders'."

As the old lady passed by, he bowed to her in respect. She gave him a strange look – as anyone would to a monk talking to himself down an alleyway. Jack carried off a passable Shinto chant to cover it up.

"You're a long way from home, Robert. Is it the American invasion? Is something about to happen?"

Churchill wants you out. They've a new bomb…

"Listen, the Japanese are beat. They've probably been beat since Pearl Harbor, but these guys have turned denial into an art form. A new type of bomb will just fan the flames of their defiance…"

Just one *of these bombs will match the damage inflicted in March.*

He stared. His eyes darted around as he began to think.

"Okay…" he said, slowly. "Come with me."

We proceeded, emerging upon another temple even more impressive than the Kanda Shrine.

"The Yushima Seido," he explained. "Confucian temple. Don't ask me how that makes it any different from Shinto or Buddhist temples." He chuckled to himself again, adding, in a bad Japanese accent, "Confucius say, 'War does not decide who is right; war decide who is left!'"

We reached the Kanda River and crossed at the Hijiribashi Bridge, to be greeted by what looked like a Greek Orthodox Cathedral, with a green patina dome – an unexpected burst of the Byzantine in the middle of the Orient.

"The Holy Resurrection Cathedral of the Japanese Orthodox Church," Jack commented. "Built last century by a Russian Archbishop."

A reminder that the Japanese and the Russians were still at peace. I wondered whether it would be allowed to stand once the Emperor found out what Stalin was planning.

The streets were alive with pedestrians and vehicles; it was a cosmopolitan area, with concrete buildings of several storeys that would not look out of place in New York or Paris. It felt a million miles away from warfare. I gathered he was getting twitchy being away from Cassie, who was deep in trance back at the Kanto Shrine – he didn't like leaving her unprotected.

What did you mean when you said the Japanese have probably been beat since Pearl Harbor?

"If you're going to cripple a fleet, you've got to pulverise the hell out of it, but the American aircraft carriers weren't even at Pearl Harbor when it was attacked – and they barely tickled the Yanks' subs. The Japanese admirals' obsession with taking the Pacific by battleship means they were wrong-footed when the Americans used aircraft to reach their mainland and submarines to critically curtail their import of oil and supplies."

We walked for some time before crossing another river, to find ourselves in sight of the Palace Castle. Jack was breaking a sweat over more than just the heat – the closer we got to the Imperial Headquarters, the heavier the military presence.

"They've hardly dared whisper to themselves that their strategy was wrong from the outset," he continued. *"The Japanese military have this mentality that they're* entitled *to glory; even now, they're holding on for inevitable victory in one great, decisive battle."*

In the shade of a nearby tree, he sat and drew out his lunch from his carryall. To passing sentries, here was a Shinto priest enjoying a picnic while watching the world go by.

"This is where I leave you, old friend," he muttered under his breath. "When are they dropping this bomb of yours?"

I'm to insist you leave the country by August.

He nodded. "Don't worry about us."

I'd thought he would have qualms.

"Cassie will," he agreed, picking up my surprise. "So, I may not actually tell her."

I'd never heard Jack talk about deceiving his wife. They'd always been the most symbiotic couple I'd known. He rested his head back against the tree with a heavy sigh.

"I'm exhausted, Robert – to a level I can't begin to put into words. So is the entire human race. You know the March bombing of the docks here? Those were working people, like the people I used to be; it would have been like splashing napalm all over Merseyside, all my loved ones and every single person I even knew…

"This war needs to end."

But we're talking about tens of thousands of civilians in one push of a button…

"One bomb, a hundred, a thousand – the outcome's the same. Coventry, Dresden, Tokyo, so many more. Maybe we need a grand, insane gesture to put it all into perspective. The bigger toys we get, the further civilisation is going down the toilet. You know what? This has been a *shitty* century…"

I watched a squirrel creep down the tree, freezing as it saw Jack. It'd never occurred to me there were squirrels in Tokyo.

"Listen, Robert," Jack began, his tone grim, "you achieve more than I ever will, because you are a raving idealist and you believe in people. And I'm married to the world's most extraordinary woman, who has that same stuff going on. I'll follow her to the ends of the Earth, even though I'm nothing like that and I think you're both naive. If this experience has done anything, it's confirmed what I already thought: that the human race is essentially brutal and feral. All we'll ever do is damage one another. People like you and Cassie – with your happy-clappy belief that we can be better than this – are wonderful freaks, mate, but you're fated to die disappointed."

I held Jack in high regard and here he was speaking with such conviction that it challenged my faith. He looked up and nodded across the moat towards the palace complex.

"Right now, she's in there dancing with the Devil. Makes me nervous as hell."

The Devil, Jack – really?

"The things they've done, the horrors they've wreaked. Nanking's just the beginning. And you're telling me their Commander-in-Chief is not complicit? Pull the other one."

I was starting to understand why Jack was so twitchy. But Cassie knew how to handle herself…

"Oh, if anybody in Japan can turn Hirohito around, it's Cassandra Mayfair. As we speak, her mind's in there somewhere. When it returns to her body, if there's the slightest hint that she can get him to budge, maybe I'll tell her about the bomb – otherwise I'll whisk her out of the country."

What about Sachiko?

"Sachi? She's not even in Tokyo."

How did you find her?

"She found us. She's incredibly powerful, Robert – sensed we were in the country almost before we *were* here. She's already taken the Blood, by the way."

I was surprised. Although I hadn't set eyes on her yet, she sounded very young – it would mean she would take decades to even start to mature.

That's unusual. Any idea why?

"Same sort of deal as my girls, I gather – she'd been dangerously ill as a child."

He finished his lunch and rose to his feet. His next words melted with sarcasm.

"The Japanese are 'unique' – we already know that. They're 'special'. But did you know that apparently the Japanese are *better*? Now, the Germans were better too, but not as better as the Japanese. Need I remind you that, thirty-odd years ago, the Austrians and the Germans were better than everyone else as well – and look at how that worked out for them...

"Well now, *there's* a lesson the Japanese didn't learn when they were studying world history – oh, hang on, they don't study world history. Governments don't like history. Unless they've written it."

As he started to head back the way we'd come, head down into the crowd, blending into any shadows in his path, he left me with a parting thought.

"These people, a disease has taken root in their hearts and minds. I don't like the waters I've been bathing in. You remember I mentioned those 'mere mortals'? Go have a surf in the memories of these soldiers."

Pretty soon, he was just another Japanese amongst the sea of Japanese.

I turned to consider the Palace Castle with a growing bad feeling. This complex was extraordinary: from above, it looked like a square mile of parkland in the middle of Tokyo, but I was soon drifting through Zen gardens, over koi-heavy streams and the private Shinto shrines of the Emperor, past castle donjons shattered by recent bombing.

Throughout, I found the army men. Many were young and not yet blooded in battle, though even these were fiercely idealistic and consumed with a zealous rage for their nation and their Emperor – simmering with a fervour for greatness. It was contagious. Suddenly, I wanted to change the world for the greater good, create enlightenment for all time. I wanted to charge into battle beside them, singing joyously of the new world we would make together…

Amongst these, however, were the men who had seen service. They'd been fighting now for eight years, since 1937. Theirs had been the longest war and always righteous. Some of them had an inkling of what they'd been a party to, at what their eyes had seen and their hands had done; but they had no choice but to stave off such thoughts and bury them deep in their subconscious – where they were slowly festering.

It had been ordered. It had been endorsed by their superiors and was divinely justified. The Emperor himself coursed through them in every act performed for the greater good of their beautiful, *favoured* country – and their ancestors were watching with pride.

Their ancestors had watched with pride in the December of 1937, when they had taken Nanking; they must have rejoiced at the massacre. In the name of Imperial greatness, they'd hacked down the defenceless in unimaginable numbers…

There were flashes of memories: this sentry here had dug ditches and blinked as the bound were machine-gunned into them; this one had used a living, bound Chinese man for bayonet practice; this sergeant passing me just now had been a party to the rape and butchery of several generations of one family. The violence perpetrated upon the women and children – including babes in arms and still in the womb…

I reeled. Somewhere in the back of my mind, my own part in all this called out to haunt me…

Their ancestors had watched with pride in April 1942, when they had marched seventy thousand prisoners of war under a blazing sun across the Philippines following the Battle of Bataan. Nearly thirty percent of these died from random execution, beatings, starvation, dehydration or disease due to poor hygiene. To stumble and appear weak could be fatal, resulting in being quickly dispatched as human litter by bayonet or sword.

I looked into the mind of an officer who had been there and in a blinding moment of realisation grasped how all this was deemed to be okay. These prisoners had not been human beings, you see; they were sort of subhuman. He had absolutely no perception that it might have been he who had acted as a beast. For the moment these creatures had allowed themselves to be captured, the moment they had surrendered, they'd lost all dignity…

"Have you ever heard of Kazuo Sakamaki?"

It was Cassie. Her tone was warm and gentle, a breeze on a humid afternoon. I drifted away from these disturbed minds and allowed myself to be the moth drawn to her light.

I'm afraid the name doesn't ring any bells.

"Nor will it to the good folk of Japan. Sakamaki-san has been POW since the December of 1941. He was the sole Japanese soldier captured at Pearl Harbor and the first Japanese prisoner of the war. The poor man will be tainted by his failure to die for the rest of his life. It is a great shame to be captured and dishonour your country, your loved ones, your ancestors, your Emperor – that's a lot of people peering over your shoulder, don't you think?"

Floating through the gardens, I passed more evidence of the bombing. Yet the watchtowers of the ancient keep were untouched – a teahouse, ponds and bridges and many cherry trees – it didn't take much to imagine the blossoming colours in spring. I listened to the wind rustling through the black pines and the twitter of swallows and wagtails.

"Isn't it stunning, Robert? The Japanese seem so spiritual, so much closer to peace. For them, the seasons pass and all is inevitable."

So somehow that stoicism has been their downfall? Something slipped in through the back door – and took hold…

"Shinto has been exploited, turned into a tool for worship of empire by clever men looking to rouse 'one hundred million souls' as one spirit. Their great legends too have been used, twisted to enflame their young men; they all dream now of

being Samurai, of dying with honour. As their slow defeat begins to strangle them, they are lining up in their masses with Seppuku *on their minds."*

And to take as many of us as possible with them…

"Time and again, these past eight years, their military commanders have ordered a 'scorched earth' policy – kill all, burn all, loot all. If enemies may be pretending to be local people, then all local people are enemies; if a Chinese male civilian is suspected of being an enemy, the suspicion is enough – better safe than sorry. In Nanking, it is said that Prince Asaka's command was to 'kill all captives'. A common word that comes up in reference to fighting the Americans on the beaches of the Pacific islands is 'annihilate'."

I had no illusions about the heat of the battle. In war, you have to kill and there is no prettiness for either side. I started to understand the American position better: they'd seen the evidence of the Japanese soldiers' treatment of civilians. In Britain, we could rest easy now, but the States had only the Pacific between them and an enemy who was so alien.

"No pretty way to kill, indeed. And we will one day spend hours debating whether any of this would have taken place in a matriarchy…"

Thank you for sparing me that one.

"My pleasure. Right now, it's all about Hirohito. In a nation where 'surrender' is worse than death and they are in deep denial about the condition their war is in, there's only one man in this entire country who can end this."

The sense of her presence was intensifying. To engage with her would be very different than, say, looking at physical Jack; physical Cassie was across town in the Kanda Shrine, but *psychic* Cassie was somewhere in the air here…

Etheric travel is the travel of the mind across the physical plain; to engage with another floating soul would require shifting up a gear. I could feel that my body was under great strain now and wondered how much longer I would be able to safely manage this…

Slowly, the world faded and there she was. Cassandra Mayfair: Liverpudlian of birth, born at the end of the eighteenth century; wife to Jack, mother to Alice and Nellie; extraordinary empath, fiercely determined and idealistic. To the mind's eye she looked like the physical Cassie I'd lifted from the cholera-infested docks in 1832 – blonde with deep blue, kind, kind eyes, beautiful but unconventionally so, wrinkles weathered into her face from years of hard graft, fused with a dazzling inner light.

"Hello, Robert." I could feel her smile. "Any news from the west?"
"You and Jack have to return immediately. PM's orders."
"You work for Attlee now?"
It was official, then: Winston was no longer PM. Clement Attlee's Labour Party was in.
She read my surprise easily.
"Seems like telegrams travel faster than psychic adventurers. When did you leave Berlin?"
"The eighteenth," I replied, in consternation. "Why, what's the date?"
I had lost all sense of time in Halcyon. All the turbulence, the clamour of lost souls, had been extremely disorientating.
"Well since you left," she continued, "the Allies have served Hirohito up with an ultimatum. We're calling it the Potsdam Declaration."
I slipped from consternation to outright alarm.
"What's the date, Cassie?" I repeated urgently.
Disconcerted, she replied, "It's the twenty-ninth of July."
Oh, hell. Eleven days. It had taken me eleven days to get there…

- CHAPTER FOUR -

Descendant of the Gods

The Emperor often spent time meditating in the afternoon. The Imperial Castle gardens used to be the place for this but following the bombings of May he had taken to retreating to his library – which was underground, housed in concrete.

Where better to build a 'mind palace' than around books?

Hirohito was highly intelligent and well read, with a passion for natural history and marine biology; he took a great interest in the flora and fauna of the palace complex. In 1921, he'd toured Europe for six months. Three years later, he had married his distant cousin, the Princess Nagako; they'd had seven children together, though one – a daughter – had died in infancy. He was the first Emperor to eschew the tradition of court concubines, favouring fidelity and constancy in his marriage to his Empress. As a young man, he'd been given high-ranking commissions in both the army and the navy.

The one hundred and twenty-fourth Emperor of Japan in his line, he had been reigning since the age of twenty-five.

He was waiting for us.

A dry rock *karesansui* garden acted as an antechamber, with a miniature landscape of rocks and sand raked to represent ripples, water features trickling quietly over moss and pruned bonsai. The garden opened via sliding partitions onto a bright yet intimate tea room, where the reader could sit cross-legged on a woven grass mat and sip green tea while engrossed in their book.

Beyond this, slender paper doors gave way to a vast, two-storey library, supported by pillars and overlooked by an arched roof, which looked to stretch on forever in a long tunnel. On the ceiling were painted the stories of the Japanese creation myth and their folk legends, as well as the many *kami* spirits found in Shinto. Against each of the long two walls were mounted numerous suits of samurai armour and helmets, each with a *katana* sword at its side.

I never knew what the real 'concrete library' looked like. This was the astral plain. Halcyon. And essentially, we were now guests inside the Emperor's head.

He was a modest-looking man, relatively small in stature – at about five and a half feet, I noted, shorter even than Mussolini and Hitler. Despite his outward appearance – he could have passed for a bank clerk or an accountant – and his comparative youth at only forty-four, he radiated power.

This was a big man.

Sat at a table with a book on jellyfish, his hands folded before him, Emperor Hirohito peered at us impassively through round glasses. He seemed to be experiencing polite curiosity.

"Do you like my garden?" he asked.

I followed Cassie's cue and bowed. *Retain humility,* she reminded me. *Let me lead.*

"It is most beautiful, Your Imperial Highness," she replied.

"The rock garden is very strange to western eyes, I imagine? It is intended to represent one's intimate relationship with nature, particularly the transience of all things – and to serve to enhance one's meditations in pursuit of true meaning."

She nodded in understanding, replying that, "It is important to take time to consider things deeply and not to squander our time as mortals in the rush towards daily life."

He blinked at her then indicated the ceiling.

"Here is the story of our creation. Our first gods, called *Kotoamatsukami*, appear at the birth of the universe; they are followed – upon the formation of heaven and earth – by the *Kamivonanavo*. Of these later generations, I would bring your attention to these two: *Izanagi*, who is male, and *Izanami*, who is female. In their love, they create beautiful *Ōyashima* – our great country of many islands.

"Here we see that Izanami dies in childbirth and that Izanagi goes on a quest into the underworld to save her, but she denies him. In his grief, Izanagi seeks to purify himself of the underworld by bathing. As he washes his left eye, the goddess *Amaterasu* is born and rises to inherit the Sun and the stars…"

He turned to consider us. I had a feeling that he was baiting us.

"*She* is my ancestor."

Meeting his gaze, Cassie said simply, "We are not here to debate your divinity, Your Majesty."

He cocked his head to one side, revealing nothing – except perhaps vague amusement.

"Are you here then to assassinate me?"

"We are here only in peace."

"Ah. A diplomatic mission then. I see." He seemed vaguely disappointed.

"My name is Cassandra Mayfair and this is Robert Tulliver."

His attention was returning to the book on the table. Distractedly, he said, "I was in England once and was most enchanted with the way in which your leaders will talk to those below them. Alas, in my country, the Emperor does not speak with subordinates."

Jack would have seen red at this. Cassie only bowed and turned to leave in dismissal. She said, "Very well. We shall take our terms with us…"

"Wait."

Clever girl.

"Who is it you represent?" the Emperor asked.

"We are here for Churchill."

He snorted. "He is no longer in power."

"Churchill is *always* in power. And he has Attlee's ear."

Considering me, the Emperor gestured to the other seats at the table.

"The same Tulliver who nearly got King George and Prime Minister Asquith killed in 1914? Who was a party to the assassination of Archduke Franz Ferdinand at Sarajevo?"

"That would be me," I replied. "You know your Society history."

"It's a wonder you show your face, Tulliver." There was an element of dry humour there.

"It's true," I conceded, "that in your culture I would have fallen on my katana long ago."

Hirohito's right eyebrow shot up.

Humility, Robert…

"If His Imperial Majesty does not welcome complete honesty," I countered. "I should leave."

There was a moment of tension, then the Emperor threw open his arms.

"This promises to be an entertaining distraction."

We sat.

"You westerners," he added, as if we were lovable rogues. "Your directness is refreshing. In this country, even I must watch my words." Then he turned to Cassie. "These *terms*?"

She shrugged. "Surrender – unconditional on the part of the military. Allied occupation of Japan. You must renounce your divinity. To provide a focal point of stability for your people, you will be retained as Emperor. There will be no war crimes proceedings against yourself or any member of the royal family, the official line being that you have been to all extents and purposes a prisoner in your own home. Your senior military officers and statesmen will be stood accountable. No reprisals against your person or people."

The two of them, without moving an inch, were circling one another.

The Emperor said, "These terms are different to those of the Potsdam Declaration."

Issued on the twenty-sixth of July, just nine days after Truman had known for sure that the power of the atomic bomb was his to wield, the Allied ultimatum had pulled few punches. Signed by Truman, Churchill and Chiang Kai-shek, it demanded ("We will not deviate… no alternatives") the occupation of Japanese territory and that Japanese sovereignty be limited to a much smaller group of islands; it talked of "irresponsible militarism", demanded the elimination "of the authority and influence of those who had deceived and misled the people of Japan" and insisted that justice be meted out to "all war criminals".

In some ways, it was generous: Japanese soldiers were to return home and lead peaceful, productive lives; democratic tendencies, such as freedom of speech and respect for human rights, were to be revived; Japan was to return to industrial and economic participation on the global stage. Once Japan had a peacefully inclined and responsible government, the Allies would withdraw.

I'd scrutinised the telegram for any reference to the bomb. It was there sure enough, but *way* too implicit: the Allies were "poised to strike the final blows upon Japan… until she ceases to resist"; the might that now converged on Japan was "immeasurably greater than that applied to the Nazis"; the Allied resolve would mean "the inevitable and complete destruction of Japanese armed forces and… the utter devastation of the Japanese homeland".

As a document that sued for peace it was feeble; as a set-up to give you an excuse to use your new weapon, it was on the money.

Here was a piece of paper denouncing reckless militarism and warning of retribution for war crimes, sent to a government that consisted of military men – the very men upon whose heads the ultimate responsibility for said crimes would almost certainly fall, and who would be facing certain execution. It demanded surrender from the very people for whom surrender was deeply abhorrent. It was saying, "Do that thing that will most humiliate you and we will kill you anyway."

Crucially, through the omission of all references to Hirohito, the Japanese people were left to infer no mercy for their Emperor – a complete desecration of their identity. By not mentioning him, it was fatally grey. Reading it, I'd wondered at the omission of any reassurances for the Japanese people that the God who walked among them would not be made to pay.

An omnipotent being simply cannot be brought to task by heathen…

Hirohito himself needed only look to the fates of Mussolini and Hitler to draw certain conclusions.

Surely the Allied leaders knew all this. Surely, they had *some* understanding of the psychology of their enemy? Churchill understood only too well the ferocious tenacity of the enemy – the Allied threats would inevitably ring hollow to those who did not know the truth of Japan's predicament; and for those who did, they offered little hope.

I could smell Stalin's influence. He'd been at Potsdam, where his commitment to joining the war against Japan was an open secret. He was not yet officially an enemy of Japan, but Truman, Churchill and Chiang were no idiots – they knew how much Japan was counting on the Soviets' continued good will. Why omit Stalin from the declaration? With his name attached, surely Japan would have had no choice but to accept the inevitable eventuality of their defeat.

There could be only two reasons. The first was that Truman wanted to win the war without Stalin; that he was afraid that the Soviets, under the pretence of war with Japan, might gain a greater foothold in Asia – and therefore on the Pacific.

The second was that the Allies were only making a token, half-hearted show of bidding for peace…

"I think," Cassie was saying, "we can both agree that the Potsdam Declaration is unsatisfactory…"

"It is entirely unacceptable," he cut in, his voice rising. There was cold fury in his eyes. "It is an insult and a veiled threat to our person."

"Why not seek clarification through diplomatic channels?" I suggested.

He glared at me. "Their terms are *unconditional.* Anything else is begging."

"They are only unconditional in reference to your armed forces," she countered. "It does not specify unconditional surrender on the part of His Imperial Highness. I believe the Allied leaders have deliberately omitted such reference to allow you room to manoeuvre."

He considered this for a moment then shrugged. "This is irrelevant. We have already made discreet entreaties via Marshal Stalin."

This was the first I'd heard of any such thing.

"Really? Via telegram?"

The Emperor seemed to sag a little. He spoke carefully. "We are mindful of the great evil and sacrifice the present war inflicts upon the peoples of all the belligerent powers and desire from our heart that it may be quickly terminated. Before the opening of the Potsdam Conference, we employed our Minister of Foreign Affairs to approach our ambassador in Moscow and signal the Imperial willingness to make concessions."

Now his rage threatened to spill over.

"But they wish to *pulverise* us. They insist upon seeing us subservient and enfeebled, placing the future of our glorious nation – a legacy that has never been besmirched by the breath of a *gaijin* in one hundred and twenty-four generations of rule – in their hands!"

Suddenly, as if reflecting his anger, every one of the samurai statues stepped forward and drew their swords.

Having taken them for decorative, I suddenly saw them in a different light.

Cassie threw me a nervous glance.

Hirohito's eyes were blazing. "They have continually sought to insult us – from the very beginning. You know of the Americans' previous ultimatum, I assume?"

Cassie nodded. I had no idea what he was talking about.

"The American Secretary of State, Cordell Hull, demanded Japan's complete withdrawal from China," she said in my head. *"This was eleven days* before *Pearl Harbor – by which time the Japanese fleet was already on route.*

"The Americans had for several months been openly funding and supplying the Chinese and had imposed crippling trade sanctions upon Japan…"

Hirohito appeared to have been listening to us, adding, "That was a declaration of war, pure and simple – they withdrew their trade and supported our enemies. How else were we to perceive their actions? When the Americans protest at our 'unprovoked' attack, they lie – they had for months been seeking to provoke us. They knew war was coming."

While personally I felt that Pearl Harbor had been a violation of international law, I could see how – if the Japanese thought they were essentially already at war – it could have been a reaction to the signals sent by the States. Perhaps even a justifiable 'preemptive strike'.

The Emperor was pacing, like a wild cat trapped with no escape route.

He said, "It will be *my* failure for all time. My ancestors will forever look to me and say, 'There, *he* is the one who desecrated our memory.'"

Cassie stepped towards him, causing the samurai to advance and raise their swords. She opened her palms to show that she meant no harm.

"Your Majesty, please – I know that this goes against all you hold dear; but consider, there may be some occasions in which there can be great dignity in a show of trust."

He met her eyes with a look that said he wanted to listen, that he was desperate for a way out. I wondered whether the Emperor had ever known a lack of self-confidence before. Perhaps this truly was virgin territory for him.

His voice wavering slightly, he insisted, "My armed forces await yours on our mainland. Here, you will see a final battle the likes of which you cannot possibly imagine. Let me reassure, our blow will be devastating."

How could he be in such denial? Their cities were smashed, their naval and air forces crippled, they had no oil left… He was desperately clinging to the illusion that one final, glorious confrontation would definitively establish, once and for all, that the Japanese Empire would never stand down. He believed we would be forced to make concessions.

But he did not know how much the game had changed – the Allies no longer needed to put a single soldier on Japanese ground…

"You are not Chancellor Hitler," she continued, softly. "That man took his country down with him. Through his delusions, he brought his people low."

He was listening. The samurai took a step backwards and lowered their swords.

Cassie breathed a sigh of relief.

"You truly believe my family will be spared?" he asked.

I saw him then as a mortal man in the finest sense: a loving husband and father. It must have been a terrible fear for him, the thought that Tokyo might be ransacked and her people butchered, her women raped…

He nodded, reading my thoughts; but when he met my gaze there was resentment there.

"Nowhere is the saying 'history is written by the victors' more starkly true," he said, "than when it comes to the matter of 'war crimes'. Do you think the Soviet soldiers who raped in their thousands will ever be made to stand to account? What about the British and Americans who mutilate the bodies and take the skulls of my soldiers for keepsakes? Will they be punished?"

Hirohito was growing angry again. I looked to the samurai, warily.

"I imagine they will christen Pearl Harbor a war crime," he continued. "They may even classify their military dead as civilians because 'they were not at war'; but nobody will talk of their aggressive and provocative actions in embargoing our oil. And the bombing of my civilians: one hundred thousand dead in *one night* here. When did I rain that much fire and destruction upon you?"

The rage was coursing through him again. His samurai took a step forward, their katana slowly beginning to creep up into the air again as his rant escalated. But there was a glint in Cassie's eye – she'd read something in him.

"The truth is," she countered, "your generals always aspired to cast a Japanese blanket across East Asia. Their desire to drive out western influence was motivated by *conquest*, by the hunger for superiority. Why did you not rein them in, Your Majesty?"

She pointedly walked across to stand next to the samurai and defiantly met his gaze.

"Or was it in fact *you* who personally conceived of a long-term plan to extend the influence of the empire? Was it really you, after all, who ratified the use of chemical and biological weapons against the Chinese, oversaw their brutal subjugation, even perceived the necessity of a preemptive strike against the Americans – all as part of a vision of greatness, a dream of glory you have nurtured since you were a boy?"

Cassie gestured up towards the myths and legends, the bold, romantic tales of adventure and derring-do, depicted on the ceiling.

"Is it possible that your head has been spinning with the need to make your mark like the shogun of old? Imagine such an emperor – the master of Asia. He could stand proud beside his ancestors. But of course, such an emperor cannot exist in these days of mechanised, wholesale slaughter…"

He had stopped in his tracks, eyes bulging – the Emperor was little used to being to being challenged, and certainly not by a western woman.

"With a world view like that, such an emperor would be badly out of step with time…"

Her meaning was clear – time had caught up with Hirohito.

"No," she added finally, "it seems far more likely that the Japanese people's beloved, benevolent idol and beacon has been exploited as a figurehead by a despotic military hell-bent on war, wouldn't you say?"

The samurai stayed where they were, their swords poised; they too had frozen.

When he spoke again, his tone was measured and careful.

"How can you possibly hope to understand the pressures I am under?"

"You're right," she conceded. "As a mere mortal, free of your burdens, I cannot begin to imagine. Were I to try, I might perceive a man who did not choose to be born a deity, a loving husband and parent only too aware of the precarious nature of his power. He must have often read of the likes of the Romanovs, for example – not so long ago – a family who were never perceived as divine, but whose fate certainly offered parallels for a father to fear.

"I might look to the rise of militarism in his nation in recent decades, the assassinations of its opponents, violent uprisings amongst the ranks of his soldiers – they are often out of control. He himself has seen at least one attempt upon his life. In such a context, one might better understand the silence and distance he has always exercised – for to be aloof and removed better preserves the impression of his sanctity."

He stared at her, started to say something, thought better of it.

Instead, he replied, "I was alone in this castle when the great earthquake hit in 1923, my father – the *Taishō* Emperor – being fortuitously away at the time. The earth shook the city apart and triggered a firestorm. Cracks appeared in the palace walls. But the people fled here for the safety of the open space.

"They looked to me."

Slowly, Hirohito subsided back into his chair and began leafing through his book on jellyfish.

Almost absent-mindedly, he added, "I think that to be truly great, the Emperor must always ultimately be unknowable, don't you?"

By the time Cassandra Mayfair emerged from her trance state, into a fog of incense and the deep guttural resonance of meditating Shinto monks, it was dark outside. She sat there rocking, cross-legged, for a while, coming to slowly and collecting her thoughts.

She knew I was there beside her.

"I'm missing something. Hirohito has signalled his interest in terms; he wants to surrender. That's a big deal to him, they must know that. Yet instead of acknowledging this, they issue the Potsdam Declaration."

Maybe the chain of communication broke down?

"The Foreign Minister in Tokyo to the Japanese Ambassador in Moscow, to Stalin, who attended Potsdam – where do you imagine the chain broke?"

A matter of the Imperial will and so grave a matter – they would make doubly and triply sure the message reached its destination. Of course, the Japanese pride had been their undoing: Stalin being deemed an ally to Japan, there was no perceived humiliation in discreetly broaching the subject with him. Whereas to telegram London or Washington would be abhorrent.

Perhaps Stalin withheld the information of the Japanese peace approach?

Her eyes still closed, Cassie nodded.

"Maybe he wants to go to war, take a huge slice of Japanese territory for the Soviet Union."

The Soviets had denounced their neutrality pact with the Japanese back in April. China would have little time for 'conditional' surrender. The very existence of the Potsdam Declaration meant that Japan's attempt at diplomacy via Stalin had failed.

In which case, the Allies are determined – it's unconditional, or nothing.

She opened her eyes.

"I'll urge Churchill to reconsider. Our intel will reinforce what he may or may not have heard from Stalin. Hirohito wants an end to the war – they will have to help him save face."

I noticed that several of the monks had broken from their meditation and were peering her way – Cassie had been so distracted, she had dropped her psychic mask. The Shinto priests were seeing a western woman in their midst! Consternation was sweeping through the temple. Oops.

She was up and on her feet in an instant.

"Jack..."

"I'm on it."

As Cassie made for the door, the room was erupting with shouts. The alarm was being raised. The chief priest at the shrine may be friendly, but there would be little he could do for the Mayfairs now.

As she passed through the door, Jack was there to slide it shut and roll a cart in to block the priests' exit. She'd reinstated her disguise now and his was still in place, but the Kanda Shrine was lost to them as a place to hide.

The monks had the door open but were struggling to clamber over it the cart. I used what little power I had to hold it in place.

Jack took her hand. They ran across the courtyard through confused onlookers, turning left out of the gate. I jumped ahead and was able to warn of approaching soldiers; they had black chevrons on their uniforms and white armbands on their left arms – all were armed with pistols and bayonets.

"*Kempeitai*," Jack said, tersely. "The Japanese Gestapo. Seems your Emperor has worked out where we've been hiding."

Floating overhead, but weak now, I saw that there was a quiet alley nearby, which led into a peasant area of the city. They took it. Helping them this way, I was able to lead them to comparative safety – but they would need new disguises.

"What we need," Jack snapped, "is to get the hell out of Japan." He looked at her, imploringly. "If the secret police are onto us, the stakes just got massively raised. There will be Kempeitai psychics – you know that. And they'll be here any minute. Tell me you got some big concession out of Hirohito?"

She couldn't.

I came in with Jack. *Churchill wants you out of Japan. Let's get you two to our contacts in Korea and maybe you can telegraph from there.*

She considered this and shook her head.

"That will take days. We're going to need Sachiko."

I'm here, Cassandra...

Sachiko's sudden presence was unexpected – she must have been listening throughout. In her astral state, Sachiko was an extraordinary blaze of colours. We all, all of us, emit light; psychics more so. Sachi was a beacon amongst psychics, burning brighter than most.

I understand that a message needs to be sent to Winston Churchill. It should read, 'Our friend responsive. Needs help to save face. Urge you to accept hellos via Moscow. Tulliver concurs.'"

"Yes, that should do it."

Leave it with me.

Suddenly, the kaleidoscope of light had vanished. I wondered how a young Japanese girl could possibly get a telegram to a British politician...

"Your own light is fading, Robert," Jack said. "You need to head home."

I knew he was right. Back in Berlin, my body was becoming severely weakened by intense psychic activity. Nurse Gertrud would be working overtime to keep me up and running.

And yet there was still the question of Hiroshima...

Jack's eyes flashed a warning.

Let it play itself out. Don't be naïve: they will never *listen. The war must end.*

Neither of us said anything to Cassie about it.

I left them there, clandestinely slipping out of Tokyo. People had helped them in, Jack said; the same people would help them out. Cassie seemed unsatisfied, puzzled, as if she sensed a missing part of the equation. The real endgame was just out of her reach.

Would Jack tell her? She might violate national security to warn Hirohito.

I doubted that Hirohito would have listened and believed her anyway. We were all so smothered in lies and propaganda that he would just hear a bluff.

Only a demonstration could ever earn his complete attention…

Meanwhile, perhaps Sachiko's telegram would swing Churchill to a change of heart. I'd been successful in my mission – the Mayfairs were on their way home – and in my failing state, there was little more I could do here.

But a little reconnaissance wouldn't hurt.

- CHAPTER FIVE -

The Forty-Seventh Ronin

I'd never pushed myself so hard, but somehow I needed to see that city. I found it on the mouth of the Ōta River, where its six channels create a delta onto the inland sea at the south-western end of Honshu. As with Tokyo, its industry had grown up around the docks of the river; but this city was free of bomb damage – a healthy, bustling, untouched oasis, blissfully far from the war.

Every one of the four hundred and twenty miles west from Tokyo to Hiroshima had sapped my energy, so that I arrived there feeling like a wraith. But to my surprise, I was greeted by an old friend.

Terasaka Kichiemon had been eighty-three when he died in 1747, but I'd met him as a much younger man, forty-four years earlier. The Terasaka I knew had been an *ashiguru* – a foot soldier to the samurai – but his life had taken on a mythic dimension due to his being the only survivor of the Japanese people's celebrated 'Forty-seven Ronin'.

A national legend on a par with our own Robin Hood or George and the Dragon, the forty-seven were samurai whose master was compelled to commit the ritual suicide of seppuku following his assault upon a court official, Kira. Now leaderless *ronin*, they'd returned to restore his honour by killing Kira – after which, in turn, they'd had to present themselves to the authorities as murderers. In recognition that they had acted according to the precepts of Bushido, the warrior's code, forty-six of them were allowed to commit seppuku by falling upon their swords. Only my friend Terasaka had been spared this honourable fate.

Westerners have tragic heroes, yes, but not who would stoically 'accept their fate' in mass suicide The Japanese embrace death differently. We find their relationship with honour and noble death exotic and attractive, but ultimately alien. It was an elegant ideal that had somehow metamorphosed into something terrible.

Having witnessed those events, I had an understanding of how the samurai mind ticked and a deep respect for those leaderless men of honour. There have been periods of my own life when I felt like a ronin of sorts, wandering the world in search of a cause. It was I who had restored to Terasaka a sense of purpose following the mass seppuku of his comrades – being instrumental in making him one of my opposite numbers in the Japanese chapter of the Society.

Like me, he was a Society recruiter and keeper of the Blood.

In the years since the events of 1703, his adventures had often been as spectacular as my own. Though he'd taken the Blood at eighty-three, his mind was as sharp as ever – with the power of a two hundred and eighty-one-year-old.

As I was of him, Terasaka was aware of the immediacy of a strong, incoming psychic before he realised it was me. The joy in his voice was moving.

"My English friend! Is that you after all these years?"

Terasaka san? I hear you, but I do not see you.

"The larger island in the western part of the bay. It is called Miyajima*, the 'shrine island'."*

As I swooped low along the sea and towards the island, I knew immediately that my friend had chosen to settle in a very holy place. There was a huge Shinto *torii* gate in the water marking entry to the sacred site, a frame of vermillion-coloured pillars supporting a curved lintel, devised so that it appeared to be floating. Passing over the beach, pagodas and the piers and jetties of the *Itsukushima* shrine, I headed up the densely forested Mount Misen.

The picture-perfect wizened Japanese wizard, Terasaka was waiting for me at the Daishō-in temple, a flurry of stacked roofs, eaves and cantilevers; he took me on a guided wander through their gardens, occasionally pointing out a statue of particular interest. It was reassuring to be with him again and, even after two centuries, we fell easily into banter.

"It is a shame you cannot be here in person," Terasaka declared. "My issue with the psychic plain is the distinct lack of alcohol. Sake is all well and good, but I have a bottle of genuine Japanese Scotch whisky I am waiting to share."

I snorted.

It is either genuine Scotch or it is Japanese whisky. Scotch is from Scotland.

"Bring your body with you next time you visit," he countered, "and I will make you choke on your words."

He shook his head at the thought that we were enemies.

"I am unhappy at the state of my country. It starts with a slow, creeping dismay, then one day you realise something has taken root and you are too small to do anything other than hide until the madness has burnt itself out."

I dared to suggest that such stoicism amounted to complacency. He flared his nostrils at me.

"Tell that to the loved ones of Tsunesaburō Makiguchi, of Takuma Dan, of Makota Tomioka, of Kanō Jigorō, of Hara Takashi. The reputations of others such as Takigawa Yukitoki, Kijūrō Shidehara and Tatsukichi Minobe have been dragged through the mud. Satomi Hakamada, Kyuichi Tokuda, Jōsei Toda and Hitoshi Yamakawa are imprisoned as dissidents. Do not go thinking all Japanese follow blindly."

We came to a breathtaking panorama of the city. It was just after dawn and Hiroshima was stirring.

"Such beauty and yet only two nights ago, the sky was burning."

Where? The city seems relatively undamaged.

"The city itself has been lucky. I refer to Kure, the naval base a few miles to the east."

The people across the bay were waking each day feeling blessed at their luck, but the truth was far more sinister. Far, far away, men had sat in a darkened room with a map and very deliberately singled their little dot out.

"You do not look well. Where do you lie?"

He was referring to my 'aura'. I shrugged it off.

Berlin.

His eyebrows shot up. "No wonder you are ill." Terasaka cocked his head in suspicion. "Is this not a social call then?"

It's reconnaissance. But I mean to use the information I gather to dissuade the Allies against further bombing.

"They bombed for three days. The naval district was host to one of our four key shipyards and our remaining capital ships. Your planes sank pretty much everything we had left, most notably the *Amagi* and the *Ōyodo*, the flagship of the Combined Fleet. In addition, you have crippled three battleships, two heavy cruisers and a number of warships."

I was astonished. *How do you know this in so much detail?*

"Like you, I often let my soul fly. I flew with Nakajima Ki-84s and Boeing B-29s and saw the American planes triumph three-to-one. Let me reassure you, we have been paid back for Pearl Harbor many times over."

The Allied commanders must already know this, I thought – aerial recon would have firmly established their victory. Surely this negated any need for the bomb…

Terasaka gazed at me, searchingly. Then he turned away and bowed his head.

"So, they have split the atom."

I was not surprised that he had read me so easily – he was nearly three centuries old and knew most of the tricks by now. Even if I was the older man.

Is Hiroshima a legitimate military target, Terasaka san?

He looked to the city and sagged with sorrow.

"We have the Fifth Division of our Infantry garrisoned here at Hiroshima Castle. Shunroku Hata's Second General Army is also headquartered here, as is Yoji Fujii's Fifty-Ninth. Hata is a very big player with key responsibilities for the anticipated battle for the mainland. Yes, there are tens of thousands of soldiers here. It is an army city…"

Terasaka's voice dried.

"Then there is our logistical and industrial importance: the Mitsubishi Shipbuilding factory is here. We have stockpiles of fuel and supplies. We are a communications centre. Our children are in the factories building bombs… Ah, the *children*…" Composing himself, he continued, "Until the day before yesterday, I would have said yes. Yes, yes, yes – we are a legitimate target. But the naval base lies devastated – we cannot field a fleet. Japan is no longer a naval power and poses no significant direct threat to the States."

There needs to be surrender. After all that has passed…

"Retribution, I think you mean." He gestured to the panorama with a bitter chuckle. "And so you bomb my view." Then he fell very quiet and after a moment whispered, "I wish you had never told me this. I wish you away."

Tearing his gaze from the city, he walked into the trees – eyes on the ground as if he could no longer bear to look out that way. Quietly, he asked, "Have you witnessed the destructive power of the bomb with your own eyes?"

The flash was seen ten miles away. A soldier ten thousand feet from the detonation was knocked down. The force of the explosion was equivalent to several million sticks of dynamite.

"When will it fall?"

All I know is August.

"That's tomorrow."

I will try to reach Churchill via telegram…

He laughed. "You are so old and yet still so blinkered. Can you not see that it is written? You know that our Prime Minister, Suzuki, declared *mokusatsu* in response to your Potsdam Declaration?"

I don't understand what that is.

"Neither will Truman. The word is composed of two characters: *moku* for 'silence' and *satsu* for 'killing'. It essentially means to kill with silence. He may have meant simply that he had nothing to say at this time, but his ambiguity is fatal. Sozuki has shown only contempt for the Allies' half-hearted demands for surrender. Not his cleverest move. You do not offer your back to a snake."

You think Truman is a snake?

"I think that any man handed the greatest power in history will inevitably have to fight temptation. Such a thing would possess the greatest of us. He will look only for reasons to unmake his mind – and Sozuki has offered none." His whole body shuddered with a sigh. "Hiroshima is dead."

With that, he walked to his quarters near the temple and began to pack. I was taken aback, thinking that if I were in his position I would have chosen to stay…

"Should I run into the city, to desperately administer the Blood to as many of the Gifted as I can find? How many could I save, do you think, in the time given me?"

Not thirty years earlier, I had found myself in a similar predicament in the trenches of Europe. I had saved precious few. I remembered all too well the anguish.

"A precious few, Robert?"

He could not see me and yet I had a feeling that he was looking right through me. His eyes were dry now and there was great patience in them.

"They were *all* precious. As is every dog, bird and insect that will be eradicated here. I am no connoisseur of human suffering and do not propose to witness it; but we live in seasons, my friend. We are the sea that becomes the mist, that becomes the cloud, that becomes the rain, that becomes the sea. Today we may feel the heat of summer, but this is the coldest hour of Winter – and the Spring will follow.

"Hiroshima will rise again and she will prosper."

There it was: the Japanese stoicism, so deeply enshrined in their hearts. I admired their essential existentialism; the Shinto and Buddhism philosophy that we are all but leaves in the wind. For the first time, I saw its dark side. We might call it fatalistic, but they would see it simply as bowing down to 'what must be'. Though they deplored surrender to an inferior enemy, they joyfully embraced the surrender of their free will. And this had been usurped, hijacked by their military leaders.

Ultimately, as with every country, the ordinary people had been encouraged to misunderstand one another to make them easier to manipulate. The propaganda whitewash had been too effective.

I followed Terasaka down the white stone steps and through the temple. He nodded to friends and acquaintances. One or two stopped him to ask after his journey and he talked of pilgrimages. As we approached the shore, he gazed briefly upon the city again.

"The soldiers who are unblooded, the good people – particularly the children. I shall return to do what I can for those who survive.

"But among the soldiers, some have committed terrible acts. Where once there was a small minority of warrior nobles, now every child of Japan aspires to be a samurai with the Emperor as his master; the Government have bastardised the Bushido code to manipulate them. Ours was a moral way, of chivalry and wisdom; prisoners were treated with respect, we would never rape or butcher children. These soldiers think they will be purified by war, but they have dishonoured their ancestors.

"I shall not mourn for these men."

Terasaka stepped onto a boat and pushed away from the island, indicating that I should not follow.

Where will you go?

"I was ronin once, but now I have two masters – Shinto and the Society. I shall wander freely until I hear their call."

I remained on the shore long after his boat was out of sight, listening to his thoughts. The world spun and I vaguely knew I was in danger of forgetting my name, of dispersing into the universe. I thought of the mindless sleepers in Berlin and wondered whether I was one of them now.

Terasaka Kichiemon's voice came to me one last time – a distant echo.

"We believe that all humans have a reikon *– you would probably call it a 'soul'. If a person should die with violent suddenness, their reikon is said to transform into a* yūrei *and haunt the Earth in purgatory until its pain can be resolved.*

"I think there will be many yūrei here soon..."

- CHAPTER SIX -

Enola Gay

I thought I heard sirens. The pieces of my mind drifted slowly back together. I was ready for a new start after six years of madness. As consciousness reasserted itself, I realised I'd been dreaming of a warm, just-pulled pint, locally brewed and supped in my favourite beer garden – taken ideally with the smell of freshly cut grass and the soft hum of bees at work in a nearby lavender bush.

But Berlin wasn't as I remembered it. I wasn't coming to in the basement of a bombed-out library, but in a small room that seemed to be made of paper and wood, which glowed with the silver sunlight of dawn.

Sat cross-legged on the floor before me with intent, piercing eyes was an eighteen-year-old girl. Her long black hair pinned up in a bun; she wore a pure white kimono. The whole effect was so ethereal I could imagine I was waking up in Heaven to find a Japanese angel waiting for me.

"Welcome back, Robert Tulliver," she said.

Sachiko?

She nodded, smiling warmly – exuding a sweet benevolence. But she seemed troubled. "Your soul light was very subdued, like only smouldering embers. You have been very weak."

I stirred and tried to 'spread my wings', but back in Berlin my head was thumping.

"I sent your message. Anticipating that a telegram from Japan would not be trusted and would draw a great deal of unwanted attention, I flew to the Allied air base at Tinian in the Mariana Islands and possessed the mind of an American telegraph operator…" Sachiko frowned. "There is a great deal of activity there. Mounting excitement."

Of course. Tinian was host to possibly the largest air base in the world, with upwards of five hundred B-29s based there.

I was becoming more alert by the minute.

What's the date?

"It's August the sixth, why?"

Did the Mayfairs get out of Japan alright?

Sachiko nodded. She was watching me very closely. "Safe and sound with friends in China. Why?"

With a growing bad feeling, I passed through the nearest door to find that I was in a humble family machiya: a long but narrow abode, perhaps twenty yards in length but barely seven yards wide, partitioned by *fusuma* sliding doors – lattice-framed wood coated in paper, painted with woodland scenes and particularly cherry blossom. There were more painted scenes on the decorative folding screens against one wall, which stood on earthen floors covered in tatami mats.

Sachiko's family were sat here at their breakfast. There were grandparents in their eighties, their son and his wife in their fifties, *their* son and his wife in their thirties and their children – two boys aged ten and seven and a girl aged three. They looked up as I entered – but of course they weren't seeing me, they were seeing her behind me. She fell easily into early morning hellos, but telepathically she was talking to me.

"These are my grandparents. The younger man is my uncle. The children are like brothers and sisters to me. I have been staying with them for four years, since I became trapped in this country."

You are not born Japanese?

"I am Nisei *– second generation Japanese American. My parents immigrated to California before I was born but sent me here for a traditional education and to learn about my ancestry. Since the beginning of the war, it has not been possible for me to return home.*

"However, I understand there is no home to return to at present."

I understood the reference – many first generation *Issei* were now interned in camps in the States.

Are there many Nisei in Hiroshima?

"Numerous. In the decades before the war, many Japanese emigrated."

Hibakusha: this is the name given to the survivors of the atomic bombings of August 1945. Long afterwards, I learnt that three thousand Japanese American hibakusha returned home to the States after the war. If that is the number who survived, the perished are estimated at eight thousand.

Harry Truman killed more Americans at Hiroshima than were killed by the Japanese at Pearl Harbor.

I thought I heard sirens…

"It was a false alarm, triggered by the sighting of an American plane. I went out to see it. I like to see the B-29s – they are like friends and angels from back home."

I'd heard the all-clear. The plane that passed over without incident had to be the reconnaissance plane. It would be reporting back on the weather. I bolted through the door into their tranquil garden courtyard and looked straight to the sky.

It was a clear blue, beautiful day. A virgin day. The kind of day where you step out with a strut in your stride and everything seems possible. *Damn…*

She was right beside me. Beyond her, her family were framed in the doorway, startled at her sudden exit. The little three-year-old toddled out after her and did a double-take my way; I think she could make out an outline. Children often manifest the Gift before it is brainwashed out of them.

Sachiko picked the girl up and cooed reassuringly at her in a stream of chattered Japanese. I gathered the girl's name was Keiko. But while her words were light and happy, her eyes bored into me. "You never answered. Why?"

Get them out, Sachi. Your family. Any friends you can reach in a hurry. Run. Get them the hell out of Hiroshima as fast as you can…

That was enough for her. After what she'd seen at Tinian, I think she'd already put most of the pieces together. I sped through the city, mind racing – wanting desperately to be wrong. It was coming alive: people still emerging from the bomb shelters, confidence in their safety renewed. Hiroshima always avoided the worst of the bombings. It felt blessed. On the sixth of August at eight in the morning, the middle of the Monday morning rush hour, it was the absolute picture of blissful ignorance.

Please be wrong. Please. Be wrong. There'll be more air raid sirens. Everybody will have time to get back to safety.

But somehow the American mission had slipped through the net. At six minutes past eight, the Matsunaga Monitoring Station at Fukushima reported a sighting of enemy aircraft; the Japanese military was by now running so short of staff, it fell to a fourteen-year-old school girl named Yoshie Oka, who was working at the Chugoku Military District Headquarters, to raise the alarm.

This was at thirteen minutes past eight.

I was by then at the heart of the city, near a modern, domed concrete building – the 'Prefectural Industrial Promotion Hall' was the name I snatched from the minds of passersby. Some had visited its exhibitions. Already there were a handful of cleaners and keen officials at work in there.

Nearby, the Ota River flowed beneath an unusual three-way bridge, spanning the Ota before it split two ways to become the Hon and Motoyasu rivers on its way to the sea. By providing a link to the island district of Nakajima, the Aioi Bridge formed a distinctive T-shape.

A perfect target from high overhead.

The city was bustling with people just getting into the day, who had no concept of themselves as aggressors. Amongst the trams, cars, rickshaws and bicycles, there were soldiers – yes, many soldiers – but all I could see was young couples in the flush of love, geisha girls smiling shyly out from beneath their parasols, somebody's beloved grandpa, many children on their way to school…

I took to the sky, climbing higher and higher, searching with my mind not for flying metal but for the presence of human beings at altitude. I found them at thirty thousand feet.

By now, the air raid sirens were sounding again; but the Americans met with no resistance. Compared to missions over Germany, where they were lucky to get through enemy air space with their lives, some would later remark how eerily undefended the skies over Hiroshima were.

There were three aeroplanes to the south-west, heading in from the sea. I had a minute, perhaps two…

I soared to the nearest and passed through the fuselage, seeking the minds of the crew, finding the pilot – Captain George Marquadt. I learnt quickly that George, son of a veterinarian, had been brought up in the small community of Golconda, Illinois; a star player in his high school basketball team, he'd interrupted his scholarship to Illinois Wesleyan University to join the Army Air Corps; he'd just married his sweetheart Bernece in Salt Lake City and was twenty-six.

I also learnt that this plane, designated 'Victor 91', was carrying photographic equipment. It was an observer only.

In the aftermath of what followed, they would give Victor 91 a new name: 'The Necessary Evil'.

Dropping through the floor, I made for the next plane. For a fleeting moment, my heart leapt elated – I was flying with B-29s! Not for nothing were these graceful silver birds known as Superfortresses. The air rippled with the waves of power from their four propeller-driven engines. Any other time, I would have surrendered to the joy of coasting alongside such magnificent feats of engineering.

I rolled and slid through the fuselage of the next plane, 'The Great Artiste'. There were thirteen men here, three of whom were scientists on board as observers. Skating through a few minds – radio operator Abe Spitzer, tail gunner Albert 'Pappy' DeHart, bombardier Kermit Beahan – I finally alighted upon the man in charge: Major Charles Sweeney.

At twenty-five, Sweeney was a Massachusetts man, the son of an Irish-American Catholic; an avid pilot for as long as he could remember, he'd been married to Dorothy going on for five years. He was very proud to be responsible for the blast measurement instrumentation for this historic mission…

From the cockpit of B-29, I could see the third plane was marginally leading the way. As I watched, we began to veer away from it to put some distance between us. The Great Artiste's observers were gearing up to watch from safety. I thrust myself through the air, again feeling my strength weakening – my body desperate to wake up in Berlin. I spun dizzily and below me Hiroshima was a kaleidoscope. Then I corrected and swam for the final plane, close enough now to read her name.

Enola Gay.

Such a pretty name for a monster.

Entering from the rear, the first man I encountered was the tail gunner, Staff Sergeant Bob Caron. A fresh-faced twenty-five-year-old from Brooklyn, his thoughts never far from his wife Kay, to whom he'd been married for less than a year, Bob's head was still buzzing following the exchange he'd just had with their aircraft commander, Colonel Tibbets.

Aside from some relatively low-risk bombing missions over the Japanese islands, Hiroshima was only Bob's fourth mission. Like the other crew members, his mind had been blown by their briefing back on Tinian. For only two days, he had known he was one of the chosen, the privileged few fated to be heroes for all history.

Back at base, he'd felt like a Hollywood star – what with the lights and cameras and all. It had been like the big show-biz premiere of a new Bing Crosby, or something. All that was missing was a red carpet. They'd been seen off by generals and admirals and he'd never posed for so many pictures.

As they were in the final stages of approach, Bob was excitedly checking his equipment in the gun turret for the umpteenth time. He'd been up since before midnight and in the air since three but was wired – as the only gunner on board, he was the Enola Gay's sole line of defense.

Up until a few minutes earlier, Bob had been in the waist section of the plane – it got lonely in the tail – and this was where he'd encountered the Colonel.

They'd be dropping a new kind of bomb – the equivalent of twenty thousand tons of TNT, Tibbets had said in the briefing. But back in the waist, the Colonel had challenged him to guess about their cargo. It had all been high security and need-to-know so far, but now they were in the air the mission commander was finally loosening up on his secrets.

Well, the boys had all been speculating about the presence of a few Brit scientists back on the island – chemists was the theory. But Bob had another theory: he'd been reading up on physics in his down time and had recently come across an article…

"Colonel," Bob had chanced. "Are we splitting atoms this morning?"

When Tibbets had confirmed this, it had sent one hell of a thrill through his tail gunner. Now Bob was readying his Fairchild K-20 camera. The skies were quiet and he suspected he would more likely be using a lens than a gun today.

Bob Caron was one of the regular crew assigned to the plane under Captain Robert A. Lewis, who had been skipper since she'd left the assembly line back in May. Along with Lewis and several others of the regular crew on board that day, collectively known as crew B-9, he'd seen her undergo a few name changes; but since only the day before, she was now known as 'Enola Gay'. Captain Lewis had pretty much freaked out when he'd turned up on the morning of the fifth to find that the Colonel named the plane after his mother.

Well, Bob had known Tibbets a damn sight longer than he'd known Lewis; he'd come a long way with the Colonel, who'd been instrumental in getting this mission in the air – and figured Tibbets deserved to stamp his mark on it.

I moved on, learning as much about the crew and their intentions as quickly as I could, skimming through their minds and filtering their thoughts. The oldest of the regular crew at thirty-two, flight engineer Wyatt Duzenbury exuded the confidence of a man who had seen three years active service; he often thought of his fiancée, Inez.

Radar operator Joe Stiborik thought of Texas and his immigrant Czech parents, of how he had always wanted to be a pilot but had failed the tests due to his being colour-blind; of his wife of seven years, Helen.

As assistant engineer Robert Shumard thought about Eleanor, he absent-mindedly tugged at the Saint Christopher she'd given him. As far as Shumard was concerned, this was a regular general-purpose mission; he had very little knowledge of their cargo and was happy to leave all that to the higher-ups near the nose of the plane.

At only twenty, the radio operator Richard Nelson was the youngest; he still couldn't quite believe he'd been plucked out of Radio School – where he'd shown strong aptitude – and dropped into Tibbets' outfit, without any previous overseas or combat experience. His head still spinning with the glamorous send-off they'd been given, Dick was quietly monitoring the airwaves, but – as had been the case for hours now – was rewarded only with radio silence.

As he usually did on long flights, he'd filled the time by reading a book – five and a half inches by four, pocketsize books such as these were official issues from the Council on Books in Wartime, exclusively distributed to the American Armed Forces. This one was 'Watch Out For Willie Carter' by Theodore Naidish, which featured the adventures of a gentleman boxer. It had been a good read.

They'd all been hand-picked by Tibbets, it seemed. He'd generally flown with them before – some back in Europe on B-17s. The

Colonel was held in high regard. But as a crew they weren't particularly tight: sure, Bob had flown with Duze a few times these past months, but several of the twelve-man crew had replaced the regulars. Their usual co-pilot, navigator and bombardier had all been bounced for this mission.

I knew if I was to have any chance of stopping them dropping the bomb, I needed to make my way along the claustrophobic tunnel towards the front, but on my way there I encountered two of the new additions to the crew: Jacob Beser and Morris Jeppson. At twenty-four and twenty-three respectively, these guys knew far more about the mission than the regular crew.

Alarmingly for someone who had such a critical role in the proceedings, Jacob had barely slept in thirty hours – up until their take-off from Tinian, his pre-flight duties had kept him from getting his head down. Therefore, much to the amusement of the enlisted crew, he had only just awoken from a one thousand-mile snooze – and even then, it had taken strong coffee to properly wake him up.

An expert in mechanical engineering and electronics, Jacob was responsible for the radar-related workings of the bomb – specifically, he had to babysit a fuse device on the bomb set to blow at a precise altitude above ground. For Hiroshima, this would be one thousand, eight hundred and fifty feet, which it recognised by bouncing radar beams off the ground. He also had to monitor enemy radar to ensure they weren't using the same frequency as said fuse, for obvious reasons.

It's fair to say Jacob Beser was radiating a greater sense of heightened awareness than most of the crew. For him, this was no 'milk run' or general-purpose mission. When Jacob had first been recruited for Tibbets' outfit, he'd been told there were others in the military who could do the job but they were deemed "too valuable to risk". Baltimore born, Jewish by religion, he had been heavily motivated to fight by the loss of family in Germany; but right now, with notions of his own expendability knocking around his head, Jacob Beser was feeling rather more mortal than his colleagues.

As for Morris 'Dick' Jeppson, here was a man who had travelled a long way with the atomic bomb. Having been attached to the Manhattan Project at the Los Alamos National Laboratory, under Scientific Director and genius physicist Robert Oppenheimer, Dick had been associated with the development of the electronics fusing on the bomb. Oppenheimer himself had personally endorsed Dick as a shortlisted candidate for his role on this mission, which was to monitor the electronics on route to their target.

It had been a shortlist of six, all of whom had trained at Harvard and the Massachusetts Institute of Technology to do the same job. Yesterday, the list had been narrowed to two and a toss of the coin had decided Dick was to fly. This was his first combat mission, which was why he was the only man on board who was wearing his parachute.

It would be his only combat mission.

He wasn't officially in the know, but – while as far as most of the crew were concerned, they were dropping a bomb of extraordinary power – he'd figured out they were carrying a uranium-based device.

I hesitated here for a moment.

Of all the men I'd encountered on the Enola Gay so far, Dick Jeppson had the most access to the bomb. On the journey, while they were still flying low at eight thousand feet, he had been regularly checking the circuits to make sure the batteries, timers and radars were all talking to each other. Half an hour earlier, it had been his responsibility to swap the green 'testing' plugs for the red 'firing' plugs – after which the Enola Gay had begun her ascent to thirty thousand feet, with an armed titan in her belly.

This had made him the last man to actually touch the bomb.

Dick's job was now essentially done, but he was brimming with tension: the bomb was live; he had enabled a destructive power greater than tens of thousands of tons of TNT. But Dick was waiting, going over the math in his head, working out how long after the bomb dropped he should see the flash of detonation inside the cabin, how long after that he could expect the shockwaves – a primary then a secondary, as the primary was bounced back up again from the ground.

Because it needed to detonate above the ground, not on impact…

It occurred to me I might try to get under Jeppson's skin, climb into his head and possess him. Maybe I could get him to climb into the bomb bay, swap the plugs back around…

But it was too late, because a voice came over the radio declaring they had commenced the bomb run, the bay doors swung open before me – and I laid eyes on the atomic bomb for the first time.

Little Boy.

They had given it a cute name.

I caught a glimpse from Jeppson: one of the scientists had chosen to name it after a character from 'The Maltese Falcon'. This was a theme, apparently – an earlier, aborted plutonium-based bomb had been named 'Thin Man' after another of Dashiell Hammett's books; and their other bomb was also called 'Fat Man' after a Hammett character…

My God. They had *another* bomb…

I didn't have time to digest this, as I was already making for the cockpit.

Caron, Duzenbury, Stiborik, Shumard, Nelson, Beser, Jeppson – highly skilled, yes, but ordinary men. Here now was Theodore 'Dutch' Van Kirk, Tibbets' chosen navigator. At twenty-four, he was already a veteran of dangerous air missions and had often flown with Tibbets – his mind occasionally wandered to fifty or so sorties he had made across Europe and North Africa.

He was thinking this one seemed much easier than most – they were so high they were unlikely to hit flak up here. His thoughts drifted to his wife, Mary Jane, and his month-old daughter, Connie. He wondered if Connie was sleeping through tonight. He had little perception of this as being any different a mission than the others he'd participated in.

But here was Captain William 'Deke' Parsons, the man in charge. At forty-three, the oldest on board, Deke was a modest, well-liked, conscientious man who had been with the Manhattan Project since 1943; his track record in ordnance had seen him recruited by Oppenheimer to be his Number Two. It was Deke Parsons who had been instrumental in building the military machine around Oppenheimer's science.

Over the previous weeks at Tinian, Deke had seen several B-29s burn up after crashes on the runway. Alarmed at the prospect of an Enola Gay crash that might detonate its cargo and take out the entire American base, he had – just the day before – volunteered to personally arm Little Boy once they were safely in the air. Thus, he'd had the unique distinction of spending most of the last eighteen hours in cramped conditions, practising how to finalise the assembly of a nuclear bomb.

Deke had spent a lot of the long flight thinking of his wife, Martha, to whom he'd been married since 1929 – and of their daughters, Peggy and Clare, a ten-year-old nerd and a seven-year-old tomboy. But now he was rerunning the insertion of the powder charge and detonator over and over, doubting himself like Beser and Jeppson – had he got it right?

For the briefest of instants, I considered somehow using him to deactivate the bomb – but I saw in his mind that we were only seconds away.

Then I was in the cockpit, thinking, *"Who the hell do I stop? Which one is it?"*

As the pilot and co-pilot raised their heavy Polaroid goggles in preparation, I saw they were ill at ease with one another. Having dropped the regular navigator, bombardier and co-pilot from the crew for this mission, Paul Tibbets had taken the pilot's seat from Bob Lewis; he'd named the plane after his mother.

A keen footballer and a ladies' man, Lewis generally felt left out of the loop – having only just learnt from Tibbets they were ferrying an atomic bomb. Of all the men aboard, he would struggle the most with a sense if remorse.

As aircraft commander, Colonel Paul Tibbets answered to their mission commander, Captain Parsons – but in many ways felt this moment belonged to him. He was a driven man, consumed by a sense of purpose, who was held in high regard by his superior officers – both as a pilot and a leader. At only thirty, Tibbets had been made commander of the nine-month-old 509th Composite Group, the USAF's task force for the waging of atomic warfare; he was in charge of fifteen B-29s and nearly eighteen hundred people.

Shining with determination and feeling indestructible, he was piloting a plane crewed with men he had chosen on a mission that would go down in history.

Naming the plane after his mother said everything about how this man ticked. When Paul had opted to abandon a career in medicine to join the army and fly, Enola Gay Tibbets had supported her son in the face of his father's opposition. In Tibbets' mind, that moment was directly linked to this one. The dropping of the bomb would vindicate her support and the passion for flying his father could not understand; it would justify the displacement he'd put his wife, Lucy, and their two sons through.

As a boy growing up in Miami, during his attendance at the Hialeah Race Track, his mother had allowed him to fly on board a Waco 9 bi-plane and drop parachuted Baby Ruth candy bars into the crowd – from that day he'd had the flying bug. The sense of riding a magic carpet over the mere mortals below had stayed with him ever since. Since then, he'd been Patton's personal pilot, been amongst the first Americans deployed to Europe and to bomb the Germans in occupied France, been the guy selected to fly Eisenhower to Gibraltar and had survived forty-three combat missions.

Deep inside, Paul was a twelve-year-old dropping a bomb-shaped candy bar that would save millions of American lives.

At that moment, Paul Tibbets was bracing himself to get his crew safely out once the bomb had dropped. He'd spoken to Oppenheimer about their chances and knew this bomb was a very different beast to those they'd used to drop in Europe. To fly any lower than thirty thousand feet would be fatal. There could be no flying straight ahead; if they were above the explosion, they'd be incinerated.

Without her heavy burden, the Enola Gay would naturally want to lift away. They'd need to veer off in a one hundred- and fifty-nine-degree tangent to the shockwave, *fast* – and get the hell out of Dodge…

With seconds left, I realised it wasn't Paul Tibbets who'd been charged with the final act. Beneath them in the glass bubble in the nose of the B-29 sat their bombardier, Major Thomas Ferebee – focused intently on the Norden Bombsight before him.

Tom Ferebee: aged twenty-six, a farm boy from a big family in North Carolina, he'd tried out for the Boston Red Sox but hadn't made the team; abandoning dreams of professional baseball, he'd found his place in the Air Force – paarticularly at Paul Tibbets' side. He, Tibbets and Dutch Van Kirk had flown together many times and the Colonel thought of him as the best bombardier in the air.

As a veteran who knew his instruments and job inside out, Ferebee was less nervous than some of the greener crew members; in fact, this seemed like one of the easiest runs he'd ever had. There was the small matter of the cyanide tablets they'd all been issued with – but it was well known how the Japs treated their prisoners.

Ferebee had snoozed for some of the journey, spending his waking hours consulting with Dutch – after so many sorties, the bombardier and navigator had developed a form of verbal shorthand. He'd also watched Parsons and Jeppson assemble the bomb. Now it was coming up to nine-fifteen American time, eight-fifteen Japanese time, and it was all about him and his Norden Bombsight.

What a freak of history this man was. I caught slips of his childhood; his home town Mocksville back in Davie County; his Mum and Dad, William and Zella; of his love of the game; of Ann. But mostly he was thinking about ending the war. Tom had gazed down a lot of sights and dropped a lot of bombs. It was a distant, detached way to kill people, but he didn't like to think about that.

The brass said this could bring it to an end and that was all he needed to hear.

The Norden Bombsight was deemed so top secret it left the plane at the end of each mission to spend the night secured. There wasn't a lever to pull or a button to push; properly pampered, the Norden finished the job and all Tom had to do was make sure it kept on ticking. From some angles it looked like a large movie camera, but it essentially consisted of a gyroscopic stabilisation platform, a mechanical analog computer and a sighting prism mounted with an eyepiece.

As they'd left Tinian, the bombardier had calculated his drop point by inputting altitude, velocity, range and heading, making allowances for the unique weight and aerodynamics of the bomb. Somewhere over Iwo Jima, he'd switched on his sight and the device had come to life, seeking out its target – at this point, he'd been in constant contact with navigation and radar.

On approach, he'd fine-tuned for the effects of wind and drift, with his sighting point crosshair slowly, tachometrically zeroing in on the target crosshair.

Now he was looking for a confirmed visual of the primary. In theory, he could have trusted the Norden to decide when to drop for itself, but Tom had to be sure – and there it was! After so many hours poring over photographs, there was a thrill in seeing it with his own eyes: a T-shaped bridge where all the fingers kind of came together, like the wrist of a hand.

The Aioi Bridge.

With the target virtually motionless in his sights and the crosshairs moving into alignment, all that remained was for Tom Ferebee to finally release control to the Automatic Flight Control autopilot; the bombsight would essentially guide the bomber for the final seconds and automatically deploy the bomb.

Which is where I stopped him…

I don't know if Tom Ferebee ever knew I was there inside his head. In that instant, I was a schizophrenic thing: the naïve idealist my friend Jack Mayfair despised so lovingly; an Allied soldier and very human; and I was of the Society, alien and removed from the obsessions of mere mortals.

I saw a horrendous precedent. It wasn't just the staggering numbers; it was this hideous idea that was finally taking hold, that so long as there was some sort of lens involved, you could detach yourself from causing suffering to people who will never know your name. It had become acceptable to view our fellow humans as ants. We had flicked a switch and engaged a species-wide empathy bypass.

Jack's words came back to haunt me – perhaps this is just what we were. Perhaps this was the beginning of the end for us and good riddance. I thought back over the wars I'd seen, the barbarity visited upon so many. My heart bled and I knew Jack would have scoffed at that, exasperated, and that many like him and worse would perceive me is weak.

I still had to cling onto some sort of faith, that beyond all this there was still an impetus for good much stronger than our nihilistic need to wreck our own playground.

Looking down that sight, through Tom Ferebee's eyes, I confronted demons of my own – from a moment, mere months ago, when I had been in his position. I'd been riven with regret ever since.

These men weren't here to conquer; all they wanted was to end this. They'd flown out of Tinian, fully aware they might not return, in the belief that ending the war would save thousands of lives. In their minds, this was about striking out in the name of freedom.

It seemed absurd to end killing by doing lots of killing; but this was where we'd come to – the most grotesque peak of human stupidity.

The only question was: would it work? If this really was to end the war, *could* it be justified?

There was a wave of conviction behind this mission, from a lot of very intelligent, compassionate men, that *this* was the way – and if this mission were to fail, they'd try and try again. They all believed a ground invasion of Japan would cost far more lives; they'd all been briefed that Hiroshima was a military target – and, sure enough, down there was what was left of the Japanese army.

I knew I couldn't hope to be on every plane they sent.

How could we possibly begin to anticipate the repercussions of that in the coming decades? Perhaps the human race needed to drop the bomb in order to learn not to drop the bomb…

I'll always wonder whether that crucial moment of indecision cost me what little energy I had left.

"Bomb away!" Ferebee declared – and Tibbets immediately threw the Enola Gay into a sharp angle, initiating a descent that would see the twelve men safely miles away in the forty-three seconds they had before detonation. But while they counted, I followed Little Boy out of the bomb bay doors.

I owed it to the people of Hiroshima to witness the truth of this and ensure it was shared.

Little Boy was a squat, ugly, bulbous thing ten feet long, weighing ten thousand pounds. Once it was clear of the aircraft, timers kicked in and circuits closed, activating the radar altimeter firing command circuit. Once the radar altimeters had detected optimum altitude, a firing switch closed, setting off a charge of four silk bags each packed with cordite – an explosive made from nitroglycerine, nitrocellulose and petroleum jelly. In what is called a 'gun method', this shot a uranium bullet along the barrel of the bomb at an enriched uranium target, instantaneously causing a nuclear chain reaction of rapidly intensifying energy.

As this was all happening inside it, Little Boy and I soared. It was a stunningly beautiful day and the view of Hiroshima contained in her valley bowl, left deliberately pristine and untouched by the war, was astonishing. Virgin soil, there wasn't a lick of damage on her. She was a perfect guinea pig.

The question of what might happen to that side of my consciousness that was falling with Little Boy had barely occurred to me. I distantly thought I might die now.

We fell twenty-eight thousand feet together, Little Boy and I. At nineteen hundred feet from the ground, the altitude chosen to cause the most destruction, the sky turned to fire; nanoseconds turned to milliseconds and wave upon wave of gamma rays coasting on a plasma fireball reached out to the rooftops of the city.

I remember it like it was yesterday.

I remember it like I am still there.

- CHAPTER SEVEN -

I Have Become the Rain

My soul is shattered into thousands of tiny fragments and scattered everywhere.

There are many, many people with me, suspended between breaths. We feel no fear, no time to feel resentment or bewilderment. Then we are gone, dissipating into the burning wind – sixty thousand of us, deleted from existence. There isn't time to blink, let alone register our passing; we leave no signature other than dust.

Little Boy has been taken ever so slightly of course. It has missed the bridge, detonating over Shima Hospital and instantly vaporising everybody within. The hospital is the first of Hiroshima's seventy-six thousand buildings to go.

After the explosion and the resulting firestorm, only six thousand will be left.

First comes the light – white and celestial, but vicious – ripping into my retinas, pounding at my brain. The blast follows instantaneously, as Little Boy's yield tears into the city's densely populated machiya communities, devouring flimsy wooden townhouses like an immense rabid beast – every inch of narrow street and alleyway engulfed in one wrathful gulp. For a radius of several miles from the hypocentre, the city simply folds and life capitulates to thunder, rolling relentlessly through it at a velocity greater than the speed of sound.

The heart of the explosion is a fireball burning at six thousand degrees centigrade.

One fragment of me makes it back to the Enola Gay and finds gunner Robert Caron – because of his vantage point in the tail of the B-29, the first man to witness the mushroom cloud which signalled the eradication of Hiroshima. I watch through his eyes as it bubbles up behind the turret, white on the outside and a sort of purplish black with a fiery red core towards the centre. Looking down upon the city, Bob thinks of bubbling molasses spreading out, up into the foothills – the foothills that are containing and refocusing the heat and fire back onto the city, as Little Boy's wards have always intended.

From his window, Jacob Beser thinks the cloud looks like sand billowing up in shallow water. In the cockpit, Paul Tibbets sees the sky lit up with the prettiest blues and pinks he has ever seen in his life; Tom Ferebee thinks he can see dissolving buildings boiling up inside the cloud; Bob Lewis sits in shock as the city is consumed by fire – never having expected anything like this.

On board Victor 91, George Marquadt feels it is like the sun has come out of the ground and exploded.

For a moment, I am with Shuntaro.

Attending a patient in the nearby village of Hesaka, four miles away, Shuntaro Hida – who would normally be on duty in the military hospital in central Hiroshima – witnesses from ground level the rise of the mushroom cloud. Through his eyes, it has many colours and is strangely beautiful, but gives birth to a black tidal wave that is coming his way – until the shockwave hits and he blacks out.

The hibakusha are born – and the horror begins.

Across the city, we are thrown from our feet by an immense force. Those who will survive are mostly indoors, partially shielded; one moment we are in offices at our desks, or at home doing chores, the next we are weightless. Coming to, we find we have been blown to one end of the room, or into another room entirely, that the glass from our windows is now embedded in our bodies – and we are being roasted alive.

One by one, we come blinking back into the world, to find that it has been turned inside out. Where a breath before there has been blue skies, now the sky is stolen from us. It is as dark as night with a half moon. We are beneath a rising mushroom of ferocious heat and unearthly power, sucking up the debris of consumed buildings and the detritus of consumed people – above us rising the ashes of everything we've ever known, our lives, our loved ones.

I am Eizo Nomura, forty-seven, a worker for the Fuel Rationing Union at the Prefectural Fuel Hall.

Moments earlier, I'd been under stairs in the hall basement, looking for documents. I don't know it yet, but at little over one hundred and seventy yards from the Shima Hospital, I am a small miracle.

I stumble out of the wreckage of the hall with my friend Hirose, who like me is also bleeding. Together we turn to take in our desecrated city. At the nearby Motoyasu Bridge, my eyes fall upon a naked man lying on his back and pointing to the sky with trembling hands; his clothes have been burnt off of him. Everywhere people are emerging near-naked, their clothing having been incinerated off their skin. Some are rolling on the ground to put the flames out.

Finding a patch of earth, Hirose and I sit and peer through the black smoke to see that the Prefectural Industrial Promotion Hall is still standing, it's dome now a shattered husk. The shells of other structures remain partially intact, but these are only the newer reinforced concrete buildings, built with earthquakes in mind. The flames are spreading now – before long we see our workplace go up.

All I can think of is the faces of my children, wonder how they will manage without me.

Others from the Union have escaped to join us – four women and two more men. All injured, we watch in silence until the stifling heat becomes too much and we flee the sparks and burning rubble being spat upon us. The smoke is stinging our eyes and scalding our throats. As we flee, we witness the Motoyasu River spiral up into a column, its water being whipped up into the air in a tornado…

I am twenty-year-old Akiko, a worker at the Bank of Hiroshima – three hundred yards or so from the hypocentre.

One minute I'd been dusting desks, the next there'd been a flash like white magnesium in my head; then came the dark and the heat. Now there are many wounds on my back. I convince my badly injured friend Asami to flee the flaming shell of the bank, thinking to escape to the parade grounds, but everywhere we turn the fire is eating our oxygen.

It feels like we are just breathing in hot smoke.

My friend and I collapse in the street, two girls watching helplessly as a whirlpool of fire whips at us from the south, consuming everything in its path. Feeling my own skin starting to burn, I watch in shock as the fire devours dead bodies nearby. It seems to start by melting their fingertips then engulfing their hands – and all I can think is how painful it is to know that they should burn away so easily, these hands and fingers that should be holding babies and turning pages…

I am fifteen-year-old Taeko, a third grader from the girls' junior high school.

As one of the many students mobilised for the war effort, I've been working in the central telephone office, half a kilometre from the hypocentre. As I recover consciousness in the rubble of the office, I struggle to make sense of this new world around me. I can hear people calling for help. I can't move. There is a smell like Sulphur, the smell you get around volcanoes; the smell of the Earth ripping open.

Where has the sun gone? Have I fallen asleep and this is a nightmare?

Finally, our class teacher Mister Wakita calls for us to pull ourselves together. Managing to free myself, I stumble with him out into the dark. Where there should have been a bustling city, there is only flame and silence and smoke so dense it's hard to get our bearings. Passing the burning bridge, we wade into the river together; it is running very high and I'm out of my depth. Half way across, I begin to struggle and I'm losing consciousness again, but he gets me across. He saves my life.

Panting for breath on the far bank, I can see little in that hideous smoke; but I can hear. I'd thought at first that a bomb had been dropped on the telephone office, but I realise now that this was something much bigger. For my mobilisation, I'd been working indoors, but many of my fellow students have been assigned to widening the streets and creating firebreaks in the area of Tsurumi Bridge and the City Hall. They'd been outside when the bomb was dropped, all these high school students. Now they are burnt and dying in the streets; some are crawling into the river and drowning.

And this is what I hear: many, many of them crying for their mothers.

Half a mile from the hypocentre, near Hatchobori Station, I am clambering out of a shattered streetcar – one of seventy such streetcars that had been running in the city only moments before, all packed tight for the morning commute. My name is Eiko; I am twenty-one and I am on my way to Funairi to acquire a wagon for my impending house move.

In my arms is my one-year-old son, who was beside the window – now his face is bloodied from the glass, but he manages a dazed smile for his mother. Such a good boy.

He does not last the month.

I am seventeen-year-old Tomiko, travelling with two classmates to a holiday at a friend's in Funairi; the other girls are both badly burnt and in great pain, so I am looking for water to tend their wounds. Although my face is bleeding, somehow I am not burnt.

Perhaps this is why I will live, while they will die two weeks later.

I am Akira; at seventeen, I am training to be an airman. This was to be a day off with my elder brother, who is beside me now. We feel lucky to have survived and join others in fleeing along the tracks, as someone is warning of a second strike.

Lucky, yes, but my brother's luck runs out in September.

My name is Tsutaichi; I am a thirty-seven year-old factory worker, travelling with three co-workers. We have survived the blast, but they will all be gone within three weeks.

I am Keiko, aged fourteen, on my way with friends for a day out at Miyajima, since we have no mobilised labour today. I have never known heat like this. I touch my skin and it peels right off. One of my friends is worse than me so we set out to get her seen to at the first-aid station at Nukushina.

She doesn't make the day.

I drift again, finally finding the classroom at Zakoba-cho, half a mile from the hypocentre, where I am a thirteen-year-old boy named Yoshitaka. I've come to in terrible pain, trapped under debris and breathing sandy dust. All around me, my classmates are recovering consciousness too. Frightened, sobbing and calling out for our teachers and mothers, after a while about ten of us bravely start singing our school song. It's a way to draw our rescuers to us.

Nobody comes. Slowly, I realise mid-chorus that I am the only one still singing.

With all my strength, I push and struggle and at last shuffle my way out from beneath my prison, out into the dark and the distant threat of what sounds like a storm on the ground. Although I am bleeding, my injuries are not terrible; I look around for someone to help and find a friend who is still alive. His skull is cracked open, his flesh is dangling from his head and he has lost an eye. He looks back at me with his remaining eye and tries to tell me something; he manages to reach to his chest pocket, to his notebook there and I promise to find his mother and give it to her. I am unable to pull him out.

The remains of my school are ablaze now and I try to get to the playground. As I run, my friends are grabbing at my ankles. I am horrified at so many hands trying to grab at my ankles, but I am in such pain and terror that I kick them away.

Of all things, this will stay with me forever.

I make it to the Miyuki Bridge, my throat desperately dry now with the heat and dust. The water is dead people. I push the bodies aside to drink the muddy water. Above me, the mushroom cloud rises – so bright, rippling with every colour of the rainbow, it is beautiful. I wonder whether I will ever see my mother again, or my little brother. I slowly lose consciousness, and this is a comfort. Much later, when they start to load the bodies like sacks into the trucks, I am very lucky. A soldier drops me and, picking me up again, finds I have a pulse…

I am Shoji; dragging myself from the rubble of my home, I hear my mother calling. Only thirteen, I am not strong enough to lift the beam that is pinning her down. Soon the flames are licking at us and weeping I beg her forgiveness. As she releases my hand, her last words are, "Study hard and be a good student."

I am Hiroko, eighteen, fleeing with friends from the remains of the Bureau of Post Communications in Hakushima. We are all making for the river, but it is a stampede now to escape the flames and we tumble down the cliff like dominoes, where I have to squirm and wriggle out from the growing crush-pile of screaming people. Managing to get free, I swim across towards the opposite bank in relief – but it is becoming a growing struggle and I am being spun around and then I realise I am caught in some sort of swirling tornado in the water. I am slipping beneath the water again and again, swallowing a lot of it; I am drowning. The faces of my family come to my mind one after another – my mother, my sister, my two younger brothers.

Miraculously, I find a friend and – so glad to see one another – we help pull each other from the whirlpool. Escaping the panic, we dare not look back. I set out to find my loved ones.

A man comes running by with a camera…

For a time, I am Yoshito Matsushige, thirty-two, photographer for the Chugoku Newspaper. I am trying to take pictures, but keep failing – it feels wrong. The people are so pathetic, wretchedly stripped of their humanity. There are some children who have lost their shoes and have burnt the soles of their feet where they've had to run barefoot through the fire; I want to capture this moment, but I can't push the shutter and the view finder is clouded with my tears.

Coming across the burnt-out streetcar, I peer in to see fifteen or so people lying dead on top of one another. I can't take the picture. There is no dignity in their death and I will not record it.

I am an American airman, Normand Roland Brissette from Lowell, Massachusetts; I'm nineteen. Airman Third Class, I was combat gunner for my pilot Lieutenant Ray Porter when our Curtiss SB2C Helldiver – flying out of the aircraft carrier Ticonderoga, as part of a thirty-nine plane strike on Kure Naval Base – took a hit. Forced to ditch, we took to a life raft, were picked up by the Japanese and have been POW for the past ten days in the Chugoku Kempei Tai Military Police Headquarters.

As it was barely a quarter of a mile from the hypocentre, the Police Headquarters is pretty much a wreck now. Ray bought it in the blast. We weren't the only prisoners there: the Japs were also holding John Hantschel, pilot of a downed F6 Hellcat from the USS Randolph – as well as another six guys, most of the surviving crew of the B-24 'Lonesome Lady'.

They're all dead too now except from Ralph Neal, a Kentucky boy who was ball turret gunner on the B-24. We were lucky; we managed to survive the worst of it by submerging ourselves into a cesspool. Well, I call it luck. We've already fallen straight back into enemy hands and maybe that's lucky too, because I wouldn't want to be an Allied soldier on the streets of Hiroshima right now. But my skin's burning up and already I'm feeling sick to my stomach.

I'm thinking about my folks, about my kid sister Connie – so proud that I'm fighting for my country. From what I'm hearing out there in the smoke, sounds like the end of the war. Only two years since I left High School. Feels like a lifetime. Can't wait to get back to the States, to Lowell. I'll be a hero. Bet there'll be a parade.

My God, the things I'm hearing out there…

I am a prince. A member of the declining Korean Royal Family, a shadow of its former glory these days since the Japanese annexed my country, I am grandson and nephew to emperors. There are very few of my like. At age thirty-two, my name is Yi Wu; I am a Lieutenant-Colonel in the Japanese Army and I am dying.

Lying here not far from the river, between the Honkawa and Aioi bridges, barely conscious, I am so badly burnt and the pain is so ferocious that I know the end is near. We are so many, the nearly dead, stumbling mindlessly until we drop and die.

I am thinking of the Unhyeon Palace, of Seoul, of the home I will never see again; of my wife and my two boys. I think of the tragedy of my friend and adjutant, Yoshinari Hiroshi, who will most certainly commit seppuku in despair at his failure to protect me. Men are coming now, lifting and carrying me. I wonder how many more of my countrymen have been claimed by this bomb.

For a while, I am Robert Tulliver – or some part of him at least – gazing down at this soldier as he is rushed away. Tulliver thinks, *"He was our legitimate target."* A high-ranking officer, who has served against the Chinese – surely, he was guilty of terrible war crimes. Surely, he deserved this. There are many combatants amongst the dead. When the dust – the loaded, radioactive dust – settles, their corpses will number some twenty thousand.

Combatants…

Was *this* how we would be defining combat now? Tulliver reminds himself of the alternative, but his conviction is a flickering candle in this relentless wind.

What of the Koreans? Much later it will transpire that they make up another twenty thousand of the dead. The Prince is unusual in that he is treated with respect by the Japanese; most of the Koreans present in Hiroshima this day are cheap labour in the factories.

Tulliver comes across a party of priests, Jesuits, who have apparently emerged unscathed from the ruins of their church, the Assumption of Our Lady at Nobori-cho, barely a kilometre from the hypocentre. It seems that all four members of the Central Mission in Hiroshima have miraculously survived. They are hastily placating an agitated Kempei Tai, who is seconds away from shooting them dead – for they are not Japanese and a Caucasian face is a dangerous thing to be wearing today.

There are rumours of an American airman having been tied up and beaten to death near the Aioi Bridge; also of the angry stoning of American POWs. But Tulliver sees no sign of this.

"We are Germans," they desperately assure him. "*Allies.*"

Although they are not burnt, upon second glance they are in a bad way. Father Schiffer has sustained a head injury and his skin has been lacerated; he is losing a lot of blood. Father Superior Lassalle is slowly succumbing to the wounds on his legs, so painful now that he will soon be unable to walk; his entire back is riddled with glass. Father Cieslik has minor cuts and bruises and will recover well, but Father Kleinsorge will ultimately suffer greatly from the after-effects.

As the policeman stalks off, appeased, Tulliver circles the Jesuit party for a while and reads their minds to learn their story – all four emanate a powerful force for good, but Hugo Lassalle is an unusual Gifted man with a great interest in Zen Buddhism. The four priests are accompanied by a young seminarian called Takemoto, their housekeeper Mrs Murata and Kanji Fukai, secretary to the vicar apostolic, a former Anglican priest now converted to Roman Catholicism.

Fukai is demented and has clearly lost his mind.

Their church has been levelled, as has all the houses around them; all that is left are the contorted remains of a few concrete structures and their battered residence, which was sturdier than most as it had been constructed recently using lessons learnt from the 1923 Tokyo earthquake.

Since climbing from the rubble of the priests' residence, they have endeavoured to help as many people as they can. They've pulled out the family of Mister Hoshijima, their resident catechist, from beneath their collapsed home – alas, Hoshijima himself and his son were on their way to work at the prefectural offices when the bomb fell. The priests have also freed the children of the church kindergarten and their teacher.

It is quickly becoming apparent that, though many of the buried are not badly injured, rescuing them in the face of the swarming flames will be impossible. Instead, they have had to flee here, to the open expanse of Asano Park, along a hellish route flanked by the desperate – and yet tragically formal – pleas for help of a trapped congregation only seconds away from burning to death.

These Catholics are the Central Mission; there is also an additional Novitiate of the Society of Jesus housing more priests on the outskirts of the city at Nagatsuka. The Jesuit mission to Japan has been largely driven out of Tokyo by the air raids there. In contrast, the Fathers at Hiroshima have lately become so used to the constant air raid sirens and presence of enemy planes – and yet no actual bombing – that they had stopped making for the bomb shelters.

Now the Allied bomb has visited upon the parish of Hiroshima an exorcism so fierce as to purify it of any naivety for a lifetime.

Stumbling over a gruesome sea of the dead and dying, past soldiers whose faces have melted and children who are quietly slipping away, the priests manage to find a patch of grass on which to collapse. They dispatch the student Takemoto to try to reach their colleagues at Nagatsuka. In the chaos, they lose track of Mister Fukai – who seems determined to consign himself to the fire.

Young men, passionately devout, Cieslik and Kleingorge set about tending to the injured, many of whom have also fled to the park. They do much good, bringing water to those in need and receiving tragically polite bows of gratitude for their trouble. Soon the flames are nipping at the trees of the park and the priests join in with the fight to repel them; but the crowd, growing newly fearful, presses towards the river – driving the weakest into the waters to drown.

A whirlwind tears through the park, ripping trees out at the root and spinning debris high up into its funnel, to crash it down into the river. It's as if the elements themselves have been tortured into deranged, abnormal behaviour, in wretched anguish at the atrocity we have rained upon them.

Tulliver retreats from this, numbed by the insanity… Tulliver… *I* am *Tulliver. I'm going mad. I must leave this place, or it will suck me up like those uprooted trees and drown me forever in wretchedness and horror.*

I retreat into a priest, hoping to find solace there. Clutching his Rosary and praying, channeling the message of Fatima so that he may heal and survive this day, he believes that he has been spared by the grace of God; having been so close to the epicentre of this terrible cataclysm, he can only conclude that they were shielded from the worst by the Blessed Mother to whom they have devoted their lives.

I recoil. There's no "grace" here! Brought up a Christian these past five hundred years, I have always kept the faith; but what manner of

God would allow this? I want to scream at Him, "Where was your purpose in this? You abandoned us this day!"

Some will smell a miracle in the survival of these men, but the priest is just one of the hibakusha – there are many who have been much closer to the hypocentre. Turning from him, I witness instead many small miracles of humanity in Asano Park – neighbour helping neighbour. The Japanese are already looking for ways to rebuild and to restore order.

Drifting through the firestorm which is now gulping in any surface air, anything flammable to feed itself into an inferno, I come across the shadow of a man imprinted on a stone steps – just an outline, remembered by the now-bleached stone. On I wander amongst the growing ocean of revenants, shuffling deliriously in stunned streams as if sleep walking, holding their hands away from themselves because it hurts less if they are raised, their faces swollen or blistered, their skin hanging in strips like tattered rags.

Many are begging for water.

I float wraithlike, detached and numb – unable to tear my eyes from them, yet desperate to get away. Here I see a mother wetting a towel and wiping the soot and dust from her baby son's face; she sings him a lullaby and bounces him in his papoose, then sets off in search of a lost husband she will never find.

A badly burnt mathematics teacher passes by leading the survivors of her mobilised class to find a hospital; they seem to be in a trance but are softly singing hymns together.

Nearby there is a woman, trapped by the flames and calling from a rooftop with a babe in arms; she's imploring the sea of people below for someone to catch the child, but nobody listens.

Then I come across a small girl crying and asking passersby to help pull her mother from the rubble; they try to lift the heavy fallen beam, but the fire drives them away. Weeping, the would-be rescuers bow deeply with clasped hands in apology and retreat. The mother is burnt alive and the child is lost in the crowd.

Here is a boy aged nine. His elder sister, who is twenty-one, is collapsed under their house and imploring, "Please move this pillar so I can get out. My legs are trapped. Give me a saw." Just a child far out of his depth, he looks about helplessly for a saw. His mother crawls out from nearby rubble. Numbly, she sees the oncoming fire. There is another daughter trapped as well.

Were it not for her son, the mother would just lie down and burn with them. Taking the boy's hand and silently leading him away, she closes her ears – but she'll hear their cries again every night for the rest of her life.

For a time, I walk beside an eight-year-old girl as she tries not to look while clambering over the dead. Hands grab at her legs and time and again there is a cry for water, but she needs to live. Once or twice, she hesitates and wonders whether she might just have the strength to lift some of this fallen wall or that roof beam, but I whisper in her ear, "Keep walking home. Ignore the cries. Don't look down. You should never have had to know this."

Soon I come across a contorted, blackened creature, her body frozen in paroxysms of fury and savage pain, emanating wave upon wave of strangled psychic distress the likes of which I had never known before.

And then I am Sachiko, whose name meant 'child of bliss' and could also be taken to mean 'happiness'. I am Sachiko, who knows this Robert Tulliver and glares at him in accusation.

You knew. You knew this was coming and you said nothing.

I turn and stumble into the river, sliding beneath the surface of waters now choked with the dead – and I am gone.

After a while, it begins to rain. We are so thirsty, we turn our faces to the sky and drink it in. But this is rain the likes of which the world has never seen before – similar to the rain following a volcanic eruption, perhaps, but never before has the rain been full of people.

The rain is black. It falls in drops so big they hurt our sore skin. Soon we are all drenched and, unbelievably for the height of summer, shivering. But even as our teeth are chattering, the downpour hardly seems to dent the firestorm. It just coats and stains our faces, hands and bodies in a sticky tar-like substance.

We don't know it, of course, but this is the harbinger of a new death mankind has created. It will become known as 'fallout' and the death will be radiation sickness. The heat generated by Little Boy has vaporised large amounts of earth, water, living creatures and buildings, which has been absorbed into the cloud to become irradiated and return to ground mingled with carbon residue from the fires – and now we are desperately imbibing it.

Those of us lucky enough to have avoided serious injury begin to try to turn the tide.

I am Yosaku, a thirty-two-year-old fireman; I was on a streetcar one and a quarter miles from the hypocentre, heading home to Sakaemachi after a long night shift. Thankfully, my family have all just recently been evacuated. Now I race back to my station at Ujina, hopping straight onto a fire truck as my colleagues set out; but the wall of fire is too intense, and it beats us back.

Dowsing ourselves with water from the tanks, we give up fighting the fire and set out instead to help the most heavily injured. At Miyuki Bridge, we find many people dying. All are calling to us for help. We try to lift as many as possible onto the truck, but it's difficult as their skin keeps peeling off as we move them. Once the prefectural hospital is full, we start ferrying the injured to the Akatsuki Military Hospital.

Coming across a small fire station in the city centre, I find a burned-out fire engine with a dead man inside – scorched to death behind the wheel.

I am Hiroshi, an army doctor aged twenty-eight, stationed at Ujina – two and a half miles from the hypocenter. It begins with a strange noise, like a distant flock of mosquitoes. Looking out of the window towards town, we see that the people of Hiroshima are coming. They look strange. Their clothes and skin have been burnt off of them. Holding their hands before them, they look like ghosts.

While I understand that these must be the wounded from the explosion, I wonder why so many are coming our way when there are Red Cross Hospitals and much bigger hospitals in the centre.

At first, I haven't realised that there isn't a centre any more.

I don't know it yet, but of the upwards of two hundred doctors based in Hiroshima, less than twenty are left to service the flood of suffering that is coming; out of nearly seventeen hundred and eighty nurses, only one hundred and twenty-six are left to assist us. Before the bomb, Hiroshima had forty-five civilian and two large army hospitals; now only three are usable.

Setting one room for the heavily injured and one for the less injured, we begin to work through the onslaught in a mechanical manner – having to improvise a lot, as we are only a first aid facility. As I am working along the throngs of the injured, a pregnant lady reaches to my leg. She says she knows she is going to die, but she can feel her baby moving inside her; if it is delivered now, she says, "It does not have to die with me."

We have no obstetricians, no delivery room, but I tell her I will come back when everything is ready for her and her baby. I leave her looking happy and return to battle the deluge of patients – there are only a handful of us to treat maybe three thousand people. It feels as if the day will never end.

When finally, I return to the pregnant lady, I pat her on the shoulder but she does not respond. The person next to her says that she had fallen silent just a short while ago. I am glad that I was at least able to talk to her, calm her worries; but so sad that I was unable to fulfil her last wish.

My name is Toshiko and I am twenty-six; as I have been staying in Yasufuruichi, I and my children were safe when the bomb hit.

But now I am heading into Hiroshima to search for my family. I'm running along the main road when I start encountering survivors, but I can't get any sense out of them as to which part of the city has been hit. A mad, naked man, badly burnt, comes running up the road, hiding his face as he is embarrassed by his nakedness. Also embarrassed, I venture to ask him for news of the explosion. He lowers his hands and his face is so horribly swollen I can't even make out his eyes. But he says my name…

Only then do I realise it is my brother.

Telling me that he was engulfed by flames and barely made it out alive, he says that mother was upstairs when the bomb dropped – but he could not find her afterwards. He believes she was killed in the blast. It is mid-afternoon as I arrive in the city to continue my search…

I am Kinue, a widow; my son is away fighting, but my daughter Yatchan was commuting to work at the Industrial Research Institute when the bomb was dropped. I was at home just over three miles from the hypocentre when the explosion shattered all my windows and threw me to the floor; now all I can think of is finding my daughter.

On my way to the train station, I encounter a naked girl Yatchan's age. Her skin is dangling off of her and she mutters, "Mother, water… Mother, water…" But she is not my girl and I do not give her any water.

I shall always be sorry for that.

Hiroshima Station is heaving with the dead and wounded. Many call for their mothers. None of them are my girl. I can't get any further than Tokiwa Bridge, but now I think perhaps she will return home and I have missed her somehow. I run and run to get home, but she is not there. So, I open the windows and wait…

I am Yasu, mother to four daughters and wife to a soldier, praying every day to have him safely back home. My youngest girl has been safely evacuated, but my other children are students and therefore must work to support the war effort: my oldest, Kuniko, works at a savings bureau; Mineko, our third, is working a domestic evacuation today. My second daughter has a day off today and was with me at home when the blinding flash came.

We seek medical attention for our wounds at the Sumiyoshi Shinto Shrine – a head wound and extensive burns in my case, while my poor little girl has had a mirror shatter all over her. They are overwhelmed at the shrine and we are separated for treatment. As I can walk, I have to make my own way to Sumiyoshi Bridge to catch a boat to a nearby island, but time and again I am unable to get aboard and boat after boat leaves without me.

Finally, I succumb to unconsciousness. Too exhausted to move, I wonder about my children; but I have lost too much blood, I've had no water and the burns hurt so much…

I surrender to sleep, barely caring whether I'll ever wake up…

I am Father John Siemes, a Jesuit priest at the Novitiate of the Society of Jesus housed on the outskirts of the city at Nagatsuka, about three miles from the hypocentre. Like many, my fellow priests and I initially formed the impression that we had been hit by a localised bomb; then we saw the fires and explosions breaking out in the city below. Now a rapidly thickening procession of people is streaming up the valley towards us.

Our Superior, Father Pedro Arrupe, attended medical school in Madrid. Taking his lead, we give first aid where we can and rest the victims on straw mats in the chapel and library. When we are struggling, we kneel to pray and ask for guidance. It gives us the strength to continue in our insurmountable task. We have iodine, aspirin, bicarbonate of soda and room for one hundred and fifty – yet there are tens of thousands in need.

With our bandages and drugs rapidly consumed, we set to cleaning wounds. The houses of the local farmers are filling up quickly and we are soon inundated by requests to take the worst cases. We begin to realise that these wounded are from the *outer districts* of the city – and wonder what has happened to those in the centre.

Some of the Fathers set out to help those who are struggling towards the village school, which has been set up as a temporary aid station – but mostly we seek to save those beneath our roof. It is all we can do. As there are many uninjured young men among our students, we send them out to gather up food: fortifying our patients against the oncoming danger of infection is an essential part of Father Arrupe's approach.

The Japanese seem almost fatalistic about this catastrophe and as a result unable to show much in the way of initiative, but they respond well to instruction.

The day wears on and I regularly fall back upon prayer.

Father Arrupe shows us how to treat the various different kinds of wounds: fractures and gashes caused by falling tiles and roof beams are flecked and clogged with dirt, splinters or glass fragments. They need cleaning, but are raw and we have no anaesthetic.

Our patients suffer in a dignified silence I will never forget.

It is the burns which trouble Father Superior the most. Often these have been suffered while escaping burning death traps, but in many cases the victim can only cite the "flash of light" to account for the blisters which are arising upon their skin. Where an ordinary blister might yield a little weeping upon being lanced, these blisters cover whole bodies; they must be punctured for the poison to be cleaned, but the discharge is enough to nearly fill a cup.

In the late afternoon, we receive the seminarian, Takemoto, who tells us – much to our relief – that our colleagues at the Central Mission are alive and taking refuge at Asano Park. Several of us set out to retrieve them, taking with us two hastily improvised stretchers.

The journey is like a descent into Hell.

Night falls as we make our way. This is a blessing, as it shrouds the dark, inert forms lying on the periphery of our vision. The shattered outskirts still vaguely resemble communities, albeit crumpled, but further in the city has been swallowed whole. We stick to the river bank, sometimes wading in to steer clear of the inferno. The dark glows with a smoke-choked, flickering death.

Out of the shadows come many pleas for assistance and especially water, becoming a crescendo of begging. They are trapped. They are fading. We cannot help them all and gradually the calls for water become a ghostly, rhythmic whisper, almost a chant, that we take for granted in the background. I realise that by morning it will be much quieter here.

I encounter a child who has a piece of glass imbedded in the pupil of his eye; another who has a wooden splinter the size of a dagger protruding from his side. Sobbing, he pleads for salvation…

Salvation…

I am Robert Tulliver. The weakened spirit of an English madman. I have no power here to reach out. I am *yūrei*, cursed to haunt this earthbound purgatory, to remind myself over and over that this – this punishment, this experiment, this abattoir – is justified in the name of a greater salvation. A much greater number, Allied and Japanese lives together, have been saved.

The war is surely over. I should rejoice.

But I mourn. I mourn angrily.

Nearing the park now, the Jesuits are forced to listen helplessly to the consequences of the rising tide. The debilitated who have sought respite in the mud of the low river have no strength to fight and are drowning in droves. The air is filled with a clamour of enfeebled wailing.

In the park, there are reunions infused with joy, relief and sorrow. The priests from the Novitiate distribute the food they have brought and do what they can to bring water to those calling for it. A Japanese Methodist minister named Kiyoshi Tanimoto is helping transport the injured upstream by boat; he first ferries away Father Schiffer, whose condition is becoming more critical by the minute. Returning, he enlists the Jesuits' help to rescue two young girls who are struggling in the water – the children, who have lost their parents, are badly burnt – before heading off with Father Lassalle.

The fires are gradually dying now.

Watching Reverend Tanimoto's boat disappear into the smog, I turn to consider the refugees of Asano Park. Father Kleinsorge has elected to stay with the injured until his colleagues' return in the morning. He comforts the housekeeper, Mrs Murata, and others. Although it is still very hot, the younger of the girls rescued from the river cannot stop shivering and the Father gives her his jacket then finds a blanket to wrap her up in; but finally, her body gives out.

I wish I knew how to be numb to this. But after all the horror, this touches me the most – a beautiful little girl, who just that morning had been playing on her way to school, slips away in the darkened shadows of the park she has played in a hundred times. Her parents have led the way into death, but this would be no comfort to them, as they'd surely never have wanted to leave their cherished one to face her end so frightened and alone and in such pain.

It feels so wrong that she never got to play again, or find young love, or have babies of her own.

Father Kleinsorge feels the same way, I can tell – and for a moment, I want to reach to him and tell him how much I admire him and Tanimoto, and Arrupe, and the other priests for their work to ease the suffering here today. For a moment, I see the extraordinary power for good that can burst from men and women inspired by their religion and wish that somehow it could be always be about the good.

But I can't do this any more.

I turn from them.

I try to take flight, to leave this place and find an astral highway, to swim into Halcyon and return to my body in Berlin. Any release would do. I'll go anywhere. I am Robert Tulliver. *I am Robert Tulliver…*

I am Kinue, waiting with the windows open for her daughter to return. I am Toshiko, scouring the city for my mother. I am Yasu, separated from three of my girls, barely conscious and on the edge of embracing my death.

I am a nameless spirit, seeking respite where there is none. At least, as a ghost, there is somewhere I can hide where they cannot go. Fleeing these stories, I crawl into the flames – and burn painlessly until I am surrounded only by ashes.

The sun returns and the hibakusha reach for the future.

Inspired by their faith, Father Arrupe and his Jesuit brothers stir themselves to make a difference and salvage who they can in the face of this holocaust. Having arrived back at Nagatsuka at five in the morning, following an arduous twelve-hour trek which would ordinarily have taken two, they have rescued and treated Fathers Schiffer and Lassalle; they have freed families from collapsed homes and marshalled the local Japanese to begin to manage their casualties; they are tending to two hundred casualties in their own buildings and many more across the neighbourhood.

Later, they will successfully find and reconcile patients with their loved ones.

Among the refugees who arrive now at the Novitiate are a number of nuns from the convent of the Society of the Helpers of the Holy Souls. Accompanied by the German Jesuit, Father Kopp, they number three French, two Italian, two Japanese and one Irish sister – fifty-one years-old Julia Canny from Galway.

The numbers being cared for continue to rise, but Father Arrupe sets to systematically cleaning their wounds; he manages to find time to "do the rounds" across the local farms. The chances of survival are considerably increased here. The Novitiate of the Society of Jesus is the place to be in Hiroshima on the seventh of August.

I realise that things have improved for me. I am no longer scattered across the city, but now refocused in one place and one time. However, I still cannot pull away. Somehow, I remain tethered here.

Making time for Mass, Father Siemes and several of his colleagues head into Hiroshima to seek Father Kleinsorge and other surviving acquaintances known to be injured. Saying Mass fortifies them and, feeling closer to God, they resolve themselves to face the sights that await them in the light of day.

I envy them.

Stark in the baking sun, the city is one gigantic, burnt-out scar. Only outlines in the ground mark the buildings that yesterday lined these streets. Only a very few of the sturdiest structures are left and these are mere skeletons. The river banks are flooded with corpses and those still lingering. Pushing their hand cart before them along the broad street at Hakushina, the priests see many naked burned cadavers. There are survivors here too, seeking to curl up and die in private by crawling beneath wrecked trams.

Frightfully injured forms beckon to them and then collapse.

They place as many wounded as they can on their cart and wheel them to a nearby burnt-out hospital. But every corridor is already clogged with bodies and the few doctors here are woefully under-supplied. Even as they deliver these people, they know most will die untreated.

The task is endless.

Reaching the park, they load Mrs Murata and a mother and two children onto the cart. Father Kleinsorge walks. On their route back to Nagatsuka, they distribute water where they can. After a short break to eat, they set out again to go back for those wounded they noted on their first excursion; by now, they are encountering many more individual rescue missions and a growing presence of the army. Returning again to the park, they are able to locate a six-year-old boy and twelve-year-old girl Father Kleinsorge has asked them to watch for.

I drift away from the park. At a nearby elementary school, I encounter Toshiko still scouring the city for her mother and stay with her for a while, willing her success. Just as with the hospital, however, the hallways are jammed; they ring with mournful cries. In many cases, it's near-impossible to identify people by their faces. Out in the playground, she desperately inspects the mounds of bodies – not just human bodies, but animals too – but they are piled so deep that to sort through them is unimaginable.

I drift away from the elementary school. Soon I encounter Kinue, running once more towards Hiroshima Station – but this time with several of her neighbours close behind, imploring her to go carefully in case she should fall. Kinue has stayed awake all night waiting in vain for her daughter to return; but just now the father of one of Yatchan's workmates has found her with the report of a sighting.

At the station, there are many more dead than yesterday. Beyond this is the River Ota, where Yatchan has been seen. Kinue calls out, unable to see past the burns on the survivors' faces.

After a while she is rewarded with a call back: "Mother!"

Yatchan is in a pitiful state. Barely recognisable, her skin is peeling off and a sticky, yellowish pus is oozing out of her wounds. Because of the summer heat, maggots are flourishing in these. At a total loss, Kinue hesitantly tries to pick some out, concerned that this will hurt her daughter.

When Yatchan asks what she is doing, Kinue shrugs it off.

"Oh, it's nothing."

"I don't want to die," Yatchan says.

"Hang on," her mother replies. Yatchan's brother is at war; Kinue urges her to hang on so that she may see him again. She pulls her child onto her lap, takes her in her arms.

"Mother, it took you so long," Yatchan says.

Kinue apologises and promises not to leave her again. She does not know what to do, dares not move to fetch help – and anyway, there is no help. She can only keep her promise to stay.

Yatchan is in great pain and she cries a lot. After a while, she says, "There shouldn't be any war."

Kinue holds her like that for nine hours, until she has gone.

I wish there is something I can do. I try to get into their heads and soothe it all away, but I'm not even a shadow to them.

I drift away from the Ota River.

The healthier survivors and those from the outskirts are more in evidence now, trying to pick up the pieces. Many are wandering the ruins searching for signs of missing loved ones. Sometimes I am privileged to witness joyous tears of reunion.

Among the soldiers who are slowly drip-feeding into the city, I overhear many whispered snippets of conversation. Only the furthest outlying districts to the south and east are untouched. Somebody talks of a place where eighty Korean labourers were barracked; only twenty have returned. Of six hundred students of the Protestant girls' school, who were working at a factory, only thirty have returned. Every family has lost someone. The Mayor and his family are all dead.

The army has been wiped out.

A few whisper that President Truman has made an announcement to the world. It's only rumours, as very few of us have any contact with the outside world. One day they'll read that Truman has talked of "harnessing the basic power of the universe" and that "the force from which the sun draws its power has been loosed against those who brought war to the Far East". This they'll understand.

Especially in the hospitals.

I spend some time with the family of eight-year-old Reiko. She'd been lining up for drill in her school playing ground when the B-29 flew over, a silver dart in the blue drawing a white arc of vapour behind it. She'd thought it looked pretty. Afterwards, she'd staggered home through streets clogged with the injured to find her house flattened but not burnt.

Thankfully, Reiko's younger sister was off sick yesterday, as not one of her school mates – the whole class having been mobilised to clear fire lanes – has returned. Her father has been rescued from beneath a collapsed building and has made it home, but his skin is full of glass. Her eldest sister was at the railway station, just under a mile from the hypocentre, when the flash happened; having been burnt on the neck and back, she has just made it home.

They have no medicine to treat her, but Reiko's mother uses slices of cucumber to try to cool the wounds. The cucumber rapidly spoils because of the heat and draws maggots. The smell is bad and soon there are many flies, but the family take turns to fan the girl's sores.

In the street outside the remains of Reiko's house, I encounter what looks like a moving black lump. It crawls into a nearby home. The five children there, who have been waiting for news of their mother, take it at first for a black dog. I catch the briefest glimpse of the mother's relief that all five have survived. And then she passes.

As evening sets in, the silent cremation begins. The valley glows from thousands of private funeral pyres. On the eighth, in response to the swarms of flies, awareness grows of the dangers of disease – across the city, pyramids of bodies are raised and set alight. In Reiko's playground, ditches are dug out and the dead are piled up high, dowsed with gasoline and cremated anonymously in their thousands.

I try to pull away and for a moment feel that my spirit is taking flight, but I soon realise that these are not the clouds of the psychic plane – instead, I am adrift in the human ashes floating over Hiroshima.

Now there arrives in Hiroshima a significant man. Trying to wander far from these horrors, I encounter him at Yoshijima Air Field, amongst senior military and scientific representatives of the Japanese leadership – all sent here to verify the incidence of an atomic bombing. He's a very clever and Gifted man and might easily sense my presence.

His name is Yoshio Nishina and he is the Japanese Robert Oppenheimer. Lurking at a safe distance, I dare to probe his mind – and I learn stuff I never knew.

This slight, studious man of fifty-four is a contemporary of Einstein, known the world over for his work in nuclear physics; like Einstein, he'd recognised several years ago the danger of a belligerent enemy nation developing powerful atomic weapons and had raised his concerns with his military superiors. He had been authorised by Prime Minister Tojo to actively research nuclear weapons back in 1941, which puts him running in tandem with the Manhattan Project.

Since then, with a team of over a hundred at his research facility at the Riken Institute in Tokyo, he has been making significant progress towards uranium enrichment – with the army sourcing ore from Korea – though he has recently suffered a major setback when much of his laboratory was destroyed in the bombing of Tokyo.

As chairman of the Committee on Research in the Application of Nuclear Physics, two years previously, he had ruled the production of an atomic bomb to be feasible, but Doctor Nishina has – until today – assumed that the Americans were a long way short in the race to build one.

Nishina's personal interest has always been nuclear power, but he has little doubt that his army-financed project could achieve the bomb within the next couple of years. Furthermore, he is aware of a rival navy-financed project to develop nuclear weapons under Bunsaku Arakatsu, based in Kyoto. There are even rumours that Arakatsu is only weeks from a nuclear test – although Nishina doubts that he has the capability to deploy such a weapon.

Either way, the Japanese are barely a year behind us.

Perhaps in some alternate universe, there was no fire-bombing of Tokyo, Nishina's work was not set back by months and the Japanese were the first to wield an atomic weapon.

Yoshio Nishina has a sharp mind. He knows that his very presence here is a poisoned chalice.

It's a bad sign that his superiors have even allowed him to see the full translated transcript of the President's speech: it means they are rattled. They want to believe the Americans are lying about Hiroshima.

If Doctor Nishina can give them that, the pressure to win the atomic race will increase dramatically. But before the war, Nishina was a personal friend of Niels Bohr, the Danish genius, last seen fleeing war-torn Denmark for Britain and almost certainly, the United States – he has no illusions of Bohr's brilliance, nor that of other Allied scientists.

If Doctor Nishina has to confirm that the Americans are telling the truth, it will mean that he personally has been outclassed by Allied minds; it will mean he might just have lost his country the war. It will mean harakiri.

Just viewing the city from the air has been enough for Nishina. In his mind, he has already decided that the damage is a result of one massively destructive bomb – and there is only one way that could be achieved. Final confirmation will come once his people have conducted tests at Ground Zero; but he is already preparing to notify the Japanese leadership that he has failed them.

Nishina takes a deep breath. Tonight, he will make an unofficial report, though his official report will not follow until the tenth; then he must face his maker. He laughs grimly to himself: despite all this murder, it was in the laboratory that the war has finally been won…

As the eighth of August fades, I am once more wandering the hospitals – although now I see them in a different context, having read in Yoshio Nishina's mind the contents of President Truman's speech.

Apparently, Truman has declared that we – the Allies – have destroyed the city's "usefulness to the enemy". The naïve pacifist in me cannot help but wonder just how much use all these women and children could be.

Jack would point out that, given time, Japan would have militarised every boy child in the city and turned them into the worst killers on the planet.

I spend time with a nurse called Kikue, who is twenty. Typical of her generation, she has been a fervent patriot since school – while the boys trained to be soldiers, she dutifully aspired to nursing Japan's wounded heroes. When the war with the West broke out, aged just sixteen, she was already training at the Ujina-machi Joint Army Hospital. Until this day, she has always believed that dying for one's country was a great honour.

Lucky enough to have been away on the sixth, Kikue has returned to find her hospital wrecked, its ceilings caved in and all the windows shattered. The corridors ring with grief and the ramblings of the deranged, trapped in the moment when they lost everything. One man stares wide-eyed, blinded – face transfixed with the expression of a man seeing the magnesium flash over and over again.

Her patients are piled everywhere, the wards being full to bursting. Mostly she just separates the corpses from the living. Without medical supplies, treatment consists of brushing their wounds with oil provided by the army and distributing a mush made of flour and water, served in lengths of cut bamboo, for food. There aren't enough nurses to hand-feed those who can't feed themselves.

She provides what comfort she can.

On this third day, they are dying in droves. Kikue spends more time with the dead than the living, helping to unceremoniously haul away the dead ones like baggage and to hook bodies out of the shelters, to cremate them using gasoline on a grill of steel beams in a huge pit beside the hospital. At night, as there is no power for their lights, the constant bluish glow of this fire is all she has to work by.

As Truman declares that the Japanese have been "repaid many fold" for beginning the war from the air at Pearl Harbor, Kikue is called to on her rounds by a person so horribly burned she cannot at first make out their gender. Unable to move, this person asks her to reach for the train pass in their pocket and look at the photograph there.

They want to know if they still look like their photo.

The pass reveals a clever-looking, fourteen-year-old girl with bobbed hair, named Kazuko. Kikue tells Kazuko that, yes, she still looks like this, knowing the truth is too horrific to tell. She promises to contact Kazuko's mother and helps her take a little water, but before the girl can swallow she is gone.

The anger wells up inside me. I'm angry at the Japanese leadership for bringing their people to a point of such derangement that other nations consider this can be the only available course of action. And I'm angry at my own leaders for doing this in my name.

How can this be anything other than a war crime? But we are trading war crimes now, determined to out-kill one another to prove our superiority – this madness may bring the war to an end, but what a last word to have.

Could it be worth it, if this cataclysmic act ends all wars? If the United States sets this evil power aside forever, relinquishing it to lead the world in laying down its arms, might the horror be worth it?

The whole speech oozes wrath – and I fear the United States will never let such power slip through their fingers. After all, this is how you rule the world.

Far away in his oval office, Truman talks of a production line, of the Allied willingness to "obliterate more rapidly and completely every productive enterprise the Japanese have above ground in any city". He talks of how the Potsdam declaration was designed to spare the Japanese people this fate; that if their leaders do not now capitulate, "they may expect a rain of ruin from the air, the like of which has never been seen on this Earth".

As Truman talks in congratulatory terms of great scientific gambles, declaring the atomic bomb to be "the greatest achievement of organised science in history" and the size of the enterprise and its secrecy to be marvels, Kikue on her rounds stops in her tracks and stares. She's seeing a screaming baby trying to nurse at the breast of its already dead mother.

The leash that holds me here is weakening, I can feel it. I can taste escape. And yet a facet of me will never truly be able leave Hiroshima.

I spend the night drifting, revisiting old friends: Kikue on her rounds, silently renewing her vows; Reiko taking her turn to fan her sister's wounds and pick away the maggots, while the fires burn in her playground; Normand Roland Brissette from Lowell, sick to his stomach now in his prison cell; Toshiko, still searching for her mother; Kinue, still feeling her daughter Yatchan's last clinging embrace – waiting, waiting now for the return of her soldier son and haunted by the memories of their sweet childhoods.

Eighteen-year-old Hiroko has found her mother at the first aid centre in Ninoshima and is nursing her through her last moments; she still hasn't found her sister, who was a mobilised student, but at least her brothers have survived. It will be her job to take care of them. She cannot afford to bend herself to grief.

I encounter Doctor Kaoru Shima, returning to Hiroshima having been away assisting at an operation in a nearby town. He and his nurse are the only survivors of the entire staff of the hospital that bore his name, the first building to fall before the might of 'Little Boy'.

Returning to the site, he can find only bleached bones to mark that the hospital has ever existed.

By chance, I come across the nephew of Yasu, the mother of four daughters, last seen succumbing to her wounds near the Sumiyoshi Bridge. He is searching the hospitals for her. A little of my strength has returned and I am able to encourage him to look for her at Sumiyoshi.

I make a last trip to the Novitiate. Father Arrupe is feeling increasingly disturbed by the arrival of more and more new patients who suffered no apparent initial injury on the sixth, but are now fading fast while complaining of "a terrible interior heat"...

As it enters the morning of the ninth of August, 1945, Hiroshima feels like a distant outpost of the Japanese Empire. Little in the way of aid has made its way here. An official has broadcast about the "horrible and inhuman air raid", urging the people not to lose heart – apparently, we must resign ourselves to such suffering in times of war.

Then at last I feel it – that familiar lifting sensation. My body heeding my call to draw me back. A terrible shame consumes me, a feeling that I am somehow abandoning them, but I feel... I don't know what I feel... Cowardly. Morally exhausted. Like everything I ever called a belief has been beaten black and blue.

I just want to go home. I want to climb into my own bed and weep this out of my soul.

At long last, I withdraw from Hiroshima. Leaving the distraught searchers to desperately comb the ruins for their lost loves. Fleeing the ranks of those trapped inside agony-riddled prisons they used to call bodies. The sun is rising from the mountains, but it will take a long time for dawn to represent the promise of the future again here.

I rise higher and can see that the fires of the bombing are all extinguished now – only the fires of cremation still burn, dotted around this scar in the landscape. Higher and higher and soon the city is barely a dirty white smear between the forest green of the mountains and the dark blue sea. I'm thinking of Arrupe, Kikue, Taeko and all the others, wondering whether they ever felt me there beside them.

Perhaps I was just another ghost to them.

I spare a final thought for Sachiko, who guided me here, and who in her final moments thought me complicit in this atrocity – perhaps I have been. Perhaps I should have been wiser. Perhaps I turned a blind eye for too long.

The sky today is overcast. I'm flooded with relief as I break away, reaching for the clouds, heading south-west – my intention being to skirt the southern shores of Korea and make for China. My spirit is literally lifting! I want to laugh, though I know it will be laced with a bitter hysteria.

As I fly, my mind is simultaneously entering Halcyon. The mists of the combined human subconscious are just on the periphery of my vision, calling to me to not just *etheric* travel – out of body in the physical world – but to *astral* travel, out of body in the celestial plane.

But I'm afraid to go there: Halcyon right now is a twisted place, populated with the psychic waste of a demented species. It was bad enough over the Germany of Nazis and 'the final solution'; I cannot bear to think what it must be like after the atomic bomb…

It is nearly eleven in the morning Japanese time and I'm thinking now there must be something I can do to make sure this never happens again, some way to bring the plight of the people of Hiroshima to the attention of the world. I'm thinking this must never happen again – when it does.

Away to my left, down by the coast, there is a white flash.

Simultaneously, a prolonged, high-pitched, ear-splitting scream sears through me. Somehow, I don't know how but I know: this is Halcyon.

Halcyon is screaming.

A wave of psychic distress buffets me, the aftershock of forty thousand people suddenly blinking out of existence. Turbulence increases rapidly and I realise that my mind is being sucked down towards the ground. I kick away at this in dread, appalled that it may be happening all over again. I daren't look back, but the briefest of glimpses reveals a dark mushroom cloud reaching up for me like a colossal hand. I am a drowning man, swimming for the surface with all his might.

Anything would be better than going through this again. I swim for the mists of Halcyon. I choose to leave this physical plain altogether and become pure energy.

Up ahead, a figure takes shape.

It is my friend of two and a half centuries, Terasaka Kichiemon – samurai, ronin, hero of Japanese folklore, lately Society recruiter – who, it seems a lifetime ago, pushed himself away from Miyajima, the 'shrine island', so that he might not have to watch Hiroshima suffer.

At first, I think he is beckoning to me.

I want to call to him, "My friend! You are a sight for sore eyes." But the words die before I can offer them when I see the sorrowful expression on his face. He looks disappointed. Even as he begins to speak, he is fading away and I know him for a ghost.

He says, "I have become the rain – but the rain is black."

The great Terasaka Kichiemon, you see, had sought refuge in Nagasaki.

- CHAPTER EIGHT -

Echoes from Japan

They say I awoke screaming and that for the first month all I did was rave, streaming gibberish, my eyes wide and dead. They say I was a haunted thing, jumping at shadows, constantly having hushed conversations with imaginary presences. There were visitors, friends who sought to help me heal: I have half-memories of Churchill, Tolkien, Emily Wilding Davison, among the faces.

The first time I began to make any sense again was when the Mayfairs reached me – word having made its way to them on their long journey home that Robert Tulliver had emerged from his trance having taken leave of his senses. I remember blinking and Cassandra coming into focus before me. Somehow, she had reached inside and found a way to jolt me out of my frenzied gibbering. I think it had been the word 'Sachiko' which had penetrated my hysteria.

"She's gone, Cassie," I replied. "We incinerated her. She wandered bewildered for a while, burning. Then, like the good, obedient Japanese she was, she folded up and died."

Cassie and Jack stared at me in horror.

"What sort of creature are we, that we dowse our neighbour in Hell? How distinguished we are, compared to the other animals we share this Earth with." I turned to gaze at Jack and, unforgivably, said, "It must be nice, my friend, to have your world view validated so."

She learned then that her husband had not been entirely honest with her. I think that Jack's cheek is still humming with the strength of the slap.

I would be unable to find the courage to return to Halcyon for three years. I took to using whatever sedatives and anaesthetics I could find to numb my Gift. I did not want to read minds any more, as I always found something there to remind me of what I had seen – a random kindness from a stranger could send me scurrying down the nearest alleyway struggling to catch my breath.

I spent the rest of the year in a state of panic.

There are not words to describe the things I witnessed on the psychic plain after I left Nagasaki. There is a word we human beings created which neatly allows us to excuse our worst actions and tendencies, offload all the blame for them onto a supernatural scapegoat: 'Evil'. Well, in Halcyon, everything we've ever imagined has a manifestation - and in the summer of 1945, whilst adrift in the universe of the subconscious, I encountered true evil.

It was cold winter in England when Cassie came to ask me to relive it all. She was talking about going back, to see what aid could be brought to the victims of the bombs. Without hesitation, my response was, "I'm never going back."

"This is not the Robert Tulliver I know – the man who showed us such compassion one hundred years ago…"

Refusing to communicate psychically, I spoke only out loud.

"That man rescued a family who had the Gift. It was his job. If they'd been a merely ordinary family, he'd have walked away. That man, with all the time in the world at his disposal, has no time for the masses – they are so short-lived, you see."

When she persisted I turned on her, like a cornered animal.

"I thought I knew what we were capable of, Cassie – but this century has really raised the bar!"

She stepped towards me, reaching out in sympathy.

"Let me help you with your pain."

"You don't want in on this pain, trust me," I growled. "You don't want to be in here. And this is *nothing*, this pain, compared to what the hibakusha went through…"

"It's survivor's guilt…"

"What did I survive?" I bellowed. *"I wasn't even bloody there!"*

Then she advanced upon me – and I let her in. Showed her everything. Until I sobbed myself better. When she finally pulled away, I could see from her darkened eyes that she'd taken the poison into herself.

Cassandra Mayfair leant forward, planted a kiss upon my forehead; then she left for Japan.

Gradually, my friends guided me back. In early 1946, I began to engage again – and found my thoughts returning to the Japanese. With my Society credentials and contacts high up in the CIA, I was able to access confidential governmental reports and learn about what had happened after I'd left.

Hiroshima, it turned out, had been deemed a failure in comparison to Nagasaki. As opposed to the uranium-based 'Little Boy', 'Fat Man' was born out of plutonium; instead of having a gun-type design, it was an implosion-type device, which basically meant that it had a plutonium core packed into the centre of a ball of five thousand pound of high explosives. The Nagasaki bomb was the most efficient of the three atomic devices exploded so far: it required less fissionable material and successfully fissioned twenty percent of that material, as opposed to the less than two percent fissioned by the Hiroshima bomb. Its explosive yield was twenty-one kilotons, as opposed to the fifteen of Little Boy.

If Fat Man had been dropped on the sixth of August instead, unbelievably, things could have been even worse for the people of Hiroshima.

Fate had softened its cruel grip on Japan on the ninth of August. Although the events of the day were horrendous, elements of chance came into play to offset the blow.

The Enola Gay, piloted this time by George Marquadt, had once again been stalking her skies – but as the reconnaissance plane over the town of Kokura, the primary target that day, due to its importance as a munitions centre. The Great Artiste was once more in the air to monitor the blast. The honour of weapon delivery this time, however, had fallen to *Bockscar* – piloted by Charles Sweeney. His radar specialist, Jacob Beser, was the only man to serve on both the Hiroshima and Nagasaki bombing flights.

Unbeknownst to Kokura's population, their chances of survival at the outset of the day were slim. But upon arriving at the primary target, Sweeney's bombardier Kermit Beahan – due to weather conditions and the drift of smoke resulting from an Allied raid on neighbouring Yawata – had struggled for a visual.

Sweeney had made three passes over Kokura, but the local anti-aircraft fire was far worse than that encountered three days previously – and Beser had warned of incoming fighters.

Bockscar bailed on Kokura and, with fuel supplies dwindling, had made for Nagasaki – only to find that target also masked by clouds. The briefest of breaks in the cloud cover allowed Beahan to snatch a glimpse of features at ground level. Just short of eleven in the morning local time, they'd released Fat Man onto the industrial centre of the city.

Because this was in the Urakami valley, in northern Nagasaki, the impact of the blast was mitigated by hills: the Nakashima valley – the south-eastern half of the city – escaped devastation. A disruptive terrain of ravines and river valleys meant there was not so much of a contained firestorm as at Hiroshima. Of the fifty-two thousand residential buildings in the city, only about thirty percent were destroyed.

Reports estimated an immediate death count of forty thousand, with a similar number injured, consisting mostly of factory workers, particularly at the Mitsubishi plants for steel, munitions and the shipyards. Many were mobilised students and Korean work force. Six hundred out of eight hundred and fifty students at the Medical College died.

In marked contrast to Hiroshima's military losses of twenty thousand, barely one hundred and fifty soldiers were killed.

But the bombing hadn't been the only major development that day to affect the course of the war: overnight, the Soviet Union had declared its intentions. By dawn, a million and a half Russian troops were wading into Manchuria on three fronts. The Japanese could barely field two thirds that. Within days, the Japanese hold over China and Korea was falling apart. The conflict lasted just over three weeks, in which time tens of thousands of Japanese soldiers were killed and as many as half a million suffered the humiliating status of Prisoner of War.

I wondered which had the greatest impact on the Japanese leadership's choice to surrender: the atomic bombs, or the Russian invasion.

It seemed to me that a leadership that defined itself in terms of its prowess in battle might be far more concerned by an overwhelming military distraction than the loss of a few factories – especially as Doctor Nishina was yet to file his final, official report. The Americans' new dark magic was a confusing mystery, shrouded in misinformation – but the Japanese leaders understood the language of invasion.

At midday on the fifteenth of August, the people of Japan had heard the voice of their Emperor broadcast for the first time – as he announced that their government had formally accepted the terms of the Potsdam Declaration. Knowing how they revered him, this must have been close to a religious experience for them. Despite having their worldview turned inside out, I knew that they would have reacted with humble and dignified resignation.

In an imperial rescript issued to greet 1946, their Emperor formally repudiated his divinity.

In what became as his 'Humanity Declaration', Hirohito reminded them of the 'Five Clauses of the Charter Oath' taken by Emperor Meiji upon his enthronement in 1868. These had established assemblies to decide matters of government in accordance with public opinion; they were inclusive of all classes, allowing the common people the right to "fulfil their just desires" in equality with civil and military officials.

Hirohito drew his people's attention to the high ideals of this oath – he declared his wish to renew it and reaffirm its principles, abandoning the "misguided practices of the past" in favour of seeking "civilisation consistently in peace". Stressing the Japanese love of family and country, he went on to add, "With more of this devotion should we now work towards love of mankind."

Finally, the Emperor had added, "The ties between Us and Our people... do not depend upon mere legends and myths. They are not predicated on the false conception that the Emperor is divine, and that the Japanese people are superior to other races and fated to rule the world."

By harking back to a golden age when Japan had yearned for enlightenment and democracy – independently of the West and of its own volition – he had reclaimed his nation's future.

Cassie returned in the spring of 1946 – with shattering news.

In the days after the bombing, the hibakusha had started coming down with high fevers and began vomiting blood; they were losing their hair in bunches on their pillows; their gums were bleeding, their throats horribly sore and their teeth dropping out. Purplish-red spots were swelling up on their skin. They excreted a black liquid.

As the months dragged on, many who had survived the blast unscathed began to inexplicably fade away and die like this. The surviving populations of Hiroshima and Nagasaki began to pray that they might see each new dawn without the insidious symptoms. When morning came, they would examine their bodies in dread of finding the spots. Those who cared for them – Hiroshi, Kikue, Shuntaro Hida, Kaoru Shima, Pedro Arrupe and many more – were mystified.

Of course, now we know: radiation poisoning was stalking them and corroding their bodies from the inside out.

The first official case of 'acute radiation syndrome' was the actress Midori Naka, who had wandered into the hospital of Tokyo University on the sixteenth of August – a full ten days after Hiroshima. Only four of the travelling troupe of seventeen actors had survived the initial explosion, their accommodation being barely two thousand feet from the hypocentre; Midori was their last survivor. She had emerged from the ruins physically unscathed and managed to flee the firestorm on a train back home to Tokyo.

Slowly, radiation poisoning had strengthened its grip upon her. As her temperature and heart rate shot up and her white blood cell plummeted, she lost her hair and purple blotches began to appear on her skin. In spite of the best medical care in the country, she had died eight days later.

Cassie could only guess at how many were dying in this way. In the nine months since the bombing, she figured that at least another thirty thousand had died at Hiroshima and at least another ten thousand at Nagasaki.

She had news of Yasu, the mother of four daughters – whose nephew had found her in a bad way near the Sumiyoshi Bridge. After many days, Yasu had managed some recovery and set out once again in search. Her youngest had been safely out of the city and Yasu was soon reunited with her sixteen-year-old, who had been injured with her in the blast. However, she'd been overwhelmed with grief and despair to learn of her nineteen-year-old daughter Kuniko's death.

In her final hours, Kuniko had been found by an uncle, naked and unrecognisable amongst the piles of the dying in one of the hospitals; he had identified her only by the sound of her voice.

Finally, Yasu had received word of her daughter Mineko. When Little Boy exploded, thirteen-year-old Mineko had been at her school assembly; she'd been taken by truck for treatment at a school in Fuchii. Arriving there some two weeks after the bombing, Yasu had found Mineko lying on the floor of a lecture hall – her face swollen, her open wounds festering, her fingers stuck together.

Mineko had loved making dolls out of leftover cloth with those fingers; now she turned in tears and said, "Mother, I won't be able to make dolls any more."

Yasu had gently wrapped each finger in gauze. As he was under such terrible pressure, Mineko's doctor tended to be accidentally rough while changing her bandages, so Yasu would always diligently wet them with antiseptic solution in order to start the process more gingerly. She did her best, wishing she could swap places with her little girl, but after nine days of watching her suffer terrible agony, in the darkness of that lecture hall, Mineko had finally died.

As dawn came, Yasu had cleaned her child and dressed her in her best kimono. People consoled her by saying how lovely she looked.

Following the cremation, she'd carried Mineko's remains back to Yoshijima in a heavy downpour, remembering her as a toddler and how she'd once been so excited about a primary school picnic. She took some solace at how they'd been such fine, intelligent girls, so gentle and so clever at school. She'd been so sorry not to have been there at the end for Kuniko, but at least she had been able to care for Mineko.

Weeping in the rain, she'd talked to her baby softly as she'd walked her safely back home…

After this, Cassie and I had sat in silence for a very long time.

In July 1946, the United States Strategic Bombing Survey published their summary report for the Pacific War. Leafing through these pages, reading about the tunnels beneath Nagasaki, a chilling thought came to me: while during the Blitz, British civilians had received warning via air raid sirens and a chance to take shelter, with the atomic bombs the Japanese civilians received no such courtesy.

Japanese anti-aircraft surveillance were accustomed to watching for bombing missions – squadrons of bombers – so when they'd sighted the Enola Gay, Bockscar and their accompanying planes, they'd simply assumed reconnaissance missions.

At Hiroshima and Nagasaki, death had come *from a silent sky*.

The report made passing reference to this. At Nagasaki, it said the alarm "was improperly given". It also acknowledged that there were only four hundred or so people in the city's extensive network of tunnel shelters at the time, but that all those set back from the entrances survived, largely uninjured – even those almost directly under the explosion. Since the tunnels had a capacity of one hundred thousand, with proper warning the report said, "the loss of life would have been substantially lower".

The Strategic Bombing Survey people they sketched quite a picture of the power struggles inside the Japanese government. It painted Hirohito as little more than a signatory for the policies of an intimidating oligarchy of military-minded power-mongers – too removed from the realities of what was being done in his name to be held to account.

It seemed that from mid-way through 1944, key statesmen had been slowly coming to the conclusion that the war was lost: before his death at Saipan, Admiral Takeo Tagaki had publicly declared that Japan should "seek a compromise peace"; former Prime Minister Fumimaro Konoe had advised the Emperor to seek a negotiated peace; the chief secretary to Prime Minister Suzuki, Hisatsune Sakomizu, had reported confidentially that, with resources dwindling, they would be unable to fight much longer.

In testimony to the Survey, Kōichi Kido, the Lord Keeper of the Privy Seal, maintained that he had appointed Suzuki because he alone "had the deep conviction and personal courage to stand up to the military and bring the war to an end".

In June 1945, the Emperor had called the Supreme War Direction Council together to discuss closing the war on their terms. While in public Suzuki tragically declared *mokusatsu* in response to the Potsdam Declaration, in private – along with the Foreign Minister and the Navy Minister – he signalled a willingness to accept unconditional surrender. It was the Army Minister and the Chiefs of Staff who insisted upon continued resistance. Even after the atomic bombs were dropped, they maintained that further attacks should be endured.

When the Emperor finally accepted that surrender was inevitable and recorded a message for his people, there were still factions in the military who refused to back down. In what became known as the Kyūjō incident, on the night of the fourteenth of August, a number of rebel officers had attempted a coup – seeking to occupy the Imperial Palace, place the Emperor under house arrest and assassinate Suzuki. Ultimately, two officers were killed and several buildings were torched, but having failed to locate the phonograph recording, the leaders committed suicide. The Minister of War, Korechika Anami, also took his life.

The Survey had been established by Secretary of War Henry Stimson, under Roosevelt; it had been compiled with the participation of over a thousand contributors, approximately three quarters of whom were military. Initially it had reported on Europe, aiming to provide an overview of the effectiveness of the Allied bombing campaign there. This Japanese report had been commissioned by Truman in the days after the war had ended and its directors were all esteemed politicians, businessmen or academics.

They concluded that air supremacy alone "could have exerted sufficient pressure to bring about unconditional surrender" – negating *any* need for a land invasion. By air supremacy, they meant "*even without the atomic bombing attacks*".

It was the Survey's conclusion that Japan would have surrendered anyway by November – without any need for an invasion and even if the atomic bombs had not been dropped...

- CHAPTER NINE -

Vestiges of Faith

The world began to heal its wounds, but in Hiroshima and Nagasaki those wounds healed into keloid scars – and the poison in their bodies continued to take its toll. The Japanese accepted occupation with characteristic stoicism. But at the bomb sites aid was slow to trickle through

Cassie reported regularly on developments there. Her letters indicated that General MacArthur's occupation was going relatively smoothly. As the people adjusted to the trauma of their defeat and surrender, there was – she said – a feeling of relief and liberation beginning to permeate some corners of Japanese society. The new democratic reforms in areas such as education, women's rights and the unions provided stark and welcome contrast with the decade of war and ultra-nationalistic oppression the Japanese had endured.

Responding to accounts of rape by the Allied troops, the state had sponsored the 'Recreation and Amusement Association'. When the RAA had been terminated in early 1946, having become something of an embarrassment to the authorities, the incidence of rape had risen dramatically again.

There was bitterness behind the casual tone of Cassie's words – she was clearly disappointed at the Allied men. I imagined Jack at her ear, reminding her he'd warned it would happen; he'd remind her too that Japanese treatment of the women of Nanking had been far worse. She'd glare him down and reply, "Like that is any justification."

Cassie was disillusioned too with the treatment of the hibakusha by the Atomic Bomb Casualty Commission, whose mandate was to study the effects of radiation upon humans. It seemed this translated into treatment of the survivors as guinea pigs rather than patients. The Japanese doctors were increasingly exasperated with the lack of medical cooperation, given that the scientists might have valuable research to offer.

MacArthur had been subtle with the Japanese leadership, showing great respect in his dealings with the Emperor – in the meantime, Hirohito's tacit endorsement legitimised the Americans' constitutional reforms.

War crimes prosecutions began late April 1946, following the Nuremberg model; they were overseen by twelve judges from eleven different countries. No member of the royal family was indicted: not even Prince Asaka, the Emperor's uncle, who had been commander of the Japanese army at Nanking – and who had served on the Supreme War Council throughout the war.

Defence rested in September '47. It took six months for the judges to rule, at which point several of the judges dissented from the majority verdicts – the French and Australian judges explicitly criticising Emperor Hirohito's absence from proceedings, with Justice Henri Bernard making reference to "a principal author who escaped all prosecution".

It had been over three years since I had travelled on the astral plane. My friends assured me that the universe of the subconscious had returned to a harmonious state, but my nightmares told a different story.

Sometimes they were waking nightmares. I'd be walking the streets of London, only to find I was surrounded by shambling hibakusha – hands raised before their chests, skin hanging in tatters, eyes from their sockets. On one occasion, I was transfixed by a mushroom cloud over the Thames, hoovering the city up in its magnificent wake. I might hear a whispered plea from a nearby alley, begging for water or help: "Please, sir, might you lift this weight. I cannot escape and the fire is so close."

I'd acquired the opium from Byron.

It's funny how your mind works when you're at your lowest ebb. In the habit of keeping my old Enfield Mark II revolver loaded beside my bed, sometimes I'd experiment with pressing the muzzle to my chin. I knew I had to lift it slightly to get the right trajectory of the bullet… My last bullet.

After all the fighting, all the killing, of this barbarous century, this could be my last. The thought felt comforting. Never having blown my brains out before, I had no experience of how the Blood would affect things – I couldn't imagine that anybody might be able to get to me in time…

"Not tonight, Robert."

Flinching, I snapped aloud, "Get out of my head, Cassie."

"Sir Thomas would want you to begin again…"

The thought of my friend Thomas More stayed my hand. Sir Thomas had sacrificed himself to save my life thirty years previously. This would dishonour him.

"And the world needs you."

The hand holding the gun slowly dropped onto my lap.

Resignedly, I asked, "Where are you?"

"Tokyo. I have someone here who'd like to meet you."

I took a breath. "I'll meet you in the clouds."

Trembling, like a champion swimmer, born for the water, who – having nearly drowned – had lost all confidence and sworn he would never swim again, I lay back upon my bed and closed my eyes. Darkness parted like a curtain onto the swirling mists of the collective consciousness and I waded in.

It seemed almost tranquil again. Up ahead, the web-network of highways pulsed with the traffic of souls, but I was not ready for that. It was as if the wind was at my back, as if Halcyon was sweeping me along. Around me the constellations of thought, experience and imagination swept by. Then the sun burst through and, entering a skyscape of vivid iridescence, clouds shimmering with crystalline intensity against the deepest, clearest blue, I saw them waiting for me.

Three figures. Cassandra and Jack Mayfair and a tall, slim Indian gentleman I did not recognise.

"Robert Tulliver, this is Justice Radhabinod Pal."

In astonishment: "The dissenting Indian judge?"

Justice Pal was a distinguished, austere looking man in his early sixties. Managing a slight, wry smile at my consternation, he spoke softly and politely. "For my sins, yes, I am that man."

With a disconcerted glance to the Mayfairs, I said, "Please forgive my rudeness. I'm very interested to meet you, sir."

"Likewise," he replied, with a formal nod. "For Hiroshima and Nagasaki. you have my sympathy."

"I don't deserve it," I countered, not as graciously as I might have.

"I have read your Society report, Mister Tulliver – and can assure you that you are no way accountable."

Coming from someone who had read many reports and heard many witness accounts, who'd held a position of high authority, his words were oddly reassuring.

With a shrug, he said, "Regrettably, there are many who would now question my competence to judge."

I knew a little about Radhabinod Pal. Born in a Bangladeshi village, he'd studied at the University of Calcutta and gone on to serve as a professor in Law, finally becoming vice chancellor; he had married young and had nine children. He'd been advising the Indian government on legal matters for twenty years and was a serving judge at Calcutta High Court.

Publishing his ruling in a document which ran well over seven hundred pages, Pal had challenged the very legitimacy of the Tokyo trials as having been conducted "in the spirit of retribution, and not impartial justice". Essentially dismissing the entire endeavour as a show trial, he'd held that all of the twenty-eight men principally charged should be acquitted.

The Allied response was to label him a biased Asian and hamper publication of his dissenting judgement.

Cassie and Justice Pal seemed open and congenial. Jack was different; his 'body language' spoke volumes. He was going to be Jack, which is always worth the price of admission. I threw an enquiring look to him. *What is she up to?*

He just shrugged. "As usual, I can see what she's trying to achieve and I've got some issues with it."

Then Justice Pal stepped forward.

"Tulliver, you fought valiantly in two world wars, but your greatest fight is only now beginning. Though this current conflict has ended in name, we are far from resolution. This is but a suspension of hostilities – with much greater destruction on the horizon."

"Sorry, I've no fight left in me." I turned to leave.

"So, you choose to toe your masters' line?"

Jack bristled at this. I caught Cassie rolling her eyes.

"Woah, there!" he exclaimed. "You need to show my friend here some respect. He's earnt his medals. And he and I, we work for the same paymasters."

Justice Pal regarded Jack with mortification. "I did not mean to denigrate the service you men have given your country, only to sound a warning regarding its motives."

Jack stuttered, peering at the man as if he was plainly stupid. "Listen, those Japs were guilty as hell. What part of 'mass-murder' are you struggling with?"

Pal took a slightly patronising breath. "I do not for one moment deny that horrendous atrocities were committed..."

"And that these are crimes against humanity?"

"Indeed. However, those who have set themselves up to judge these crimes should be numbered amongst their actual perpetrators."

Jack recoiled. It was almost a comedy double-take. He turned to us and said, "Several teabags short of a full pot."

"Will you allow me to explain myself?" the judge asked.

The Liverpudlian threw his arms open and grinned. "The floor is yours!"

Pal was well versed in international law, but I shared Jack's outrage. There had to be a reckoning for the Rape of Nanking, the treatment of China going back to Manchuria in 1931, the Bataan Death March, the abuse of prisoners of war over the Burma-Thailand Railway – thirteen thousand Allied soldiers had died building the railway alone...

"A reckoning, yes," he began, picking up on my thoughts. "Atrocities have been committed. The world has taken leave of its senses and now we seek to apportion blame. But why? So that we might excuse ourselves..."

Eyes bulging, Jack went to speak. Cassandra glared at him.

"It is a questionable definition of 'war crimes' when one can only be guilty if one has *lost the war*. I maintain that such proceedings, even if clothed in the garb of law, represent nothing but the satisfaction of the desire for vengeance.

"A *fair* trial should be judged objectively, by those who are impartial. All of the judges, myself included, were from victor states. Amongst the nations prosecuting the accused for warmongering were two – the Soviet Union and the Netherlands – who declared war on

Japan first, *initiating* their conflict. Where was the German judge? The Japanese?"

That seemed a good point – after all, the Japanese *people* were not on trial, just their leaders.

"You talk of impartiality," Jack declared, triumphantly, "but you began the tribunal with your mind already made up. It's widely known you are anti- the British Empire! Didn't you bow to the accused every time you entered the courtroom?"

The Justice shrugged. "I concede bias. No man could witness what the British have done to my nation without a feeling of having been wronged."

"Then you are compromised! You see Japan occupied and you project your hang-ups onto the trial."

"I certainly perceive imperialism at work," Pal agreed. "However, you have made my point for me."

Jack frowned. But I saw what Pal was saying.

"Every man on that tribunal was a political animal," I said.

He nodded. "Smell a whiff of prejudice on me and consider the stench of it on my fellow judges."

Turning to Jack, he replied, "As regards my bowing to the accused, it is basic courtesy to acknowledge with respect men who have held great authority. I am not in the habit of treating people as criminals until they are found guilty."

Jack cocked his head. "What about your failure to attend?"

Pal grimaced at this. He suddenly looked very tired.

Cassie explained, "The judges came and went. Only a quorum of six was required at any one time for the tribunal to proceed."

"You were absent for eighty days, I believe?" Jack added.

Radhabinod Pal looked out across the clouds, as if gazing towards India. "My wife is dying. I regret my absences, but the transcripts of those sessions were always available to me."

Jack had gone silent. Justice Pal turned to me.

"Hiroshima. Nagasaki. Before that, Tokyo. Between them, the total civilian death count was – a conservative figure – *two hundred thousand.* How many American civilians have been killed? Twelve thousand. How many of those were killed in their beds on the American mainland? None."

"There is Pearl Harbor," Jack challenged, quietly.

"Ah," Pal said, with a touch of sarcasm. "December the seventh, 1941, the 'date which will live in infamy'. When innocent America suffered a cruel, unprovoked attack by the aggressor Japan. Except, of course, it was Japan who was the aggressed nation…"

"Whaaaat?!" Jack looked about ready to bite Pal's head off.

Cassie soothingly cooed, "It's one of them there alternative points-of-view we've spoken of, husband. What do we do around these?"

"We try not to hyperventilate," he retorted.

Justice Pal continued: "International propaganda; the making of treaties to isolate the aggressed nation; non-violent foreign policy which slowly wears down the resistance of a people, until their will is curbed to your design – these may not constitute *physical* warfare, but are damaging and represent an attack.

"How else do we interpret the gradual deprivation of a nation's subjects of those supplies they rely upon for their standard of living? Is it not the slow, insidious engineering of hardship, to abrade a nation's morale until they are essentially beaten into submission – without a shot being fired?"

Hearing it put like this, I wondered whether we were in fact *always* at war…

"Consider Roosevelt's pre-1941 'Lend-Lease' policy: the support of weakened nations he viewed sympathetically with high-value supplies on a deferred payment basis – still, from one perspective, the equivalent of supporting the Chinese, at the *expense* of the Japanese, to the tune of upwards of one and a half billion dollars."

"How about a little perspective here?" Jack challenged, his nostrils flaring. "We *owe* him." Roosevelt's Lend-Lease aid had amounted to some thirty billion for Britain and over ten billion for Russia - and absolutely been a lifeline for us.

Pal cocked his head and peered at Jack.

"Roosevelt may have had an altruistic motive; he may have seen an opportunity to capitalise on the weakness of other nations to empower his own. I don't deny the Lend-Lease aid played a key role in your war, Mister Mayfair. My point is that he gave no such aid at all to Japan.

"It is a fact that America aided the Chinese *against* the Japanese long before Pearl Harbor, economically and in the form of war materials. The Prosecution even conceded that American nationals fought *with* the Chinese."

He was talking about the American Volunteer Group, the 'Flying Tigers' – three hundred recently resigned American military men, equipped with one hundred Curtiss P-40 fighters, who were already deployed in Asia when the U.S. entered the war. But he had more.

"In August 1941, three months before Pearl Harbor, Roosevelt dispatched a military mission to China under Brigadier General John Magruder – a *Brigadier General*, mind – its purpose to assess the Chinese need for military equipment, assist in its procurement and instruct in its use. Ostensibly, this was to resist 'movements of conquest by force'..."

He peered at us, pointedly.

"A government bans the shipment of arms and munitions to one of the parties in an armed conflict yet permits it to the other. Is this not taking sides? Might we not argue that any boycott against a nation that is engaged in war is tantamount to a participation in that conflict? The Japanese leadership understandably perceived belligerence."

Jack, Cassie and I met one another's eyes.

"Following the Japanese invasion of Manchuria in 1931, the United States did more than any nation to whip up international enmity against them..."

"Somebody had to!" Jack put in, growing more frustrated by the minute. "You can't just waltz in and annex another country's territory."

"I would agree," Pal conceded. "But while the Americans protested Manchuria in 1931 – and a cost of seven thousand Chinese lives – only thirty years earlier, they themselves were occupying the Philippines, at a cost of tens of thousands of Filipino lives."

I became aware that Cassie was watching me intently.

"We can't be 'behind the curve' any more. The greatest problem we have in contemporary world affairs is selective amnesia."

"Yeah, maybe we all need to develop better radar for politician bullshit," Jack countered. "But these guys died for us in Europe!" Jack had fought in the Pacific, while I had fought alongside Americans many times these past years.

"My point here," Justice Pal began again, "is that Pearl Harbor was just part of a gradual escalation…"

Jack snorted in derision.

"The Americans sought to drive popular feeling among the League of Nations," Pal persevered, "to scrutinise Japanese involvement in China. Quite right too, but the Japanese could not help but notice the report was written by an English noble, sitting in judgement along with three other Europeans and an American. It is little wonder that when the report was read out to the General Assembly, condemning Japan's 'delinquency' before the world, the Japanese withdrew in protest. Isolated, they grew more so by American design."

"The embargo?" I asked.

He nodded. "Following the escalation in China of 1937, the United States began to tighten the noose on its trade relationship with Japan. The Japanese were developing a vision of a 'Greater East-Asia Co-Prosperity Sphere', envisaging economic freedom from Western influence: Japan, China, Thailand, the Philippines, Cambodia, Malaysia, Vietnam, Laos and Burma were to be united for 'mutual benefit'. Their slogan was said to be 'Asia for the Asiatics'. It put the colonial interests of France, Britain and America squarely in Japan's sights…"

"Burma?" Jack interceded, pointedly. "That's right next to Bengal, isn't it? A stone's throw from Calcutta, in fact."

"Yes, Mister Mayfair," Pal replied, meeting Jack's gaze. "As you have clearly noticed, I am Asian."

"Well? Would you say you feel threatened by or sympathetic with that 'co-prosperity' vision of theirs?"

Justice Pal smiled. "It's a beautiful vision. In practice, it turned out to be corrupt: Japan's intentions were ultimately proven to be imperialistic and exploitative and the ideal exposed as not nearly as magnanimous as it first appeared."

I said, "But the American embargo was a response to it?"

Pal nodded. "The Japanese design threatened to neuter American influence in the Pacific. Although Roosevelt's Export Control Act of 1940 was driven by moral outrage over China, it essentially sought to curtail Japan's expansionism. As nearly three quarters of their iron and steel came from the States, Japan responded in two ways: they invaded French Indochina to try to prevent the Chinese supply of arms by that route; and they began to look for other sources of scrap metal supply..."

"Let's not forget," Jack interrupted, "they also treatied with the Nazis."

"Recognition from a major European power gave them credibility," Pal responded simply, before resuming. "For a while, the Japanese seemed responsive to the idea of gradual withdrawal from China. Peace terms were discussed. But in July 1941, Roosevelt froze Japanese assets and embargoed all oil exports – and keep in mind that Japan, reliant upon America for *eighty percent* of her oil, would run out entirely within three years, sooner if she went to war. This left Japan with two choices..."

He left his words trailing.

"Meek subservience," I suggested, "or aggressive reaction."

"With the British and the Dutch following suit in issuing embargoes, the Japanese were blockaded. They had to gain control of South-East Asia's resources. One of the accused, Admiral Shimada, testified regarding the psychological effect this 'anti-Japanese encirclement policy' had: the Americans were applying intense pressure for a withdrawal from China that would have been such a blow as to 'stun' the Japanese people, amounting to a humiliating relegation of Japan from her status of world power to total subordination.

"Meanwhile, the American naval presence in the Pacific had increased dramatically. Roosevelt moved his fleet to Hawaii, two thousand miles closer to Japan. To the Japanese, the Atlantic Conference between Britain and the United States looked like whispers behind closed doors... Much was made in the tribunal of the Japanese 'preparing for war', yet preparations had taken place on both sides.

"We received testimony that two weeks before Pearl Harbor, the Japanese Ambassador handed to Secretary Hull a draft letter – which he proposed to sign *and publish* – that clarified his country's relationship with Germany. It declared that the Japanese government 'would never project the people of Japan into war at the behest of any foreign power' and would only accept warfare as an 'inescapable necessity for the maintenance of its security and preservation of national life against active injustice'..."

"He was lying," Jack snapped. "We now know full well that the Japanese fleet was virtually on its way."

"Untrue," Pal countered. "The fleet did not leave until November the twenty-sixth – five days later. The same day Secretary Hull, having failed to recognise any value in the proposed letter, presented the Japanese with his ultimatum."

"The 'Hull note'," I added.

He nodded. "In which the United States demanded complete and immediate withdrawal, which – as far as the Japanese were concerned – was a sudden and unexpected development. Previously, there had been implication of compromise, a gradually stepped de-escalation – for example, a relaxation of the blockade in exchange for the withdrawal from Indochina – for which the Japanese leadership had shown some good will..."

"In what way was it an ultimatum?" Jack challenged. "Show me evidence that America ever threatened Japan militarily."

"They did not need to. Their humiliation was assured. With no access to oil, their navy would soon be beached. Japan had to surrender Indochina, surrender China, surrender any standing they had in East Asia and the Pacific. You only 'surrender' in a *war*..."

He turned from the fuming Jack to meet my eyes.

"What sort of man would you take President Roosevelt for: naïve, blind to the consequences of his actions, or strategically astute? Perhaps he did not understand the Japanese, or failed to observe the cultural impossibility of their subjugation – though I find it highly unlikely.

"To a fiercely intelligent man, the signals were clear: the Tripartite Pact with Germany and Italy, the Neutrality Pact with the Soviet Union – these are not signs of a proud nation obligingly slipping into slumber, but of escalation. A wise man would observe this and seek conciliation, instead of continuously dogging his adversary..."

"Enough!" Jack snarled, his voice breaking with incredulity. "You're saying he manipulated them? That he engineered the conflict in the Pacific? These were good men."

Justice Pal was unswayed.

"I reiterate: it is agreed that atrocities took place..."

Jack turned to us. "It's like he's reading a menu!" Then to Pal he asked, indignantly, "Where is your horror? Your moral outrage at

Nanking, the Filipino atrocities, Bataan, the Burma-Thailand railway, the treatment of Allied airmen?"

Justice Pal glared back. "You westerners like to wring your hands. In our part of the world, we do not express ourselves so readily. Let me reassure you: I find the incidents you mention appalling, as I find all war appalling. And I would add the dropping of the atom bomb to the very top of that list.

"As for the behaviour of the Japanese with regards to the human rights of their enemies, it should have been addressed correctly, via an impartial court – as should any large-scale aerial bombing of civilians."

Jack rolled his eyes in frustration. "I'm sorry, but the things we saw out there – somebody has to answer for that."

Pal agreed. "Nanking was atrocious and Bataan inhuman, but there is no *evidence* that members of the government authorised these offenses – and certainly not as a matter of policy. They were far from the field, with no satisfactory means of communication. Nor was I convinced there was any inaction on their part which would indicate they desired such acts be done. They were entitled to rely on the competency of their high-ranking officers to restrain the soldiers under their command."

The hands-on perpetrators of those brutalities had already been dealt with in the lower courts. Over five and a half thousand individuals had been indicted for war crimes; nearly a thousand condemned to death.

I found his contention that the leaders in Tokyo bore no guilt troubling: the disregard for human life had been so systemic that surely leaders had to be held responsible. Surely if you send men to war, place them in a position where they slowly go mad performing acts deemed illegal and immoral outside of war – the taking of human life – the ultimate moral accountability has to be on you.

"The Japanese rank and file were completely unprepared psychologically for surrender in such numbers," Pal suggested. "The Japanese soldiers saw their prisoners as disgraced and it was bitter to them that they did not recognise their shame. The logistics of moving seventy thousand men you cannot release – a figure they could never have anticipated – seventy-five miles, without transport or appropriate supplies, speak for themselves…"

"That's no excuse," Jack snapped.

"Agreed – and with the guilty officers now punished, the question is to what extent we should find the government liable. General Tojo issued the order to employ prisoners-of-war, but does that make him responsible for their treatment?"

There was no doubt the local officers had been vicious. But I kept coming back to the principle that you can't condemn a soldier for acting like a madman when he has been driven practically mad by the position he has been placed in.

I couldn't read Cassie. She met my gaze with a soft smile.

"What about their treatment of American airmen?" Jack challenged, angrily. "Where's your rule of law there?"

The punishment was death by firing squad, or life or imprisonment of over ten years – often without trial.

"We must remember," Pal replied, "that aerial warfare still has no established rules of conduct. It is very difficult to consider the conduct of the Japanese authorities towards the air pilots, when the American authorities follow no rules of bombardment whatsoever."

And there it was: Tokyo, Hiroshima, Nagasaki.

Turning my way in exasperation, Jack said, "It does my head in that you might even buy into this."

But I thought of what I'd witnessed. How could we even talk of the Geneva Convention, the 'accepted rules of warfare' or the 'Articles of War' when we'd done *that*?

Considering Jack for a moment, Pal asked, "Why do you so readily embrace the story of conspiracy that is the Allied version of events?"

Jack frowned. "What the hell are you talking about?"

"The Prosecution talks of a 'criminal conspiracy' by the Japanese leadership extending back as far as 1928. It claims they were preparing their people for a great, illegal war of aggression upon their peaceable neighbours on this Earth.

"There is no allowance in international law that entitles a victor to sit in legal judgement over the vanquished for *all* his life's doings. There is not even a crime called 'conspiracy to wage aggressive war'. The Allies seek to bring about a retrospective trial for acts dating back to even before the perceived declaration of war! The Manchurian Incident and the Nanking Atrocities took place before Pearl Harbor...

"If the Prosecution wishes to invoke the greater Chinese conflict, then they must accept that America and Japan were essentially already at war in 1941. And if we are to allow for a crime of conspiracy to wage war, then we must ask whether the Americans were up to something similar."

This was red rag to a bull for Jack.

"You don't see the Yanks stamping out free speech," he countered, with a tone of great irony. "Or imprisoning those who challenge their policies." There was a glint in his eye as he added, "You could never have dissented the way you have if you were a Jap in Tokyo five years ago."

"No," Pal agreed. "But the Japanese people showed as much contentment with their lot as the Americans. Yes, there were political prisoners…"

"…as well as police coercion, assassinations, censorship, propaganda…"

Pal picked up on those last words.

"Over a hundred thousand were 'relocated' during the war, Mister Mayfair, due to the colour of their skin – the official line being 'for their own safety'. These were *Americans*. To this day, there remains no evidence that any Japanese American was planning a 'fifth column'-style uprising – nonetheless, an executive order saw them incarcerated…

"In America, joke 'Jap hunting licenses' were circulated; neither officially endorsed nor discouraged by the authorities, they declared open season on an animal which 'resembles a skunk in appearance' and 'has an appetite for women and children'. The holder was encouraged to aim for the stomach, since the Jap has 'lots of guts, but no heart or brains'…

"According to an American opinion poll in 1944, a significant percentage of its population favoured total extermination of the Japanese – a state of mind they did not reach all on their own."

Jack had fallen silent.

"Censorship? My own report has sunk without a trace in the States and Britain. Nationalist propaganda? A failing common to all nations, encouraged by every government on the planet. It is no great step from there to racial superiority and on to contempt for other races and peoples…

"As for the incarceration of 'undesirables', a mass relocation of Japanese Americans certainly sounds like an encroachment upon the fundamental liberties of the people to me."

Jack whistled through his teeth, slowly shaking his head.

"Is there a problem?" Justice Pal asked, blinking at him.

"Do you have children, Judge?"

"I do."

"Imagine them programmed to desire war, to hate; imagine their playful spirit saturated with the stench of racial superiority. Is that not abhorrent to you?"

"Of course."

"They had officers stationed in their schools, for God's sake – who drilled a righteous military anger into the boys and filled the girls with dreams of nursing wounded heroes, who inspected and spied on those schools."

Pal shook his head. "After the Great War, there was considerable social unrest in Japan, a frivolousness that military training curtailed. You have National Service in your own country, do you not? Is it not deemed good to instill discipline in your restless youth?"

"They killed their childhood," Jack growled, "and replaced it with the divine mission of a new order for the Empire – calling it glorious, when really their lives were just *coin*. You may be blind to how loathsome that is, but I was there and it turned my stomach." Jack was very het up now. "All your words, Judge..." Never a public speaker, Jack struggled to express himself. "They just don't apply to reality, to how mankind really is."

Pal looked appalled. "You are saying that we are essentially base? In that case, there would be no point in reaching for greatness."

Jack clicked his fingers. "There you go – you're so much better at this than me. 'Essentially base.' Yeah. You see, you talk about reaching for greatness and I get it: you're talking about striving to be better, more moral. Any minute now the word 'transcend' is going to pop up. But, mate, you've got to get over yourself...

"For most people, 'greatness' is whatever feeds the kids. It's what keeps a roof over your head. Greatness is about blending in, having a tribe. It's us over them. Your idealism, your pacifism, it's wishy-washy weakness – while you preach soft justice, they're getting in through our back door.

"At the end of the day, where you see pink fluffy unicorns, I see 'Lord of the Flies'."

There was a long silence...

Then Jack asked, "Can I go for that pint now?"

And Radhabinod Pal said, "I was rather hoping for a nice pot of tea."

They smiled at each other, as old friends might. Turning to Cassie, Pal asked, "Are you done with us?"

She broke into a smile and nodded. They looked to me.

Jack said, "There's nothing I said that I didn't believe." Then he just winked and faded away.

The Judge hesitated. "Tulliver, if you take away anything today, take this: for me, Law and Justice are sacrosanct; they are not playthings. The victors wish to whisper into the popular ear the untruth that a final few murders will resolve the last of their unspent rage, so that a new status quo may assert itself...

"No judicial tribunal should contribute to such a delusion. If Justice really is nothing more than the interest of the stronger, if it can be invoked in order to prolong vindictive retaliation, then we are lost." For a moment, he seemed powerfully moved. Then he too slipped away.

I blinked. The entire exchange had been for my benefit.

I suppose these days we'd call this an 'intervention'.

Meeting Cassie's eyes, I realised I'd been presented with two diametrically opposing world views.

"World views that, now the nuclear beast prowls that world, will destroy us all – if we cannot reconcile them."

"All war is tragedy," she added. "But there will forever be those who cannot see that – or *will not* see it. There will forever be those who find war productive and these are the people who will bring us low."

I had encountered such people more and more this century and knew them as 'The Invisible Nation'...

"Justice Pal is right," she said, "when he sees a failure of diplomacy and the gradual development of tension. They were two very different cultures, butting heads and simply failing – or *choosing* – not to understand one another..."

The courage it must have taken to publicly dissent from the judgement of your peers in plain view of the world: Pal had produced a document nearly as long as the actual tribunal ruling itself to support his views, in the full awareness that it would make him an unpopular man.

"I'm not saying the Japanese were innocent, I'm simply pointing out that when the Allies presented the tribunal as a *Court of Law*, they laid the proceedings before the world as representative of *Justice*. But true justice can never be decided by the victors… The problem is no one wants to be confronted with the blood on their own hands when there are easy scapegoats available."

She sighed and gazed out across the clouds.

"The world's attention has been misdirected, not least with misleading parallels drawn between the Japanese and Nazi regimes. We are calling it 'World War Two', enshrining it as one great battle between Good and Evil, when Europe and the Pacific were two very different wars…"

I followed her gaze, but for me the horizon was littered by hundreds of mushroom clouds – ripping into the air, consuming my faith. They blossomed like flowers turning to face the sunlight.

Looking back, I found she was regarding me with urgency.

"Humanity is in a state of agitation, Robert. It needs to sleep easier. By pointing to false causes as the fountains of our ills, attributing our present deplorable state to the actions of an 'evil' few, we escape our own responsibility – and there is no telling where escalation might take us now."

There had already been two more nuclear explosions since Nagasaki. In 1946, America had test-detonated two 'Fat Man'-type, plutonium-based bombs at the Bikini Atoll in the Marshall Islands – far closer to East Asia than to the United States.

America had chosen not to share their secrets – even with Britain. The rest of the world interpreted this either as intimidation or provocation. Outraged that America had hoarded the science despite wartime promises, London was already initiating its own nuclear programme. It was only a matter of time before Russia developed nuclear capability.

Tensions were rising again and this time it could be far worse for us all. But I was so tired of fighting…

She said, "To paraphrase something Pal says in his conclusions, the world is in dire need of 'generous magnanimity and understanding charity' if we are to counter what is coming. I think you have those qualities in spades."

I regarded her with admiration. Her self-belief and will power seemed as strong as ever. She caught the sentiment and chuckled.

"Well, I *am* three centuries younger than you – I don't tire as easily! So, what do you say? Back on the clock?"

I sighed deeply, finally feeling my resolve strengthening.

"What is your game plan?"

She shrugged, casually. "Oh, nothing too grand. We need to systematically eliminate all chief causes of war – and it's a long haul towards world union."

I laughed. At last, I *laughed* again.

She grew serious. It was her turn to sigh and seem daunted. "Japanese imperialism, American expansionism, British colonialism… Provocation leads to sabre-rattling, to escalation, the respect for borders crumbles and it's all about territory and oil. Develop an unhealthy amnesia for when it comes to bombing people in their beds, throw in religious extremism, endemic avarice and selective morality when it comes to corporate interests, start to see these as national interests, build yourself a nuclear bomb or two… You've got a recipe for the next millennium.

"The human race is brewing up Armageddon – and we're the only ones in the way."

We were never able to help Pal's scapegoats. Of twenty-eight defendants, one was found mentally unfit for trial, two died of natural causes during the trial, eighteen were sentenced to prison – mostly life sentences. Seven army generals, a minister for war, the foreign minister and the Prime Minister, General Hideki Tojo, were sentenced to death by hanging for war crimes, crimes against humanity or crimes against peace.

Much later, it emerged that the Americans had conspired to bury any evidence concerning the Japanese 'Unit 731'. Its covert biological and chemical warfare research and development unit had been extensively engaged in lethal human experimentation on tens of thousands of people – mostly Chinese, Mongolian or Korean; some

Allied POWs. The operatives attached to Unit 731 were granted secret immunity by the United States – in return for which they surrendered their data to the Americans. They did not face War Crimes charges; in fact, they walked away, completely free, while the vivisected bodies of those they'd tortured rotted in mass graves.

In 1981, Judge Röling – last surviving member of the Tokyo Tribunal – would write with bitterness at how these war crimes had been kept from the Court.

I was heartened when, on the tenth of December, 1948, the United Nations General Assembly came together to issue a 'Universal Declaration of Human Rights'. In amongst its thirty articles were these inspiring, though I fear long-forgotten, words: "All human beings are born free and equal in dignity and rights. They are endowed with reason and conscience and should act towards one another in a spirit of brotherhood."

Prime Minister Tojo and the other nine defendants who had been sentenced to death were executed at Sugamo Prison in Ikebukuro, just before Christmas that year.

In August 1949, the Soviets shook the world by detonating their 'First Lightning' at Semipalatinsk in northern Kazakhstan. A plutonium-based implosion-type device, it was the 'Fat Man' in all but name. The local populace was not properly evacuated and in the process the Russians irradiated two hundred thousand locals.

The escalation Cassie had feared was beginning…

- CHAPTER TEN -

Ivy Mike, the Lucky Dragon & Sadako's Cranes

The occupation of Japan ended in April 1952, but the year took a turn for the worse in October, when Britain became the world's third nuclear power – a twenty-five kiloton yield establishing we were still one of the big boys. 'Operation Hurricane' was a test-detonation of just seven kilograms of plutonium, off the west coast of Australia.

Having retaken office from Attlee, Winnie's response to my pleas to desist had been characteristically blunt. "You claim the world has gone mad, Robert. That being so, this Prime Minister would sooner hold the asylum keys than end up drooling with his arms tied behind his back in a padded cell."

Once again, the decision to develop the nuclear bomb was driven by a not irrational fear of Stalin. It was widely known that the body count resulting from his purges and deportations edged well into the millions. This did not stop him being nominated for the Nobel Peace Prize. Twice.

Understandably, Churchill viewed Stalin very warily, which is why the Hurricane detonation took place *inside* the frigate HMS Plym: Winnie wanted to see what might happen if the Russians were to explode a nuclear bomb on board a Russian merchant ship – whilst on the Thames…

The United States raised their nuclear game in November 1952 with 'Ivy Mike'. While Little Boy had produced an explosive yield equivalent to approximately sixteen kilotons of TNT and Fat Man had produced twenty, their hydrogen bomb – test-detonated at the Enewetak Atoll in the Marshall Islands – recorded a yield of over ten megatons.

It was more powerful than all the high explosives detonated in both world wars *combined.*

Stalin died suddenly – perhaps mysteriously – the following March, but the hoped-for de-escalation did not materialise. Instead, the Soviets tried to see the Americans' hand that August with their own hydrogen bomb test. Though their yield was barely half a megaton, it was still twenty times the power of the Nagasaki bomb.

Japan began to blossom again, though the Americans retained a presence on Okinawa and Iwo Jima. To me, the new Japan seemed liberated by its introduction to democracy; but Radhabinod Pal might have seen a once great nation neutered, bent to the design of another power – essentially a satellite of American influence in East Asia.

In Washington, at the apex of that influence, things were changing. In January 1953, Truman's Democrats folded before Eisenhower's Republicans and there was a new President. We watched in hope for a sea change – but the Soviets' hydrogen bomb in August put paid to that.

March 1954 saw operation 'Castle Bravo', in which the Americans tested the most destructive nuclear device they would ever set off. With a yield equivalent to nearly fifteen megatons of TNT, it was a *thousand times* more powerful than the Hiroshima bomb. They called it 'The Shrimp'.

With the detonation once more taking place at Bikini Atoll on the Marshall Islands, the Scientific Director of the 'Operation Castle' tests was Alvin Graves – a Manhattan Project and Los Alamos veteran. Like Ivy Mike, Shrimp was again a hydrogen bomb – the difference being that it used dry fuel instead of wet to aid fusion. Shrimp's fuel was solid at room temperature, while Ivy Mike's required cooling equipment – which made Shrimp more practical for delivery in a missile.

Graves had been expecting a yield of five megatons, which turned out to be a spectacular underestimation he put down to a 'theoretical error'. This error resulted in a ball of flame four miles wide and a mushroom cloud seven miles wide a minute later, then sixty miles wide ten minutes after that; it travelled at two hundred miles per hour and reached twenty-five miles into the sky. Though supposedly top secret, it was seen two hundred and fifty miles away.

The wind shear then kicked in. Instead of blowing the growing plume northwards, it skewed east and dowsed thousands of square miles of the Pacific in radioactivity. The one hundred and eighteen islands of the Rongelap, Rongerik, Ailinginae and Utirik atolls were rapidly dusted. As the operatives of the American testing facilities scurried for cover – their instruments destroyed – a number of Americans stationed on the Rongerik Atoll were exposed, while sixteen crew of the aircraft carrier USS Bairoko received beta burns.

Reluctant to acknowledge a problem, the Americans were slow to evacuate – their response so lame that in the years since, many amongst the Marshallese have contended their exposure was premeditated. Whatever the case, even if retrospectively, they certainly became guinea pigs.

The Marshallese sat in irradiated ash for forty-eight hours before rescue. Upon examination, it was discovered that two hundred and thirty-nine islanders had been exposed to levels of radiation deemed 'significant', with the population of Rongelap suffering the highest doses. With a dose greater than one hundred rads, the point at which 'Acute Radiation Syndrome' begins to take effect, they began to vomit and exhibit burns, bleeding gums, diarrhoea and raw, weeping lesions. Their hair fell out.

Perhaps most famously, the crew of the fishing boat 'Lucky Dragon Number Five' – or *Daigo Fukuryū Maru* – were significantly contaminated, despite being in waters outside the exclusion zone eighty miles away. They had witnessed a second sunrise; the roar hit them minutes later; two hours after that, the mushroom cloud filling the sky overhead, they found their ship coated so deep in white, sleety particles they could see their footprints in it. It became so bothersome, they tried to scoop it up into bags.

Returning to port, they fell ill and were quarantined. A Geiger counter detected radiation thirty yards from the boat. Later that year, their radio operator, Aikichi Kuboyama, developed cirrhosis of the liver and passed away. Whether his death was due to pre-existing causes, or to contracting a hepatitis-related infection due to blood transfusions whilst under treatment, or directly due to exposure, is all disputed.

Nonetheless, he is widely viewed as the first Japanese victim of a hydrogen bomb – and recorded amongst the hibakusha.

An international incident ensued – beginning with panic in the fish markets. The authorities hunted down Lucky Dragon's haul: tuna found at Osaka central market sent their Geiger counters into overdrive; contamination discovered on scales and wrapping paper meant the fish had made its way into the food chain. When it was estimated that eight hundred vessels and many tons of fish might have been exposed, then revealed that fish had been dropped from the Emperor's table, the price of tuna nosedived.

The Americans issued denials. The AEC denied the ecological impact on fish supplies, claiming that there was only 'negligible hazard, if any' in eating Pacific fish – maintaining that radioactivity became harmless within a few miles of the test area. American Ambassador John Allinson supported this, in response to which a leading Japanese scientist invited him to eat some of the contaminated fish.

Well into March, fishing trawlers were arriving home only to have their catches condemned. Official guidance was issued. If, having been Geiger-tested from four inches away, fish did not measure more than a hundred counts per minute, it was deemed *safely* radioactive enough to eat…

The American authorities set about handling things well by speculating that the crew of the *Daigo Fukuryū Maru* had been Soviet spies. William Sterling Cole, the Chairman of the Joint Committee on Atomic Energy, was associated with these comments, causing outrage in the Japanese press; AEC chief Lewis Strauss talked of the fishermen belonging to a 'Red spy outfit'; John Allinson wrote in private of a 'fancied martyrdom' amongst the Japanese and that the incident had been blown out of proportion and exploited by 'neutralists, pacifists and professional anti-Americans'.

Accepting no legal liability, the United States made a donation of one million yen to Kuboyama's widow – at three hundred and sixty yen to the dollar, this worked out to be just under three thousand bucks. In January 1955, they paid out fifteen million and three hundred thousand dollars as compensation – each crew member of the Lucky Dragon saw two million yen, about five and a half thousand dollars, for their inconvenience. Essentially, this was a 'buy-out' for continued testing on the Marshall Islands.

The Americans were the kings of the world – although it had completely escaped their notice that if they carried on like this, there wouldn't be a world to be the kings of.

Cassie continued to visit Hiroshima and help in its revival. It was a bustling city again and a new generation was growing up with little memory of the war. Cassie's own girls, Alice and Nellie, often accompanied her and made friends with Japanese children.

One of these was twelve-year-old Sadako Sasaki.

Sadako had always been a healthy child: one of the fastest runners at Nobori-cho Elementary School, she'd been chosen to run the relay on their sports day. She had little memory of the atom bomb; although the family home had been barely a mile from the hypocentre, she'd been uninjured at the time. She had, however, been exposed to black rain.

In November, Sadako came down with a cold. She found lumps around her neck and ears, which persisted into the New Year, spreading onto her face and becoming mump-like. Into January, she was now presenting rashes of dark red purpura spots on her legs, a sign of bleeding beneath the skin. This led to a diagnosis of aggressive leukemia and in late February she was admitted to the Hiroshima Red Cross Hospital, where her white blood cell count was found to be going through the roof.

As all over the world politicians and scientists scrambled to up the nuclear ante, the little twelve-year-old began a programme of blood transfusions. Sadako's school friends visited often. She was presented with her graduation diploma and enrolled in Junior School.

Inspired by a Japanese legend, which says that he who folds a thousand origami cranes will be granted a wish, Sadako began folding paper...

In April, I received an unexpected visit in my dreams from Albert Einstein. Currently living in the States, I knew Albert had just turned seventy-six, but he appeared as a younger man, eyes shining with youth and inspiration. There was no mistaking his bushy moustache and unruly mop of hair. I assumed he was here to progress plans we were developing to make a very public protest. Instead, I found him agitated, his manner obsessive and distracted.

"Robert," he muttered, "I wished to call on you. Time is breathing down my neck..."

"Are you not well, Albert?" I replied, concerned.

He gave me an odd look, then brightened. "I have just signed Bertrand Russell's excellent letter! I am so pleased to lend my name to it. Let us hope the world listens."

What would become known as the 'Russell-Einstein Manifesto' was a bid to curtail the escalation of these new weapons of mass destruction by convening an international, politics-free conference to highlight their dangers.

"The world has to listen," I agreed. "Even if I have to make it my life's work."

Einstein's eyes twinkled, then he sank into thought. "I have seen my life's work subverted in a way I never anticipated."

He seemed almost distressed. I reassured him, "Only one element of it, my friend – you will be remembered as a genius, who significantly advanced the human condition."

"Will I? Not as a warmonger?"

This seemed so preposterous, I laughed out loud. As well as the Theory of Relativity, Quantum Physics and so much mind-blowing science I would never be capable of grasping, he was a passionate socialist, anti-racist and supporter of civil rights – and a leading pacifist. "Never! You could not hope to leave a better legacy."

He shook his head, despondently. "It was my letter, Robert – my *other* letter – that nudged Roosevelt towards the atom bomb."

"Leo Szilard instigated that letter," I countered. "He, Sachs, Wigner, Edward Teller – they were all involved before you."

But the scientists had needed a star name to get the President's attention… "My name," he muttered, grimacing. "My name forever attached to the conception of the American nuclear weapons programme. Hmm? How many have died? And how many more to come?"

Trying to help, I ventured, "Without the atomic bombs, we'd have ended up in a Japanese land war which would have cost far more lives…"

He cut across me, gently. "You don't really believe that, Robert, do you?"

"You were right to sound the alarm…"

"I wish I had never signed it."

I persevered. "It was always going to happen, with or without you – many were edging towards the breakthrough. And you weren't on the Manhattan Project." This was true: he'd been denied clearance on the grounds of his pacifism. "Look at Joe Rotblat," I urged. "You're in good company."

One of the signatories on the proposed Russell manifesto, Joseph Rotblat was the only physicist to walk out on the Manhattan Project in protest – upon realising that the intention was to bomb the Japanese. Like Einstein, he had only become involved to ensure they beat Hitler to the bomb.

Einstein's gaze was steady and unblinking.

"Robert," he said quietly, "it wasn't just the Japanese that Joseph was protesting about. Joseph attended a dinner of James Chadwick's while he was at Los Alamos, also present at which was Leslie Groves…"

I knew of Groves. The General in charge of the Manhattan Project, he'd driven it with a ferocious tenacity and forged a reputation for being something of a force of nature.

Einstein nodded. "Groves is a die-hard patriot. He knew Oppenheimer was the man for the job and assembled an outstanding team around him. But at that dinner, Rotblat quite clearly heard him declare that the *real* purpose in making the atom bomb was to 'subdue the Soviets'…"

I felt a chill. Mentally, I traced the line of command up from Groves. It wasn't far to the top.

The great scientist's eyes were blazing with urgency; if he could, he would have grasped me by the shoulders. "You must find a way to prevent all war, my friend. Promise me. As long as war remains a possibility – no matter how vocally they protest their benevolence – the governments of all nations will continue to arm, and arm, and arm. They will eventually and inevitably use every means of destruction at their disposal."

Alarmed at his distress, I realised he'd said 'you'. He usually talked in terms of 'we'.

"What is the matter, Professor? What has happened?"

His eyes widened. "I see ghosts, Robert. Just out of the corner of my eye." He shook his head. "No, not ghosts – *one* ghost. A girl. A Japanese girl. She stares at me, accuses me. The *rage* in her…" He seemed quite beside himself.

"You bear no guilt for Hiroshima, Albert," I insisted.

"But that's just it," he replied, desperation in his voice. "We all do. Through our continued inaction, we all do."

Jolting his head as if to peer into the shadows at an unexplained noise, he seemed much older suddenly than his years – frail, wizened, haunted.

"Until the day comes when we can confidently say 'this will never happen again', we allow for its recurrence. We implicitly invite it into our homes. Through our apathy, our indifference, we doom ourselves. Don't you see?"

He was fading. On the other side of the Atlantic Ocean, his body was calling him back. "This policy of military preparedness makes the abolition of war impossible, yet its abolition should be our utmost concern – above all others. They will forget, Robert. Promise you won't let them…"

"I promise, of course," I began – but he didn't seem to hear me and just kept talking, his eyes transfixed by a point somewhere behind me.

"I'm sorry," he said. "For my part in it, I am sorry. I should have protested so much sooner – before Hiroshima – but I was slow to see…" His eyes returned to me. "If we don't strive for peace as stridently as those who strive for war, every day of our lives, then we have turned a blind eye… You have to wake them up, Robert. Or the blind eye will end us."

He was so faint now, so wraithlike, that he could himself be taken for a phantom. Finally, he seemed to respond to someone I couldn't see. Shaking his head in refusal, he said, "I want to go. It is tasteless to prolong life artificially. I have done my share."

And then he was gone.

I awoke slowly to the sound of a telephone ringing, already in the knowledge of the sad news that awaited me. Having suffered a rupture of his abdominal aorta, Albert Einstein had passed away at Princeton Hospital, New Jersey.

It was the eighteenth of April 1955. As the world mourned the loss of an old man in one hospital, a twelve-year-old girl sat forgotten in another making paper cranes. Using whatever she could find to pass for paper – newspaper advertisements, medicine wrapping, the wrap from other patients' visitors' gifts – she folded and folded, hungry for life.

Every crane was a prayer.

I resolved to keep my promise, whatever it took – and I knew where I had to go next. For the first time in years, I was looking at considerable mileage again. But having developed something of a hang-up about allowing my disembodied mind to wander the world, this time I took a plane.

- CHAPTER ELEVEN -

The Boondoggle

As my Pan-Am DC-6B landed at Idlewild Airport, my head was swimming. Tourist-class air travel was still a big deal for me. I couldn't get over how science and technology were bounding ahead this century. On the one hand, it was easy to feel like a man out of his time; on the other, the century was doling out awe and wonder. There were *ninety* people on board that plane – and we flew London to New York in eleven hours! With a window seat overlooking the wing, I'd grinned like a kid through the whole flight.

The Big Apple had changed a fair bit. My ride skirted Queens, allowing a glimpse of Rikers Island before crossing the East River Suspension Bridge. I was excited to see the Triborough bridges completed: they'd cost more than the Hoover Dam. The city was properly reaching for the sky now: the iconic Art Deco skyscrapers, the Chrysler and the Empire State Building, were the tallest in the world. I confess to a love affair with the city and it's got to be partly down to that skyline – though the lion's share goes to Jazz.

I'd first encountered Jazz in 1929, when I would spend all the time I could at the Cotton Club and Connie's Inn nightclubs, soaking up Duke Ellington, Cab Calloway and Louis Armstrong. Despite these being whites-only days, I was more comfortable stalking the musicians to the liquor-drenched, marijuana smoked-filled basements of Harlem.

My opposite number in New York had ensured that many of the Jazz greats were recruited into the Society and well aware of their option to take the Blood. Some take it and drop out. Some take it to save their lives, due to its powers of healing and rejuvenation. This way, we'd managed to save George Gershwin from his brain tumour, Fats Waller from his pneumonia and Charlie Parker from his heart attack.

The downside is that as far as the world of non-psychics is concerned, you're dead: these guys, who have been incredibly famous in their lifetimes, have nowhere to play…

The secret Society nightclub was hidden beneath Minton's Playhouse in Harlem. Moody and low-lit, smelling of corn whiskey and tobacco, it was full of quiet, velvet-padded alcoves and a perfect venue for discreet pow-wows. I'd come to meet two old friends and drain their well-connected brains.

There were five musicians, young guys, on stage as I arrived, though as it was still only early afternoon the club had more of a rehearsal vibe. Their playing had a seductive quality, coming from a deep, intoxicating place that suggested recovery. The song was hauntingly familiar…

"A Nat King Cole original," came a voice from the shadows beside me. "'Nature Boy'. Sinatra covered it too."

Turning, I found it was the writer and philosopher, Alain Locke. "That's Miles Davis," he added, nodding to the stage.

"Ah," I replied. "Explains everything."

We embraced. Alain had been my opposite number in New York for decades, his chief responsibility being to recruit the Gifted. A modest and quiet, well-dressed man in his late sixties, he had huge, soulful eyes that seemed to radiate across his entire face. We'd first met forty-eight years earlier, when he'd come to Oxford from Harvard, as the first African American on the Rhodes Scholarship. Sadly, his reception at Oxford had been decidedly less than effusive.

Alain had returned to Harvard to lecture in philosophy. He had spearheaded the 'Harlem Renaissance', a flowering of Negro artistic expression that extended well into the 1930s – his anthology 'The New Negro Movement' had effectively been a call to cultural arms for generations of African Americans. He'd sought to move away from the centuries-long context of blacks always existing in comparison to whites, to a context independent of whites.

"How's death suiting you?" I asked. As far as the world was concerned, heart disease had taken him the previous June.

"Gets me in here," he said, nodding around the place. "And gives me more time to work. There are some very interesting developments in civil rights on the horizon. I intend to use my powerful anonymity to whisper discreetly in some ears."

"I wouldn't expect anything less," I beamed. "He here yet?"

Alain nodded. "And several whiskeys in."

With a chuckle, I slipped into the booth Alain indicated. Our friend, one of the founders of the American wing of the Society, had already poured me a generous Bourbon – it's not every day you get to hang out with a genuine cowboy.

"Now, Bob," he growled, in a deep mid-western drawl that resonated with statesman gravitas, "you know I don't so much care for being called a 'cowboy'."

'Buffalo Bill' Cody leant forward out of the shadows. "For one thing, it's unbecoming of a seventy-year-old."

Although it had turned white long ago, there was no mistaking his bushy Van Dyck moustache and beard. A flamboyant man at heart, he'd opted for a relatively sombre, if highly tailored, black three-piece suit. Though the wide-brimmed Stetson resting on the table was a bit of a giveaway, this was Bill dressed down. In contrast, Alain Locke looked underdressed in his light flannel suit.

"Bill," I countered, warmly, "I happen to know you're a hundred and nine this year; and you spent your whole life courting that image."

"That's as may be, Mister England," he retorted, "but I spent more of my life on the stage than I did on the prairies, so I'll take 'showman' over cowboy any time. There are thousands of cowboys, but very few true showmen."

I'd first encountered Buffalo Bill when he'd brought his Wild West Tour to England for Queen Victoria's golden jubilee in 1887. Although he revelled in diluting the facts of his legend, I did not doubt his prowess as a hero: he was said to have fought the Native Americans as a frontier scout for the army during the Utah War, worked as a rider for the Pony Express, fought for the Union in the Civil War and numerous battles as a scout for the cavalry during the Plains Wars. I was pretty sure that some of that was true.

More pertinent was Bill's secret life since his apparent death in 1917. No longer able to court the public, he'd instead set about fostering the Society's links with and championing the rights of the country's indigenous people.

"The country's indigenous people are not very happy right now," he declared, having picked up on my thoughts. "Particularly out in Nevada."

"Oh? This'll be to do with the testing?"

"You're darned right it's to do with the testing. You up to speed on that?"

Well, I knew there'd *been* testing…

"Forty-three and counting," he said.

I stared at him. "How do you like *them* apples? Forty-four little Hiroshimas on American soil. Oh, they started light back in '51; then came 'Operation Buster-Jangle'. You've got to love the names they give these things. A few air drops, some surface detonations; mixing in troop manoeuvres for good measure, just a few thousand of America's finest pretending to invade the Russkies – after we've shown them what-for with our atomic superiority…"

He necked his Bourbon and smiled wryly.

Alain shook his head. "Given what we are hearing from Cassandra regarding the rise in cancer in the hibakusha, we must wonder about the health impacts on our boys."

"Nah, it's okay," Bill shrugged, deliberately offhand. "Apparently, they wore badges that warned them as they were getting irradiated."

I glanced across the room, back to the entrance. Two men in grey suits and wearing fedoras had entered; they crossed straight to the nearest booth.

"Yep," Bill breathed, "that'll be Hoover's boys."

"They'll have tailed you here from the airport," Alain added.

"Isn't this supposed to be 'the land of the free'?" I suggested.

"Freer for some than for others, Robert," Alain commented. I took his point straight away.

"Still is," Bill replied. "It's just that J. Edgar's *freer* than most."

The Feds were ordering drinks and making a show of enjoying the Jazz.

"You know about Oppenheimer?" Alain asked, keeping his voice down. I hadn't. "He's had something of a fall from grace. Turns out they've been bugging him, tapping his phone, checking his mail since the early days at Los Alamos. Had him pegged as a 'Communist sympathiser' from the outset. It's true he associates with Communists and his brother is a party member. Well, the security leaks have been something of an embarrassment to the Government…"

Ah, yes – there had been a number of Soviet spies circling the Manhattan Project, most famously the German-born Brit Klaus Fuchs, currently serving a fourteen-year sentence at Wakefield for violating the Official Secrets Act. Luckily for him he'd been tried in Britain, where his relatively lenient sentence reflected an understanding that Russia had been an ally at the time of his betrayal. Extradition to the United States might have resulted in a death sentence.

"We've met with Oppenheimer," Alain continued. "He's undeniably a liberal, probably a socialist, but no double agent. Even so, the House Un-American Activities Committee have been all over him like flies and the Atomic Energy Commission have just had him up in front of a Personnel Security hearing, after doubts were raised about his 'eligibility for clearance' – which they've subsequently revoked."

I was astonished. "What's he doing now?"

"He continues to write and lecture, but he no longer has any political standing."

"Just like that," Bill added, contemptuously, "one of the Americans who won us the war is rendered 'un-American'. And what are they doing with his nuclear legacy? Oh yes, 'Operation Tumbler-Snapper'. They wanted to see how quickly they could 'safely' get tanks and choppers in – and to evaluate the psychological impact on the soldiers of charging headlong towards a deadly mushroom cloud…

"After all, the Soviets have actually now tested a bomb, which gave them a whole new shot in the arm in terms of validation."

I didn't need to ask how he knew this. Bill Cody was one of the Society's top recruiters in the States – he'd be looking to find the Gifted amongst America's scientists.

"Then came 'Operation Upshot-Knothole', would you believe – sounds kinda smutty to me. On their 'Encore' test, there were unfortunate exposures of eighty-four personnel – basically they hit their annual limit, which means enhanced likelihood of curtailed life expectancy… 'Minimal safe distance' turned out to be not that."

Alain Locke came in here.

"If I may? We know that the eighty-four men exceeded their annual safe exposure limit in eleven days. Strictly speaking, the exposure took place across eleven tests, but there's also the question of residual radiation between tests. In any case, the kiloton count over the whole operation approached two hundred and fifty."

"Which means they were essentially dancing with fifteen Hiroshimas." Bill sucked in the air through gritted teeth. "Our own people. Our own goldarned people..."

"Fortunately," Alain continued, "such levels of exposure do not lead to immediate unpleasantries – just to a slightly heightened risk of dying earlier. But there has been concern, expressed privately by those scientists who have more empathy for their fellow man, that the civilian population downwind of Nevada may also be 'taking a hit'."

"You're talking about a cancer epidemic?"

He nodded, gravely.

"Radioactive debris from 'Encore' drifted across Wyoming and reached North Dakota. Now, Iodine-131 is a radioactive isotope that emerges in nuclear fission: it's present in fall-out. The academic community is gradually starting to conclude that it collects in the thyroid gland – and will likely lead to an increased risk of thyroid cancer..."

Through gritted teeth, Bill growled, "Son of a bitch."

"The speculation," Alain continued, "is that the i-131 settles on pasture, is grazed upon by cattle and so enters our food chain as milk. I don't know how it is in Britain, but American children are encouraged to drink milk daily. There is therefore particular concern for the thyroids of the children of Nevada, as well as Idaho, Colorado, Montana, Utah...

"Eleven days after Encore came 'Harry'. Harry's cloud made El Paso, Salt Lake City and Nebraska, while the AEC itself reported sightings in Colorado, Kansas, even Chicago."

My jaw dropped. "What's being done about this?"

"We are exploding more bombs," he replied, dryly. "Rest assured: Harry will one day be celebrated for breaking new ground in downwind contamination. In the international race to expose your own civilians to radiation, Harry's a giant."

There was a mortified silence, then Bill came back in.

"For Encore, to test what a nuke could do to a forest, they built one and bombed it? Coincidentally at this time, we're at war with North

Korea, which has some heavily forested mountain ranges. So does Vietnam. I'm just going to leave that hanging in the air like a cornered skunk."

Alain dropped a small booklet on the table.

"And then there's this."

It was a public service booklet from the AEC, which was prefaced by a message of thanks to those who lived near the Nevada Test Site and who had therefore been 'close observers' of the tests. "Nevada tests," it said, "have been a vital factor in maintaining the peace of the world..."

By this point, America had exploded fifty-one nuclear bombs; Russia had test-detonated eighteen. The combined yield of the American bombs had been sixty megatons; the Russians had barely managed seven hundred kilotons.

"They provide important data," it went on to say, "to protect our people in event of enemy attack."

Bill Cody was glowering at me as if I'd written the thing. "As enemies go," he growled, "I'd say that one that has a tenth of your firepower, just maybe, is less an enemy and more of an underdog."

"Some of you have been inconvenienced by our test operations," the booklet said. It mentioned exposure to fall-out. It thanked the locals for their patriotic cooperation. It said, "In a world in which free people have no atomic monopoly, we must keep our atomic strength at peak level."

At the time this booklet was issued, Russia had slightly more than one percent of the nuclear firepower that the States had.

It went on to reassure the people about fall-out from the atomic cloud, saying, "We are not talking about high yield A-bombs or H-bombs... We are not discussing radiation from enemy bombs designed to do the most damage... We are talking only about low-yield test, conducted under controlled conditions..."

Alain was gazing at me, benignly. He said, "The combined yield of the Nevada bombing at this point is three and a half thousand times the yield of the Hiroshima bomb. Do you suppose they are lying, or do they just not have any clue what they are doing?"

He looked at me, intently. "We all live in Trinity's wake, my friend. It's funny: if the world was a rational place, the whole planet would observe a minute's silence at 5:29am every July 16th. That morning in

July '45, everything changed. Its consequences will play out and out until somebody *will* press the button…

"This is the insanity of the deterrent: as we allow it to go unchallenged, we perpetuate the simple inevitability; we bury our heads in the ground. We'll either drop the bomb, or we won't. But the longer we don't, it becomes more likely that we will. And all because very powerful men are growing rich off the back of it."

Bill suddenly brought his hand down onto the table with a loud bang, causing us and the FBI to jump out of our skins. Even Miles Davis looked up from his jamming session.

"I thought we were being clandestine, William?" suggested Alain, amused.

"The hell with clandestine!" he snapped. "What's happening to this country? Twelve more tests this year! Like I said, I'm close to the local Native Americans – the Western Shoshone, the Timbisha, the South Paiute, the Navajo – they're all going crazy about it…" He spoke the next words at the height of his voice. "Now *I don't trust the Russians as far as I can throw them*," then lowering his tone, he continued, "but who's testing aggressively here?"

I knew the Russian figures. "Eighteen so far," I said. "Eighteen to your forty-three. And back in 1953, they'd only tested three to your twenty-six."

Bill nearly spat. "Look at Castle Bravo. Our boys are basically just flicking firecrackers into the gas tank then standing back to see how big a bang they can get!"

Alain had to agree. "There's a singular absence of fine science going on." He gestured to us, opening his hands. "But you two are the fine old gentlemen of the Society! I always thought the role of the Society was to nurture and celebrate the breadth of human vision – but not to interfere."

I poured myself another drink. The whiskey and the music perfectly matched my mood.

"I think it's time to interfere," I declared.

Alain shifted uncomfortably in his seat. Bill whistled.

"You're going to have fun getting that past the Elders."

I frowned. Leaning forward, I said, "All I know is there can never be another Hiroshima or Nagasaki. We've got to neutralise distrust between the nations. And to do that, we need to think globally – *beyond* our borders."

Alain smiled, sympathetically. He seemed to feel sorry for me. "It's a beautiful ideal, Robert."

I knew what Jack Mayfair would have said. *Don't be naïve. For all our liberalism, we are still pack animals, who will turn on one another when we are hungry; no matter how we fool ourselves with intellectualism, it will always be about survival of the fittest.*

I met Alain's eyes.

"Your writings have enhanced our society," I said. "They call you 'the architect of a renaissance'." Turning to Bill, I said, "And you, Bill, you've fostered important links with the Native American. *That's* how the world should be changing! Just because they keep tearing it down, it doesn't mean we should ever stop building it up."

Buffalo Bill nodded, his eyes twinkling. He looked to Alain and they decided to break the bad news.

"We didn't get him," he said, quietly. "Einstein. I'm sorry."

I was gutted – but somehow this was not a surprise to me. I remembered how Albert had been in my dream. "He refused the Blood?"

Both men seemed properly unsettled now.

"Kept going on about some Japanese girl," Bill said, frowning. "Like she was right there in the room. Kept apologising."

"It wasn't as if he was frightened," Alain added. "Just very sad."

"What's *really* weird," continued Bill, "is that the same darned thing happened with Stimson and Fermi."

They were referring to former Secretary of War, Henry Stimson, and the nuclear physicist, Enrico Fermi. Stimson had been General Groves' superior for the Manhattan Project and presidential advisor; he'd died of a heart attack in 1950. Fermi had been a key member of Oppenheimer's team at Los Alamos; he'd died of cancer just the year before.

Stimson had remained staunchly pro nuclear weaponry into his eighties and been a key proponent of it as a deterrent. In comparison, Fermi had questioned whether humanity had the maturity and wisdom to command its new powers.

"All three refused the Blood," I asked, incredulously, "on the grounds of the imagined presence of a Japanese girl?"

"Not exactly," Alain replied. "It was Albert who first mentioned her. But the others also talked to an invisible presence in the room."

It was not unheard of for some to decline the Blood. I'd say one in five of our wards decline – usually because of leaving loved ones behind.

"A psychic attack of some sort, perhaps? Did you sense anybody?" They shook their heads. For the time being, I dismissed it from my mind. Einstein had given so much of himself in his work – perhaps, simply, he'd felt spent.

We raised a toast to him. It must have been glass seven or eight for Bill Cody. The music draped me in mellowness.

"Do you know what a 'boondoggle' is, Bob?"

There he went, calling me 'Bob' again – I don't let many people get away with that. "Sorry, a what-doggle?"

Alain leant forward, gently. "As a noun, a wasteful, unnecessary, even fraudulent endeavour; a hoax or subterfuge. As a verb, we refer to 'boondoggling' – spending time or, more relevantly, money on such endeavours."

"And this is in general usage?"

He shrugged, as if to say 'more or less'.

"Well," Bill continued, "it occurs to me this whole nuclear thing is one great boondoggle. I mean, how much are we spending here? Billions? On something – correct me if I'm wrong – we never intend to use. Now *there's* a fantastic scam! Somebody somewhere is sweeping all this public cash straight into their money bags – and laughing all the way to Vegas."

For some reason, I suddenly thought of 'The Wizard of Oz' – and knew exactly why. I drained my glass and stood up, swaying slightly as the rest of me caught up with the move. "Well, my friends, it's been a pleasure." They went to protest, but I raised a hand. "I'm heading to Washington."

"I knew it!" Bill exclaimed, clicking his fingers. "You came to see the President."

"That's what I thought too," I replied, struggling to get my overcoat back on. Then I turned and staggered over to the Feds' table. Seeing me coming, they were like bunnies in the headlights – so I gave them a big, disarming grin, which I don't think reassured them at all.

"Gentlemen," I announced. "Take me to your leader."

- CHAPTER TWELVE -

Behind the Curtain

It was some two hundred and thirty miles from New York to Washington DC and with the Interstate Highway System still at the planning stage, the Feds flew American Airlines out of LaGuardia. Our Convair CV-240 had a cruising speed of two hundred and eighty miles per hour. This gave me an hour to get my head together.

I closed my eyes and pretended to doze.

My surly, monosyllabic companions had introduced themselves as Agents Diani and Austin. Still emboldened by Bill's Bourbon, I cheerfully nicknamed them according to prominent characteristics – christening the heavy-set one with the round shoulders 'Lunkhead' and the gangly one with the pronounced forehead 'Mekon'.

Both low-level psychics. In a fight, individually they'd be no trouble; together, they'd slow me down a bit. But they'd be able to track me telepathically and I noted this: whoever was having me surveilled knew what they were doing.

Below us, the runway gave way to a flourish of the Manhattan skyline; soon, the Atlantic had faded from sight and we were crossing New Jersey towards Philadelphia. I knew the countryside down there well, having visited Pennsylvania twice before: once to witness the ratification of the Declaration of Independence in 1776 and then again to play my part in the Battle of Gettysburg in 1863.

When I'd first passed through the stretch of land that would become Pennsylvania Avenue, America's 'Main Street', it had been just following the Declaration of Independence. Back then, there had been no Washington, D.C.; where the federal city now stands, dressed along the Potomac, there had been only the port of Georgetown and the town of Alexandria. The White House had been but a glint in architect James Hoban's eye and its first resident, John Adams, wouldn't be moving in for another twenty-four years. The Capitol building wouldn't be there until 1800 either – and that would be the original, which was burnt down fourteen years later, during the war with the British.

Yes, I'd been in on that one too.

In uniform and tasked with retaining control of the colonies, I'd struggled to feel comfortable in my shoes – having been doing territoriality for centuries, the appeal had long worn off. Disenchanted with fighting people for their homes, I'd abandoned my post and entered what I guess we might call 'Tulliver's Cowboy Phase'.

There'd long been blood on my hands that I just couldn't wash off – even before the twentieth century.

That day in May 1955, under the cover of the falling dusk, a black Studebaker Starliner brought me to the front of the Department of Justice building, off Pennsylvania Avenue. Beadily stalked by Lunkhead and Mekon, and accompanied also by a third man who'd picked us up at the airport – a wiry, lizard-like Fed I nicknamed 'Reptile' – I was shown through a twenty-foot high door beneath a high limestone portico and colonnade. The building looked to have five storeys, but probably went down a couple of levels too.

It was well past normal hours now and quiet inside. Our footsteps echoed around the marble walls and a terracotta tile floor of the impressive two-storey high Great Hall, along mellow, wood-paneled corridors and through airy courtyards. In marked contrast with its neoclassical Grecian exterior, inside was smooth Art Deco – particularly with its use of torches – and extensively decorated with mosaic ceilings, paintings and murals depicting key moments in American history and loaded with allegory around themes of justice.

Eventually, we stepped into a lift, which I suppose I ought to call an elevator. It went down. My three escorts never said a word. After a brief, awkward silence, I blurted out, "How about them Yankees?"

The elevator doors slid open and I stepped into a long, vast room with a solitary desk at the far end. Ranks of fluorescent strip lighting flooded the room with a stark white light. The man at the desk stood and waited patiently.

The boys stopped. I began a slow approach. His voice echoed across the room, surprisingly high-pitched, with a slight Southern twang.

"Can I offer you some tea?"

Drawing closer, I got my first impression of the Director of the Federal Bureau of Investigation. He was sixty years old; short, about five foot seven inches; reasonably trim, with a little pot belly – I suspected he ate frugally; his short, dark hair was combed straight back, which had the effect of thrusting his face forward. It was an odd face, with big, searching eyes, a flat nose and a crooked mouth that struggled to smile. He wore a grey suit with a plain white shirt and a stripy tie, but his collar seemed tight around a long neck of saggy, leathery skin, which – in tandem with his combed-back hair – made me think of a tortoise.

I like tortoises, but J. Edgar Hoover gave me the creeps.

"Tea would be lovely."

Reptile slipped into the elevator and the doors shut with a dull ding – even the bell seemed oppressed down here. Hoover gestured for me to take the seat before his desk. It felt like a particularly sinister job interview.

Sitting, he continued, "Did you enjoy New York?"

"It's changed quite a bit."

Nodding, he said, "I'm not a keen follower of jazz, I'm afraid. The people who associate themselves with that *scene* bother me."

"Well, I guess *I* associate myself with that scene."

His lips pulled back to reveal his teeth in what I assumed was supposed to be a grin.

"Indeed you do," he replied. "Indeed you do." There was an awkward moment, then he threw open his arms in a conciliatory gesture. "But you're English, so it's tourism!"

I laughed with him; but his eyes didn't play the game.

"I'm ever so slightly English myself," he continued. "On my father's side. It's a fine country. A great ally. Shame your authorities aren't quite as stringent in vetting their people as they might be, but we can't have everything."

That was a reference to our fine tradition of producing Russian spies. I imagined Klaus Fuchs to be at the forefront of his mind; though he would also be thinking of Joseph Rotblat – the scientist who, by virtue of being the only man to walk from the Manhattan Project on grounds of conscience, had attracted the FBI's full attention. Deeply suspicious of his 'conscience', they'd compiled a dossier of evidence pointing to him being a Soviet spy with plans to defect – none of which actually turned out to be true.

Hoover held my gaze for a moment. I got the distinct impression he'd been listening to my every thought.

The tea arrived and he offered, "Shall I be mother? One pours in the milk first?"

"Actually, I prefer to let it brew a while. When I'm happy with the colour, I add milk."

"Well I never," he said, fascinated. He poured a little and waited for me to approve the strength of it, then asked, "Sugar?" I indicated that I did not. Finally, he added, "Of course, I may to have to kill you."

I took the tea. It was very nicely presented, very genteel. Had a saucer and everything.

"Good brew," I said. Leaning back in my chair, I asked, "Haven't reached our quota today, then?"

He rocked in his chair and pointed at me in a little gesture of amusement.

"You've come here in search of some sort of 'truth'. While I'm perfectly willing to have that conversation, I've formed the impression that you have *change* in mind – and my job is to stop change. We like things just the way they are…

"Why not do yourself a favour, let the boys show you out?"

He cocked his head to one side and waited.

"You were on good terms with FDR, I believe?"

"Oh," he replied, "we understood one another. I could see that his reforms would placate the masses. For his part, he knew where not to stray."

"On the subject of running mates, for example?"

Hoover raised an eyebrow in warning.

"I don't want to rock your boat, Mister Hoover," I reassured him. "I'm only interested in nuclear weapons."

Despite my best attempts to look into his mind, I was getting nothing out of him – except the heebie-jeebies. Something about this place was clawing at my instincts like nails down a blackboard.

"I am not the man you need to see," he countered, impassively. "I have no influence when it comes to our nuclear policy."

"But you are the gatekeeper, are you not?"

He blinked. After a moment, he ventured again to deflect me. "You really should be talking to President Eisenhower about this. Or perhaps the Secretary of State, Mister Dulles?"

I blinked back.

"I don't think so, sir. I think I need to speak to the people behind you."

All pretence at joviality toppled from his face.

"You really don't want to have this conversation, Tulliver. There is no coming back from it."

Time to go down the rabbit hole.

Taking a deep breath, I said, "Mister Hoover, I've lived a lot of history and it's given me a certain sense of perspective. What I see with absolute clarity is that the wars are getting worse. We may be enjoying a temporary reprieve with the Cold War, but we're on a precipice – and we need to step back." Leaning forward, I continued, "You're a great patriot, surely you can see that it's in the interests of national security for us all to live in a safer world?"

Then he did something which I took to not bode well.

He snorted.

"I was interested to meet you – you're older than my entire nation. But I'm disappointed: I expected all those decades to have worn away childish idealism, but you, sir – you're naïve. You have met many more men than me and yet you understand mankind so poorly."

I took a breath, catching the scent of a man about to talk too much; which was exactly how I wanted this to play out.

His grin was all teeth and no warmth.

"In my line of work, we're always watching for people who have a bee in their bonnet about 'making things better'. You see, I subscribe to the belief that what screws us up most in life is the picture in our head of how it's *supposed* to be."

The glint in his eye told me he'd already signed my death warrant – now I had to wait and find out why I was still alive.

"I have been in power since 1924. Already I have kept my position for thirty-one years – and I intend to stay right here until my death. That could be fifty years in office – and there are people who protest at President Roosevelt's four terms!"

"They don't realise the true power rests behind the curtain?"

"Well, I think they do – and that they like it just the way it is. They've relinquished the need to fret. All we have to do is put food on their table."

I shook my head.

"True peace of mind cannot be achieved by living in denial."

He yelped with amusement and waved a finger in my face.

"Now that's just exactly the kind of shit we don't like to hear! You start putting that stuff out there, they're going to come over all troubled." He was talking very fast now, getting pretty animated. I remembered something about his speech patterns hiding a childhood stutter. "Besides, I disagree – people are much happier in denial."

What did I actually *know* about John Edgar Hoover? Washington-born, of German, Swiss and English descent, he'd studied Law at university before embarking on a fast rise in the Justice Department; during the Great War, he'd headed Woodrow Wilson's Alien Enemy Bureau, which had specialised in arresting without trial anybody remotely German with dubious-looking intentions towards the state. From the very beginning, it seemed, he'd traded in distrust. At twenty-six, he'd been assigned to lead the General Intelligence Division of the Bureau of Investigation, where his zeal for suspicion had zeroed in on the radical left…

He beamed at me. "Anarchism is change for change's sake; it's the random destructiveness of misdirected minds. Bolsheviks, Communists, Socialists – what have their high-minded 'ideals' achieved? A revolution that saw millions dying from starvation, or just plain *cleansed*…

"You see, we must not allow our people's minds to wander. We must keep their more 'Bohemian' tendencies firmly in check."

Feigning stupidity, I ventured, "We talking about jazz again?"

He rolled his eyes. "No, sir, we're talking about the necessary pretence of Democracy."

"We… don't really *have* Democracy, then?"

"Oh, we have *some*. More than they have in the grim old Soviet Union, for sure; or China, with its labour camps and wholesale executions of landowners; or the Middle East, with its Sharia Law. That's why it galls me when people whine in this country – they have no idea how lucky they are…

"But, no, in truth we're more kind of a *partial* democracy. Think about it: we elect our politicians, but we don't elect our bankers; we don't elect our corporate leaders. And politicians, more and more these days, are transitory beasts – your Mister Roosevelt was quite an oddity with his four terms. Political office is seen by the more astute youngsters as a stepping stone into the true establishment…

"So, the people you elect have a short lifespan in power, while those you don't spend their whole lives in it. It's a watertight system, because it locks out any real change."

Reading my despair at how, in such a system, I was ever going to turn the nuclear trend around, he made a face that seemed to feel sorry for me.

"Yeah," he mused, sympathetically. "You've bitten off more than you can chew there, I'm afraid."

I tried cosying up to him by challenging his intellect.

"How would you do it?"

"Well, I wouldn't, because it's hopeless and I don't see the point. But I'll indulge you…"

He rose to his feet and paced in thought for a minute.

"The problem you have is that the nuclear arms race is in America's best interests right now…"

"Not if," I interjected, "America is laid waste to in a ball of fire."

He waved that away.

"Everybody who's anybody has their own bunker. I can get to several shelters from right here within five minutes."

I was appalled. "What about the general populace?"

"Well, obviously we'd take a *hit*."

He saw me cringe and snapped back, indignantly. "Don't you go making me out as if I don't care about the people! I *love* the American people! But the fact is that the general populace is just a part of what makes America. The public are an asset, but they break down into groups of varying value. Beyond them, we have the leadership – elected and unelected. And we have the corporations. Some of our billionaires are worth more than small countries."

Aghast, I asked, "So it's all about influencing how much of a 'hit' you take?"

"There you go," he agreed. "As I say, the problem is that the nuclear arms race is worth every penny. It creates jobs and makes a certain number of *key* people a lot of money. It also gives us a safe enemy to hate."

"How does that work?"

"We have far more nuclear warheads than the Soviet Union right now – thousands as opposed to their dozens. And yet it's the Communist Russian – and his far more dangerous ideological soulmate, the American socialist – who are the boogiemen in this country." He seemed genuinely passionate about the subject, adding a self-congratulatory, "You see what we did there?"

At my apparent confusion, he tried a different way to explain himself.

"Have you never thought about the real motivations behind what is now commonly being called 'McCarthyism', behind our prosecution of what we want the public to perceive as 'un-American'?"

He left that hanging in the air for a moment. The Republican senator from Wisconsin, Joseph McCarthy, was Hoover's close ally in the pursuit of the 'red menace' which lurked in the nooks and crannies of American society.

Many careers and reputations had been shattered in the 'witch hunt' that had resulted out of the endeavours of the House Un-American Activities Committee, which had spearheaded the drive to whip up widespread anti-Communist hysteria. Oppenheimer had suffered from the resulting purges, whilst other notable victims included the playwright Arthur Miller and movie star Charlie Chaplin.

"Note that we've pursued movie people, because they can't fight back – they have no real power. Homosexuals are easy prey too. The people love celebrity and love even more to despise loose morals. Of course, it's all a smokescreen to enable us to take the unions apart. While Walt Disney and John Wayne are happily dancing to our tune, the fish we really want to fry are the political activists, who represent ways of thinking we wouldn't want to see taking root."

This made sense – there were few bankers or leaders of industry on the HUAC hit list, if any.

"It's the 'progressives' we're weeding out. We don't want to see any subversive elements, or propaganda that might attack the form of government guaranteed by our Constitution."

"That's the Constitution which was drawn up to protect those who can't fight back, right?"

He glanced down at me, sourly.

"Very droll. The nuclear deterrent is of great value to our national security: it creates that enemy. The real threat is negligible, but the people willingly subscribe – literally paying us to increase our power over them. Because they are afraid, the nation is kept secure against their more *itinerant* impulses."

So 'national security' now meant the security of the authorities – against the more rowdy democratic excesses of its own people.

"Don't you think that paranoia is an unhealthy state of mind to keep your people in?"

He shrugged that off.

"On the contrary, paranoia's an excellent tool."

"Then you *want* a nuclear war? Because that's the end destination of all this."

He looked at me as if I was an idiot speaking a foreign language. "The United States has always been at war, it's in our DNA. If you look at our history books, you'd be hard pressed to find a year when we weren't at war with somebody." Shaking his head in exasperation, he continued, "Since the day our distant ancestors slithered out of their amoebic womb, it has always been about survival of the fittest. What eludes most people is that in the twentieth century, we have redefined what it means to be 'fit'...

"The fitness of the modern human has nothing to do with the physical and everything to do with *wealth*. It is survival of the *richest*. To be fit, to survive, to preserve one's line, one must build higher walls to shut out the wild, impoverished masses who would take our stuff. And above all, one must generate profit.

"War is business, simple as that – so sooner or later, yes, we're going to have to use these weapons. Because, quite simply, they're a revenue stream – if they don't get used, they won't get replaced. And we want to sell more."

He returned to his chair and drained the last of his tea. I set mine down, barely touched. Wincing, he said, "Biscuits. I forgot the biscuits, didn't I? You had nothing to dunk."

"Do you have anything stronger?"

"Garibaldis?" His shoulders heaved in a display of joviality. "Just messing with you. I don't make a habit of keeping alcohol, I'm afraid. We may have a cigarette in the room?"

He waved Reptile over. The Fed took out a cigarette case. I wasn't a habitual smoker, but I took one anyway – it was giving me time to think. I let him light it for me, winking at him; his face was a picture.

It would be strenuous, but I knew I could take the three suits, even all at the same time. Hoover I wasn't sure of. He was a powerful psychic – there was no doubt about that – but as to how our powers were matched, I had no sense of it. Then there was that nails-down-a-blackboard feeling, beating away in the background like a nagging migraine – something was very wrong in this building.

I had a strong feeling then that I was way out of my depth. Closing my eyes for a moment, I reached out for Bill Cody.

Bill, you'd better come find me. I think I'm in a pickle.

Hoover cocked his head, listening.

"We're not bad people," he said. "What we do here gives one hundred and forty million souls a good night's sleep. Sometimes we're forced to do questionable things, but it's understood by the general populace that's what has to happen."

"Isn't that exactly how it worked in Hitler's Germany?"

I meant this as an insult.

"Thank you! Yes. And wasn't it fascinating? Did you see how the majority turned away when hideous acts were being perpetrated on their behalf? I think it was Göring who said, in an interview in his jail cell, that of course the common people don't want war, but it's always a simple matter to drag them along; all you have to do is tell them they are being attacked and denounce the pacifists for their patriotic failings and exposing the country to danger...

"Have you heard of the Order of the German Eagle?"

"This is a medal? An honour awarded by the Nazis?"

He nodded. "It was given to foreigners, primarily diplomats and politicians, who had given valued service to the Reich. Well, Thomas Watson – chairman of IBM – was awarded it in 1937; James Mooney, a chief executive of General Motors, received it a year later, the same year that Henry Ford was awarded the Grand Cross of the German Eagle – that's the highest honour the Nazis ever bestowed upon a civilian.

"Hitler was even said to keep a portrait of Ford in his office...

"Now, I make no suggestion that any of these men were complicit in the waging of aggressive war – these awards were all given in peacetime, after all – but you must remember that many of our great corporations had German subsidiaries, which by necessity served to supply materiel to the German war effort.

"The fact is the German army drove to war in trucks built in Ford factories, and that Opel, a General Motors subsidiary, built trucks and planes for the German military…"

He leered at me.

"It's safe to say that, as Germany entered into aggressive warmongering in Europe, a number of American companies prioritised protecting their investment over challenging Hitler – these factories were highly profitable, after all. Technically, we weren't even at war – *you* were – and anyway, it might have ended at any minute. So, at least until late 1941, America enjoyed a splendid revenue stream from Germany…

"Consider for a moment President Roosevelt's 'arsenal of democracy', which was running in tandem with that revenue stream, and in which sterling work was done to fend off the dark advance of the very same regime: thousands of our firms, many of whose names you will be very familiar with – Ford and General Motors amongst them – diligently applying themselves to provide your country with steel, electronics, chemicals, gasoline, trucks, tanks, aircraft, ammunition…"

"For which we're very grateful," I interjected.

"Indeed. But not one of those companies did so at cost. If you'd taken away their profit, asked them to do it out of their goodness of their hearts – well, I fear that Hitler would long ago have opened a subsidiary of the Nazi Party in Whitehall.

"This is just the way the world turns."

"It wasn't all about self-interest – I won't accept that. There are good, honest people. *Roosevelt* had recognised that the Nazis were a threat to our freedom…"

"Roosevelt was damn near overthrown himself," he snapped, "in 1934! Some of our finest industrialists sought to hire themselves an army of five hundred thousand disenfranchised war veterans, to march into the White House and stand him down. If he'd refused, they were going to execute him right there in the Oval Office.

"These people had been getting all twitchy at FDR's liberal tendencies – remember, the President was pushing through his New Deal at the time, which was very considerate of minorities and the unions.

"Watching Hitler and Mussolini with growing admiration, they'd decided, hell, if seizing power works for those guys, it can work for us. You have to realise that in 1934, Adolf looked like an inspirational guy! In a few short years of power, he'd lifted Germany up from the ashes, from being a broken thing, and made her formidable again. I mean, no doubt about it – and I know it's not something one goes on record with these days – Adolf Hitler was a great man. He achieved spectacular things and galvanised an entire nation.

"The only reason the industrialists' coup fell apart is they picked the wrong man for their figurehead – a popular war hero who turned out to be too much of a do-gooder, by the name of Smedley Butler…"

Now there's a name to conjure with.

It almost sounded as if Hoover favoured their approach…

"Heck no," he retorted. "I favour a stable state. But those men are the backbone of America. FDR's time has passed – he made his mark – but those illustrious men and their offspring will continue to employ tens of thousands of the little people for decades yet, serving the nation through their industry. They are patriots all, with not one Communist bone amongst them."

"Of course," I countered, "in order to 'put food on the table', they are profiting from death and misery. It's not a great leap from there to murder, is it?"

He glared at me.

"We're talking about war here."

"What's the difference? Nen get to go to other countries and do stuff that back home would earn them the electric chair – and it's okay, because it's state-sponsored."

He was smiling at me, pleased. As if on cue, he opened a drawer and pulled out a dossier, dropping it on the desk with a triumphant flourish. Then he thrust his head forward.

"So, you are a pacifist?"

Feeling suddenly compromised, I said, "I fought. I served my country."

He opened his dossier, turned a few pages.

"So you did. You started on the ground at Dunkirk, I see."

"I wasn't one of the first over. I was never keen to fight. But I took up arms to get our boys back."

He nodded, eagerly. "Then you took to the air?"

I had a creeping feeling of dread at where this was heading.

"Our way of life was threatened. I fought in the Battle of Britain. With reflexes like mine, I was a natural for the Spitfire."

He turned the page.

"Goes quiet for a while after that, until '42?"

"The St Nazaire Raid, you mean? Operation Chariot."

"Nice work," he cooed. "Back on the ground for that?"

Nodding, I replied, "I went where I thought I could be most of use. The Society got heavily involved – it was clear we needed all hands to the pump."

He seemed impressed. "You get everywhere! Operation Chastise? Did we bounce bombs?"

I shrugged. "Barnes Wallis was Society."

"Then on the ground again for D-Day? Operation Market Garden? You're a bona fide hero, son. So, what turned you into such a crybaby?" He turned the page. "Ah..."

I closed my eyes, but I could sense that his were on me.

"The fourteenth of February, 1945," he declared. "Or shall we call it the date of your hypocrisy?"

I was pinching the crook of my nose, then resting my head in my hands – mortified to be so unexpectedly reunited with my memories of that day. We'd lost eight planes at Dresden: small coin for twenty-five thousand lives...

He seemed delighted.

"How many babies did you burn, do you suppose? It was the middle of the night, wasn't it? They'd have been sleeping in their cots..."

"Stop it," I whispered.

He seemed offended. "But isn't this what you're doing to us? Where's your moral high ground now?"

"I've come back from there. I avoided killing after that."

"Really?" His tone was laced with cynicism. "Even in Berlin? Even in the bunker? You *were* the last man to see Hitler, after all, weren't you? Now that was your duty..."

"I didn't kill Hitler."

This was what it had been about! From the start, this was why Hoover had tolerated meeting me, indulged my questions – I could feel him rummaging around in my mind, seeking out my secrets...

"Anyway, it wasn't the last time you killed. What about the sixth of August, 1945? The day you had control over Tom Ferebee…"

"No!" I snapped. "You don't lay that one on me…"

How the hell did he know about those few seconds on the Enola Gay?! Somehow, he'd plucked that out of my head…

"You could have stopped it, you know. But you procrastinated your chance away." He rose to his feet and came around the desk, leaning in close. "All those high school students building their firebreaks, they might be parents now if it weren't for you…"

I felt something start to give again, deep inside – something that, with Cassie's help, I thought I'd patched back together. My God, he was clever – he was picking me apart…

Erich Kästner comes from Dresden…

That night in Berlin, so long ago, as I was slipping into Halcyon, when I'd remembered that my friend was from Dresden – he'd sounded so sad: "In a thousand years was her beauty built, in one night was it utterly destroyed…"

I hadn't had the time to tell him that I was a party to her destruction, that I'd gazed on her desiccated remains as they were drenched in flame – a psychic man, suddenly swamped with the screams of those below. The screams of innocents he'd condemned to a hideous, excruciating death.

As I'd slipped away, I'd been thinking of another city five thousand miles away.

Hiroshima, I failed you.

"Yes," he whispered. "You're done now. All I need to know is about the bunker…"

My eyes snapped open.

"GET OUT OF MY HEAD!" I roared.

The power ripped out of me like a wave, washing him clear across the room. I felt the three Feds moving and spun around to deal with them. Reptile was the closest. He tried to strike at me with his mind. I dodged it effortlessly and parried, spinning him around and repelling him so that he landed in a crumpled pile several feet away – unconscious.

Mekon was reaching into his jacket. Lunkhead was charging me. In the corner, Hoover was struggling to shake himself awake. I gave myself room by leaping back over the desk, then flipped it over at

Lunkhead – the big man collapsed under its weight, but I didn't think he was down and out.

I heard Mekon's weapon being discharged. His first bullet ripped into my shoulder; the second missed. I spun the tray at him, fast, like a metal frisbee; it smacked him clean in the crook of his nose. From the crunching sound and the small explosion of blood, I knew I'd broken it. Landing disorientated, he groped for his gun again, but – reaching out – I sent it clattering well out of his reach. Furiously, I punched out at him. Although there was thirty feet between us, the blow knocked him out cold.

Lunkhead was up again and on the move, pulling his revolver from its holster, flicking the safety... I concentrated on his trigger finger, gave it a little nudge. He discharged the weapon, shooting himself in the foot. Hopped for a moment, then dropped in agony. Making sure the gun was spun far across the room, I left him screaming – and turned to confront Hoover.

Who was just standing there, composing himself – straightening his tie.

He said, "Enough now."

An instant later, I couldn't move – not a muscle. Slowly, I lifted from the ground, so that I was hovering impaled on the air. He reached out his right hand and it was as if his fingers probed right through my forehead and into my brain.

"I'm tired," he grunted, "of you and your like. It's an illness really, your delusion that we can somehow all just get along. You're all empathy and conscience. The good news is that I can knock that out of you."

Never.

I couldn't move anything with my mind either. Even my powers were clamped in this vicelike grip.

How?

Ignoring this, he sank his fingers deep into my soul. It was like being alive as a slug slithered through your exposed entrails.

"I imagine this is quite unpleasant for you. Shall I give you something to entertain your mind while I rifle through it, one last example of how pointless it is to expect the best of your fellow man?

"You'll have heard of IG Farben, I assume?"

I had, of course – once one of the largest chemicals companies in the world, they'd gone into liquidation back in '52. It had been formed back in the 1920s out of a merger of several companies – including BASF, Bayer and Agfa. Before the war, IG Farben had been huge with a couple of hundred thousand employees worldwide. Their headquarters had been in Hamburg.

"A beautiful corporate monster," he continued, "they challenged our own giants for status as the world's largest company. And just like General Motors, Standard Oil and U.S. Steel, they had interests – perfectly amicable in peacetime – that took them into murky waters come wartime, as a government contractor cosying up to the regime…

"In IG Farben's case, yes, alas this led to their unfortunate association with the pesticide 'Zyklon B'…"

I knew this. This was famous. The cyanide-based Zyklon B had been used in the extermination camps; it had been pumped into their gas chambers, which contained a thousand people at a time – those deemed by the camp doctors as unfit to work, generally women, children and the elderly, who were told they were taking a shower. It had taken them around twenty minutes to die.

At the end of the war, twenty-four of IG Farben's directors had gone on trial at Nuremberg for war crimes.

Hoover smiled. "There were three sets of trials of German industrialists at Nuremberg: six directors of the Flick Group tried first, followed by the IG Farben directors, then finally twelve directors of the Krupp Group. Flick were associated with the steel and coal industries and prosecuted over slave labour charges, use of concentration camp inmates, so on – they were looking at crimes against humanity.

"Three were acquitted immediately. Of the others, the maximum sentence was seven years, including time served – that man is now the richest in West Germany…

"Krupp's interests were in steel and munitions; at one point, they were the largest company in Europe. Their people were also prosecuted for slave labour and hence crimes against humanity, for which the maximum sentence received was twelve years and forfeiture of all assets. However, three years later, all but one of these men have been released…

"Alfried Krupp has had all his property returned and is once more the CEO of his company.

"As for IG Farben: the corporation with a controlling interest in the manufacture and distribution of Zyklon B; whose laboratories spewed forth such little joys as the nerve agents Sarin and Soman; whose operatives had tested poisons and chemicals on concentration camp inmates; who, undeterred by any regard for basic human rights, used tens of thousands of slaves at their synthetic rubber and fuels plant just outside Auschwitz – effectively making them a party to wholesale slaughter...

"Of the twenty-four men indicted, eleven were acquitted. The largest sentence passed was eight years, of which that gentleman served four. Those men have returned to work as consultants in the chemicals industry...

"Some are back on the boards of their companies.

"All these companies made a fortune out of war and that money is still out there, swilling about in their family coffers. They've paid a penalty for their naughtiness, but the banks want them back in play – there are shareholders to think of, after all.

"So you see, it always pays to be an industrialist."

I could feel him wandering through the library of my memories, going through each minute of April 1945 as if he was leafing through index cards. He'd zeroed in on Berlin on the thirtieth; now he just had to track down my remembrances of the bunker. There'd long been rumours about the FBI head's obsession with Hitler's fate. If I could only manoeuvre him into letting slip a couple of names...

"Those famous industrialists in 1934, who attempted a coup on Roosevelt – they got away with it, scot free. Had to back down, make some concessions to the President over his New Deal. But they walk amongst us still and have only grown in power. A little *moral flexibility* goes a long way..."

Hoover looked me square in the eyes, challengingly. He frowned – finding it harder than expected to break through.

How about a trade?

His eyes widened.

"You'll just *show* me what I need to know?"

You'll give me a name?

He chuckled at a private joke. His face settled into a sneer.

I couldn't see Reptile, but I heard stirring from over there. I was fairly sure Mekon was still out cold. Lunkhead was whimpering and trying to take his shoe off to get a look at the wound.

"For Christ's sake, Diani," Hoover snapped at him, "will you take yourself off to the hospital."

He waited for Lunkhead to drag himself to the elevator, then he began.

"You'll be wanting to know about the human radiation experiments, I guess? Here's what I know – none of it sanctioned by me, by the way. I just leave them to their own devices."

Them?

"It's mostly done with the approval and financial support of the Atomic Energy Commission. So, you should talk to a Doctor Hamilton, professor in Experimental Radiology, operating out of Berkeley; he was part of the Manhattan Project, I believe. He's been helping the AEC with human tolerance to plutonium. His subjects don't even know he's been doing it.

"Back in 1945, at the Manhattan Project Army Hospital in Oak Ridge, at Billings Hospital in Chicago and the University of California, there were eighteen people unknowingly injected with the stuff. These guys were all chosen because they'd been diagnosed with terminal cancer, so – hey – it's fair play…

"Studies have been conducted in Iowa City, Detroit, Memphis and several other hospitals across the country on over two hundred newborns and infants; these have been conducted by local universities but are generally funded by the AEC or health charities. The Memphis study, which was to gauge the health effects of radioactive iodine on newborns, took place at John Gaston Hospital, a charity hospital – so, you know, black kids, poor mothers – often unmarried…"

I was horrified.

What are they telling these mothers?

"I understand they're told that it's a blood test to evaluate the thyroid function of the infant."

There's a hell of a difference between taking blood and injecting i-131.

"It doesn't stop there, I'm afraid. Can I also point you to the Medical College of Virginia and their splendid work on burns victims – usually impoverished blacks – via the use of injected radioactive isotopes? Or to the doctors at Harper Hospital, Detroit, who gave the radioactive iodine orally to sixty-five babies, with a particular view on whether it affected the premature ones any differently…

"In Iowa, they gave pregnant women i-131 with a view to studying their aborted embryos. In Nashville, at Vanderbilt University, several hundred pregnant women have secretly been dosed with radioactive iron as part of, er, a 'nutrition study' – they were given vitamin drinks to enhance the health of their babies. Sadly, there were deaths.

"Meanwhile, at the Fernald School in Waltham, Massachusetts, in an experiment jointly sponsored by the Massachusetts Institute of Technology and Quaker Oats, over a hundred boys deemed to be mentally retarded have been tricked into eating radioactive cereal. They were told it was an exciting new science club, but it was an experiment to prove that the nutrients in the cereal reach all parts of the body – yes, sir, that oatmeal really lights you up!

"Now what else can I offer you…

"How about the 'Green Run'? In December 1949, the Department of Defense and the AEC initiated an experiment at our Hanford Site facility in Washington State that was designed to simulate Soviet releases of radioactive fission products – the rationale being that if you dump radioactive stuff in the air and learn how to monitor it, then you can keep a track of what the enemy is up to. The Russians had tested their first nuke just a few months earlier, so we were looking for ways to improve our reconnaissance methods…"

He took a breath.

"Well, they kinda made a hash of it. The Green Run was a particular way of processing a uranium batch at Hanford; usually, a processed batch would be allowed to cool for a minimum of eighty-three days to allow for the decay of dangerous radioactive isotopes…"

This our old friend iodine-131 again?

"As well as another called xenon-133. So these radioactive elements are supposed to decay if they sit there for at least eighty-three days, right? Except on the Green Run, in which they're only cooled for *sixteen* days – so they're anything but decayed. It was these highly radioactive isotopes that hit the atmosphere that night, to be distributed by prevailing winds across a populated area forty miles wide and two hundred miles long, containing three small towns.

"Unfortunately they accidentally released twice as much i-131 and two and a half times as much x-133 as planned…

"Once the dust had settled, they found irradiated materials on vegetation considered to be one thousand times higher than acceptable, and thyroid irradiation in animals tested to eighty times the acceptable dose."

My God, it would be in the food chain… They had irradiated a vast area and risked the lives of thousands, in order to work out a way to spy on an enemy who was nowhere near as militarily advanced as they were!

It was pure, paranoid lunacy.

"And right now, in Sonoma State Hospital, California, mentally handicapped children – sufferers of cerebral palsy and similar conditions – are being extensively tested upon. The doctors are starting out with spinal taps and irradiated milk…"

He stopped and considered me.

"Judging us again, friend? What do you think your own government is up to in Australia right now?"

The pure insanity of it. I began to laugh. He watched unimpressed as the hysteria swept through me in waves.

"This is that British irony thing, isn't it?" he said, with no note of amusement in his voice at all.

I nodded, my eyes streaming. My sides were hurting too now.

It's so sick, it's funny.

He shook his head. "Really don't get it. We had a deal."

My mirth subsided.

You may not think it's funny, but you can see it, can't you – how insane it all is? You can't tell me that Truman knew, that Eisenhower knows, about this?

"There's no man in the country has the resources I have, has a more detailed overview of the forces at work in this nation than I do – including the President. Honestly? I find it distasteful, but it makes our nation more secure, gives us stronger intelligence on this new power. As for the White House, possibly they know, but the guys at the top of the tree – they're no scientists, this is all scary voodoo to them."

A name. An entry point into the Invisible Nation. Just one name.

I knew full well he intended to kill me, but I was hoping that – as he now considered me of little risk – he might humour me…

"Oh, I have no intention of killing you," he declared, smugly. "What a waste of an extraordinary Gift." He hesitated, for a moment becoming the most sincere that I had yet seen him. "It's the money lenders you need to reach. It's always the money lenders. You know that even now there are gold bars stamped with the swastika sat in the vaults of the Bank of England – and that this is gold that once sat on the fingers, wrists and necks, and in the teeth, of Jews on their way to the death camps?

"As for names, well, they stand to reason: look to our greatest families, those whose fortunes have skyrocketed over the past fifty years. You suggest that I am some sort of 'gatekeeper'? Then think of who in this country is more powerful than I. Follow the links from man to man and imagine them all in a room, learning together how war enriches and empowers them. Patriots all. Fine men, with a common understanding of what makes America great.

"Now: we had a deal."

Indeed, we did.

Adolf Hitler had no intention of ever dying and he mocked up his death on the thirtieth of April '45.

"I knew it!" Hoover's eyes were blazing with an almost religious zeal. Secrets were his stock in trade – and he had just bought one of the best kept of recent years.

I allowed Hoover to see my memories of that day, through my point of view, as I'd set about tracking Hitler down. In that dank, subterranean, grimly claustrophobic bunker, with the approaching Russian artillery only a few hundred yards from our door, the Führer and I had played cat and mouse with one another – through the Reich Chancellery, to finally come face to face in the burning ruins of the Wertheim Department Store nearby.

"So you *did* kill him?"

No, sir, I told you: I didn't kill Adolf Hitler.

"Then who did?"

Well, that's just it – I don't think anybody did. We confronted each other. He told me home truths, just as you have done.

Hoover's eyes practically popped out. "Such as?"

He explained how he was Invisible Nation; how your bosses were angry because he'd endangered them by his actions. He told me about their plans. About the Hum.

Hoover wasn't smug any more. The sneer had faded.
"And you let him get away?"
I never got the choice. All hell landed on us care of the Soviet artillery. When I came to, he was gone. I would have made tracking him down my life's work, but stopping your slow apocalypse felt like a higher priority.
He twitched.
"Well this has certainly been instructive." Unexpectedly, he gestured beyond me in the direction of the elevator. "Allow me to introduce you to someone I know is just going to fascinate you."
Still held paralysed in mid-air, I was spun steadily around on my axis to face a young man in military uniform, his arms outstretched and shaking with the effort. He must have been mid-twenties and at first glance seemed a fresh-faced, all-American boy. Then I looked closer – and my stomach did a flip.
Keloid scars. All over the man's face, and I suspected his entire body, were rubbery lesions – the evidence of extensive healing following third degree burns.
"Hello, sir," the young man said, cheerfully. "It's a pleasure to meet you."
The tone, though cheerful, was somehow devoid of real empathy. Even as he spoke, I was realising that those heebie-jeebies – my instincts hollering at me that there was something seriously out of the norm in this building – had been fixating on him. It was he who held me so easily incapacitated.
His sheer presence was overwhelming; he just emanated power. There was a tidal wave of energy suspended just behind his eyes and it felt like it could come crashing down to consume us at any moment.
J. Edgar Hoover stepped into my line of sight, sneer refreshed.
"This is Second Lieutenant Orville Green. Before joining the army, he'd already been recruited by the Society – his Gift being evident from an early age. But Orville here, he fell terminally ill and so he was introduced to the Blood. The Second Lieutenant was devastated, as he realised that this would necessarily mean that he would soon have to drop out of the normal world; but at least he could still enjoy a few years of his career. He was damned good at his job too, ending up working logistics for General Grove on the Manhattan Project…"
Here, Hoover shook his head in mock sadness.

"But alas, a terrible misfortune befell Orville. One day in July 1945, he was working in the Jornada del Muerto desert, near Socorro, New Mexico – he shouldn't have been anywhere near where he was, but he'd mistakenly thought he had enough time to double-check a faulty instrument – when his vehicle failed him. His terrible bad luck also extended to his radio. He was stranded in the last place in the world he would want to be at that moment.

"I guess we could call it the hypocentre."

As the implications of what Hoover was saying dawned on me, I could only stare in horror.

He beamed at the man like a proud father. "This is what happens when you put a Blood-activated psychic at the heart of a nuclear detonation."

I gasped, unintentionally. Hoover was pleased by this.

"What's more, we've discovered an intriguing relationship: the greater the yield, the more supercharged the psychic."

I had only to think of what had happened to me in Hiroshima – when I was not even physically present – to understand how it could happen. I'd been shattered across the city, able to read dozens, if not hundreds of minds at once. My telepathy had been boosted astronomically.

Looking to Second Lieutenant Green, who seemed, pleased as punch, I asked, "How many of you are there now, Orville?"

"You will be our fifty-third, sir."

My stomach spun: fifty-two of these monsters walking the Earth – and counting. Then the true implications of what he'd just said hit me…

"Although," he was continuing, oblivious to my mounting fear, "the twelve we made this year are still in recovery. There are a few created out of megaton-level explosions, who are basically basket cases. And six of our guys got incinerated in the larger explosions, which was a crying shame. But I shouldn't worry, sir – the odds are pretty good for you."

"For me?" I looked to Hoover. My God, there was only one place in the western world you could make an atomic guinea pig out of a five hundred year old psychic…

"That's right, Major," Orville beamed. "You're going to the Nevada Proving Grounds. You're going to love it there – best sunrises in the world."

He reached out and I felt the ground coming up to swallow me, my head spinning. As consciousness slipped away from me, Hoover smiled down at me and, turning to Orville Green, urged, "Son, would you like to tell Mister Tulliver here what your codename is?"

Green nodded eagerly, all wide-eyed apple pie.

"I sure would," he replied – and he turned to me, his eyes glowing brightly. "Around here, sir, they call me 'Trinity'..."

- CHAPTER THIRTEEN -

Survival City

My head was banging, like somebody had used it as a pneumatic drill bit to hammer a hole into my own brain. There was no telling how long I'd been out, but I'd been dreaming some pretty weird stuff: Marilyn Monroe singing 'Diamonds Are a Girl's Best Friend', only dressed as a geisha girl in a kimono; Thanksgiving with an all-American family, except the turkey was Churchill in 'diapers' – and I had to do the carving…

I'd been smashed so hard it had driven me deep into Halcyon for a while; but Halcyon knew where to take me. Deep down in the dark id, I dredged through my guilt and grief: here was Hiroshima, here Dresden, then all the terrible things I'd been called upon to do – heroic, yes, justifiable perhaps, but they would never leave me. It had been a just war: Hitler had threatened our families' freedom. But I'd killed men who might otherwise have been tending crops, or playing with their children…

I drifted somewhere I'd never been before: a tableau of countless battlefields in a constant state of metamorphosis, stretching to the horizon. Here were all too familiar trenches, here the long grass of Pacific skirmishes; I stumbled through earth scorched with craters, a ravaged landscape of shattered homes. The night sky was ultra-vivid, with more depth and beauty than I'd ever imagined: a cornucopia of planets and constellations, astral bodies unsullied by light pollution – as if curtain after curtain for all eternity had been pulled back, to reveal the entire universe crowding in to peek benevolently down at us.

Everywhere on the ground – resting on rubble, slouched on a mound in no-man's land, leaning against a bombed-out truck – there had been a soldier, gazing up into the immortal night. Although physically exhausted, and in many cases badly maimed, each seemed strangely at peace, transfixed by the reassuring endlessness. Although they wore every uniform, side by side they were free of nation.

It seemed an elephants' graveyard of veterans, but these were the Gifted – those soldiers with psychic powers, whose bodies breathed still. They had come to rest and retrieve some human connection with those who they had once sought to kill.

One of them now stepped forward to greet me. In his late fifties and wearing the uniform of an American Marine Corps major general, he emanated mild-mannered gravitas. He introduced himself as, "Butler."

Saluting him, I replied, "Major Tulliver, sir."

This was Smedley Butler, of whom Hoover had spoken so sneeringly: the popular war hero who had turned out to be a 'do-gooder', when he had foiled a planned coup against Roosevelt in 1934. He seemed pleased that I'd heard of him.

"Surprised," he said. "I'd rather formed the impression I'm dropping out of the history books like a lead balloon."

It was surprising that Butler and the attempted coup hadn't received more coverage: he'd had the highest rank in the United States military and been its most highly decorated soldier with sixteen medals, having fought in the Caribbean, the Philippines, Central America, China and in France, during the Great War. In 1935, he'd penned a book called 'War is a Racket', which had upset some people.

"I am as experienced a soldier as you might find – and I know of which I speak. War is not what it claims to be."

"I'm starting to realise," I agreed.

"And what have you concluded?"

"It's an exercise in generating profit."

He nodded.

"After the First World War, Major Tulliver, there were many shortages; but do you know what there was twenty-one thousand more of? Millionaires. And those are the men who *declared* their good fortune to the taxman…" His eyes twinkled, but behind them I could sense great bitterness and outrage. "Clearly, there was excessive money to be made in gunpowder and munitions…"

Excessive money – now there, I suspected, was a concept the businessmen he was talking about might struggle with.

"Steel goes without saying," he continued. "And copper. The leather people did well, as did the nickel people. Sugar too. Then there was meat, cotton and coal; those who provide uniforms, knapsacks and shoes; the mosquito net people; the ships, airplane and engines people; the manufacturers of tools… Oh, and the bankers! The bankers, accountable to no one, with their impenetrable balance sheets – God bless 'em.

"Let us not forget, that some of these companies also sold to the enemy. What is certain is they were all – quite literally – making a killing."

He fell silent for a moment, looked out across the silent soldiers, their eyes fixed in a sort of prayer upon the heavens.

"For my own part, I only realised this following a career in it. I feel like a damned fool now. Back in '35, having retired, I saw this whole second Great War coming: they'd called the first 'the war to end all wars' and sent the boys to Europe with their heads all a-whirl at the glory of the thing – but then somebody looked at the bottom line...

"I warned them about Hitler and Mussolini, but nobody wanted to listen. I foresaw the war in the Pacific too: Japan was threatening American investment and free trade with China and the Philippines, to the tune of many billions of dollars. You can be damn sure those investors were breathing right down President Roosevelt's neck.

"What galls me is that it had only been decades since we'd fought *with* the Japanese against China...

"When we began 'defensive naval manoeuvres' off the Pacific coast, alarm bells began to ring for me – oh, we were told by the admirals in Washington that this was not for war, but simply to protect our coastline..."

His voice dropped. "Well, Major, there's little that is defensive about manoeuvres in the Pacific when they are nearer the Japanese coastline than the American. That's aggression, pure and simple. Our leaders are always gradually edging us back into warmongering mode – and why?"

Butler waited, testing me.

"Because the war profiteers were whispering in their ears," I replied.

"I use the term 'racketeers', but you have it."

"Do they really have that much influence?"

He laughed and shook his head.

"There are families, Major, who learnt long ago how to build fortunes from war – some of them go back to the Napoleonic Wars. Challenge them in their racketeering and they'll bite at you like a rabid dog. People get riled when you call them out on the morality of their income stream."

We gazed up at the celestial tapestry: suns orbited by planets, affecting one another's orbit in subtle, undetectable ways – each with their own satellites, moons, meteors and so on, in an invisible network of gravitational pull.

"George Washington had it right when he warned against meddling in foreign affairs. Until the turn of the century, we had few interests abroad and our national debt remained low; once we began planting our feet in other countries' business, that debt escalated astronomically.

"Our government borrows to pay the war bills while certain of its subjects grow spectacularly rich; then that debt falls to the tax payer. Our wages are stripped bare to pay taxes, to pay off debt accrued paying war bills. It will be generations before we can settle the bill – and our grandchildren will be accountable for it. If we carry on with our warmongering, the debt will *never* be paid."

One by one, the men began to hum. It was 'Pack Up Your Troubles'.

I was thinking about the new millionaires – surely, they were just entrepreneurs, offering valuable services to the state. Granted, they did not go to war in person themselves, or place themselves in any physical jeopardy – but they were a crucial part of the war effort.

"I believe," he said, "that on an individual basis, many do not realise that they are a party to perpetrating a great ill on their fellow man. They just see the money and to them it's 'the American Dream'. But this is the reality I see..."

The men stopped humming. As one, with their eyes dark pools of torment, they turned to peer at me – and let out a terrible wail. Each one cried out not just with their own anguish, but the anguish of their dead comrades – and beyond that, the grief of *their* loved ones. I heard mothers, sweethearts, children, crying for the loss of the man who had once been their prop in life.

"They were the pick of the nation," he breathed. "Boys we plucked from the fields and the classrooms and rewrote, so that we could send them abroad to murder. We rewrote them, turning them inside out, so that killing was okay now, then we discharged them and told them to do another 'about face' – dumping them back into society. We supervised them into the battlefield, but could not find the time to supervise them out of it. Our wartime propaganda drums told them how the nation loved them, but in peacetime they went quiet.

"Now these men lie forgotten by the tens of thousands in hospitals for veterans, the living dead destroyed to their core. We fed them war and told them it was God, then we cut off their supply. We took God away from them.

"Did you know, Major, that until the end of last century our soldiers were handsomely reimbursed? Then we brought in conscription – and the soldier's labour was no longer negotiated, but inflicted upon him. Conscription essentially emasculated that man. Instead of payment, he was patronised with medals, because a decorated man stands proud and forgets; instead of payment, we shamed that man by using those around him to stare accusations of cowardice; instead of payment, we fill their heads with bold ideals.

"The tragedy is that across the ocean, our opposing nations are doing the exact same thing. These boys..." He gestured to all the soldiers in their many different skins and uniforms. "They're the same."

"As we thrust rifles into their hands and pat their backs, nobody mentions the profits – that their life is now a dollar bill, folded and slipped into the wallet of a wealthy man. This is the racket, the brilliant racket, where the long game is to nudge the nation ever closer to armed conflict and find ways to stir up aggression; it is where profits are gauged in dollars... And losses?

"Well, the profiteer cannot lose.

"He deflects the loss, transfers it. While he stays at home, in comfortable shoes, beneath silk sheets, a 'lesser man' pays in a country far away in a rat-infested trench; he pays in taxes, with an eye or a limb, or his mind, or his life. The soldier always pays the biggest part of the bill – and while his blood seeps slowly into the mud, the profiteer reaches into it, draws out his dollars and squeezes them dry."

The terrible wailing had stopped. On the horizon, the Sun diffused its golden chain reaction onto the deep night and the soldiers turned to bathe in the glow.

Butler's tone changed, the bitterness and reproach fading, to be replaced – unexpectedly – by hope.

He said, "The only truly democratic way to send men to war is to cut out the old men and the businessmen and allow only those who would go to fight to vote on it. Consider for a moment a different world, in which we turn the tide – by taking the profit out of war."

I gazed at him, astonished.

With steady, implacable eyes, he replied, "Conscript the profiteers."

"What, into the army?" I asked, incredulously.

"No, sir – into the war effort."

Pay them the same as the soldiers. Let the bankers, the directors, the board members of every company, our great industrialists – all those essential to the fight – prove their true patriotism. Let them demonstrate that their love of our nation is greater than their love of themselves. Make sure they are not out of pocket, yes – pay their costs, of course. And before *we conscript our soldiers, conscript the generals, admirals and all our senators and governors too, and all those lobbyists in Congress, lest any of them should feel swayed by any financial interest in war-making.*

Give them the same pay as the men who will actually lay down their lives. *Then we'll see how quickly they rush to war.*

"Major General Butler," I said in admiration, "I wish it could be so."

Butler looked at me. "You're fading," he said. "Time to go."

I felt a distant tug at my consciousness. Somewhere far off, someone was calling me back.

"One last thing," he said, gesturing across the field of his brothers in arms.

Eyes closed as they embraced the new day, the soldiers reminded me of sunflowers worshipping the Sun's rays. So many different uniforms, creeds and skin colours…

"Across the globe, their nurses see only mad men. But here, together, they find peace – sometimes side by side with the man who wounded them…"

The feeling of being pulled away was intensifying. It felt like somebody was twisting my intestines and pulling them out through my belly button.

"But they have another thing in common: they've been given their uniforms by a rich man; they each took up arms for him in the deceived belief that they were part of that man's team. Perhaps the rich man was white and he pointed to the men of other colours and said, '*They* are your enemy'; or perhaps the rich man was Christian and he pointed out the Muslims; or perhaps the rich Communist pointed out the Capitalist, or the Capitalist pointed out the Socialist…

"In every case, the rich man stirred up those wealthless men, those men of little power, and they went to war for him, and they paid for his gain with themselves, these boys who have so much in common with one another – who, were they not divided by borders, might otherwise be friends."

They were all shades now, just vague outlines – as if a solar eclipse had shrouded the Sun. The Major General raised his hand in final salute and was gone.

Back when I had been a mortal man untouched by the Blood, when Henry VIII had ruled my country, I had never thought of myself as 'white' – that hadn't come until much later. There must have come a point when the masters had recognised the benefit of separating the poor white from the poor black – by pointing to the black and labelling him 'other'. Call them 'people of colour' and suddenly, *they* are the different ones.

It was so clever – because until that point, the two poor men had more in common due to their poverty. Divided, they were separately easier to marginalise.

The powerless men of Germany are told that they have to fight because God wills it, while across the Channel the same God is being invoked to inspire the powerless men of England. The powerless men of Japan are told that true greatness lies in glorious sacrifice for the Emperor, while across the Pacific the powerless men of the United States are inspired to die because of the threat to 'all they hold dear'. And behind it all lurk the racketeers. Men go to war over religion and borders, against difference – but they are always, always being played.

Over sixteen hundred bombs had been dropped during Operation Meetinghouse, delivered by nearly three hundred planes: how many had made money from that? The 'boondoggle' had been that an industry had sprouted around the development of nuclear weapons; but Hiroshima and Nagasaki had paid the price – straying far beyond the exploitation of battlefields, into an area where you could make money from bombing civilians.

There had been another sort of profit earnt from the deployment of Little Boy and Fat Man: America had established her supremacy for all the world to see. Few would challenge her territorial interests now. Power equals greatness equals rightness.

I heard the engines first. Opening my eyes, I had the aeroplane down to a shortlist and the Douglas C-47 Skytrain was on it: a dual-engine bird with a wingspan of about ninety feet and a maximum speed of two hundred and twenty miles per hour, I'd piloted a few for the RAF – where we'd called them 'Dakotas'. They had a range of sixteen hundred miles, which meant – given that I'd been out of it for several hours – I could be anywhere.

As I opened my eyes, however, the Dakota was already old news, taking to the sky somewhere out in the night. I could hear a radio playing in the darkness. It seemed I was in somebody's front room, as I could just make out a television set in one corner and the silhouetted figure of a man staring silently back from an armchair beside it. Beyond them was a curtained window, through which I could see moonlight.

There were others in the room with me, talking in low voices – their darting torchlight the only illumination, which seemed strange. Why didn't the house owners just flick a light switch? Were we robbing the place? All I knew for sure was that I was handcuffed to a chair – a dining chair by the feel of it – one cuff to each wrist.

As if he'd become aware that I was awake, Second Lieutenant Green pulled up another such chair and sat across from me grinning endearingly.

"How're you doing there, sir?"

"I'm feeling a tad rough, thanks, Orville."

This was true. The word 'pounding' was meant for my head.

He chuckled. "A 'tad'? I love how you English guys talk!"

"Enough to let me go?" I ventured, wryly.

"Well I would, sir," he replied, sounding convincingly earnest, "but I'd hate for you to miss the party."

"It's fine. Really. These days I'm just a pipe and slippers kind of guy."

He chuckled again and shook his head, amused. "The boss warned me you'd be slippery."

I nodded beyond Orville to the staring man in the armchair.
"Aren't you going to introduce us?"
He seemed confused at first, then he laughed and waved his torch that way – revealing a shop dummy, grotesque in the sudden, stark light.
"I'm sorry, sir – we're not on a first-name basis."
Ordinarily, I'd have taken an instant shine to Orville Green – I could tell that he was the kind of open-hearted, positive-minded boy who would make any mother proud. Orville should have been married to his childhood sweetheart by now and fixing tractors on his Pa's farm.
I'd need to get closer to him, lull him into a false sense of security – but when I tried to read his mind, I found there was no getting in there.
"Where're you from, son?"
"Iowa, sir."
"Farming family?"
Orville lifted his head and shoulders, bristling with pride at the memory. "Scott County, near Davenport and the beautiful Mississippi River! You ever been, Major Tulliver?"
"Can't say as I have."
"You should visit. My mom, she makes the finest meatloaf you ever tasted." With a wink, he added, "You just mosey on up to the front door and tell her Orville sent you, I guarantee you one content belly – yes, sir!"
"That rather assumes I'm going to live to see the day out."
Orville threw back his head and guffawed.
"Oh, sir, we're not going to *kill* you!" There was an evangelical glint in his eyes now. "We're going to fix you."
Feeling a chill, I countered, "I wasn't aware I was in need of repair."
"Oh, Major," he said, shaking his head in pity, "you so are. You know, Mister Hoover, he tells me there are three types of people in this world: those who drift happily through life, kind of in a soft, dazed wander; those who gently herd the wanderers; and then there's the contrary ones, who've got themselves all tied up in knots about how it *should* be.
"I used to be asleep, now I'm a shepherd; but you – oh dear, sir…"
He just smiled benignly and left his words in the air.

"What a waste of an extraordinary gift," Hoover had said. Then when he'd introduced Orville, he'd said, "This is what happens when you put a Blood-activated psychic at the heart of a nuclear detonation."

My stomach lurched.

"We're at the Nevada Proving Grounds."

Orville beamed from ear to ear, genuinely excited. "We sure are, sir – Area One, just west of the Yucca Flat. The place of your rebirth."

Suddenly aware that I was well out of my depth, I thought of my American minder: I reckoned he would have shadowed out of New York, probably on the next plane out. The question was had he tracked me out of Washington?

Bill Cody, if you're listening, I need you now more than ever…

From the light levels out the window, I figured it was well into the early hours. Out there was fifteen hundred square miles of the Nevada Desert: a huge, parched wilderness, dotted with low shrubs and only the occasional tree, lined with low, arid hills.

"What's the purpose of this test?" I asked, keeping the rising alarm out of my voice – trying to work out an escape strategy. If he stayed this close, there was little chance of me slipping away; but if I could just get out in the open, put some distance between us – there weren't many places to hide out there, but maybe I could make those distant hills…

I threw a quick glance to him, wondering whether he was reading my thoughts – he wasn't giving away any sign of it.

"It's a civil defense exercise. We're looking at how houses hold up to a forty-kiloton explosion, to see whether shelter areas inside and electricity cables bear up, that kind of thing."

Forty kilotons – hell's bells. Little Boy's yield had been fifteen…

It occurred to me that at heart, Orville was decent – and gullible. I wondered how I could use this against him, take the advantage.

"Orville, what does it feel like?"

He looked back to me, blankly, frowning as he tried to process my meaning. Somebody behind me flashed their torch across the room, highlighting his keloid scars.

"How does it feel now, do you mean? Or while it happens to you?"

"Well… You don't seem to be in any pain now. Now doesn't seem so bad."

He brightened a bit.

"It's not bad, sir. Not at all. It's awesome." That zeal had entered his stare again. He was a drug addict remembering his best hit. "In the beginning, it's like the world's pumping lava around your veins."

"Sounds painful," I offered, sounding not too concerned.

He nodded. "Ferociously so at first, while it's happening. The flesh blisters and spits, the eyeballs melt, but it all grows back eventually. Grows back better. And in the meantime, gradually, your soul begins to recognise the pain as kinda like *kin*, you know?"

Having concluded I was in the company of a raving fruit cake, I merely nodded.

"You were there," he was continuing. "It's like being one of those poor people at Hiroshima and Nagasaki, only you've got the Blood in you so – as long as you are a reasonable distance from the hypocentre, you can't die."

"A reasonable distance?"

He waved the question away.

"Don't you worry, sir – we've got this down pat now."

Bill Cody, where the hell are you? The clock's ticking...

I concentrated, scanned the other people in the room. There were five men in total: two military police, two civilian scientists and a Fed in a suit. These would be the only guys in the know, the only witnesses to what was going to happen to me. Hoover was keeping it strictly need-to-know. I scanned them for the Gift – they were normal people, except the suit.

From the heat I was getting off of him, I had another freak on my hands. I remembered what Hoover had said about how they'd been experimenting on my kind – that there were fifty-two more monsters like Orville walking the Earth. And counting.

I craned my neck to try to get a look at him.

"His codename is 'Zebra'," Orville said, following my gaze. "He was made out of the third detonation of Operation Sandstone, on the Enewetak Atoll back in '48. His was an eighteen-kiloton yield, as opposed to my twenty. If our test goes well, you should come out of this stronger than the two of us combined."

"The greater the yield, the more supercharged the psychic," Hoover had said. I thought back again to what had happened to me in Hiroshima, how my telepathy had been boosted astronomically.

The scientists were setting to around me. One plunged his needle into my arm, dragging out a blood sample.

"*If* your test goes well?"

He laughed. "Like I said, the few we tried to create out of megaton-level explosions are basically basket cases; and yeah, some of our guys got incinerated when we planted them too close to the hypocentre. But relax, Major – we're getting real good at this."

"That's a relief, then."

"We're working to one guy for every test, but as we refine the science there's talk of maybe more – and maybe re-exposing us successful subjects, to see if we can be boosted."

Ah, so he and Zebra weren't sticking around. In the crucial minutes before the detonation, they'd leave. Reaching into the mind of one of the MPs, I found there was a helicopter waiting outside, about fifty yards away.

"And who's in charge of the programme? Mister Hoover?"

He stopped talking and peered at me, suspiciously.

"You sure are good at keeping a fella talking, Major."

"Just being friendly," I replied, lightly.

The Gifted are all different. I was pretty sure that the two 'supercharged' psychics were not powerful telepaths – my instincts were telling me they couldn't read my mind. I set about slipping in and out of the minds of the MPs and scientists – the latter now in the closing, fine-tuning stages of setting up equipment to monitor my vital signs.

First, I drained their knowledge of the immediate environment.

I was sat in one of a hamlet-sized cluster of purpose-built buildings. This one was a two-storey masonry house, the inside being cinder 'breeze' blocks, the outside being red brick; it had a shelter in the basement but was not especially reinforced. There was a car parked outside, but nobody in the room knew whether the keys were still in it.

There were four other residential buildings out there: another two-storey, wood-clad home, redesigned and reinforced with larger concrete blocks; and three cabin-style 'rambler' bungalows – one wooden with a porch, no basement, sat on a concrete slab, another built of pre-cast concrete, the third reinforced with steel. All were furnished extensively with sofas, standing lamps, TVs and beds, as well as refrigerators and other appliances; their fridges and larders were well stocked – a study would be made of the effects on food supplies, how the packaging bore up and so on.

All the homes had radios, being broadcast to from a nearby concrete radio house – to see how quickly public communications could be reestablished following an attack.

There were two electrical substations placed at differing distances from the hypocentre and two radio towers, one self-supporting, the other of the guy-wire type. Active power lines were strung across the test site. They'd also installed liquefied petroleum and natural gas facilities, including a long cylindrical tank partially filled with propane – beside which stood a weighing and storage house.

The scientists were interested to know whether any of this would explode.

Everywhere there were mannequins: gentlemen mannequins in dapper suits, lined in a row facing the blast; lady mannequins in elegant dresses, sat taking tea; child mannequins in pigtails and baseball caps, playing with imagined pets. They were dressed in all types of textile and synthetic fabric, to see whether it would melt onto them.

Deeply eerie, they awaited their fate with blank docility.

They called this part of the test 'Operation Cue'. It was run by the Federal Civil Defense Administration and it aimed to gauge the impact of a nuclear detonation upon the civilian community, to research rescue and recovery and determine how soon normal service could be established.

The Operation Cue community was spread out at an outer distance south-east of ground zero of just over three thousand yards; at its closest end, it was only three hundred and fifty yards from the bomb.

Somewhere out in the night, maybe only a few hundred feet away, stood the tower upon which was perched – at a height of five hundred feet – 'Apple 2', the source of my imminent demise. Out beyond that, dark silhouettes in the moonlight, silently waiting in the desert sand, were various unmanned trucks, jeeps and tanks.

I reached out still further with my mind. About a mile and a half south of the tower, quite possibly closer to the bomb than we were, there were ten volunteers crouching in freshly dug trenches – just for the rush of it, it seemed.

Nine officers and one civilian, apparently none of them had heard of how well 'Ivy Mike' had gone.

The next closest people were barely two miles away: nearly two thousand troops serving as part of the ongoing 'Desert Rock VI', a thousand of whom were engaged on tactical manoeuvres codenamed 'Razor'. As a special armoured task force spearheaded by the 723rd Tank Battalion out of Camp Irwin, California, and also consisting of the armoured divisions of several battalions out of Fort Hood, Texas, their mission was to move in immediately after the detonation and seize control of the area. Sat in their tanks and personnel carriers – which admittedly were properly sealed up – some were as close as three thousand and one hundred yards.

The source of a lot of this confidential information was one of my MPs, whose name was Clyde. He had buddies on the ground – a couple of guys from Company C in the 510th – but was pretty happy to not have to be out there with them. They were supposed to be driving into ground zero within minutes of the blast and Clyde didn't like the sound of that.

There were people still further out, I discovered: nearly eight hundred Department of Defense observers, including top brass and some foreign NATO representatives, in two trenches at two and three miles; a smattering of prefabricated buildings, which were buzzing with activity. Beyond them, about six miles from us, was a convoy of headlights – reporters, commentators and news crews, observers by the busload, converging upon Media Hill.

'Civil Defense Operations' was near them. Further out still were AEC Control, where the Los Alamos people and other interested scientists were hovering in anticipation; and Yucca Lake airstrip, where various flight crews were gearing up for airlift manoeuvres in support of the Razor task force…

But we were the closest.

Clyde, I noticed, had just surreptitiously checked his watch.

"You've gone very quiet, Major," Orville said, eyes narrowing.

"I was just wondering, Orville – once I'm back up and about, what do you suppose my codename will be?"

Second Lieutenant Green visibly brightened.

"Well, sir, I'm afraid you've drawn the short straw there. Not as bad as some, mind – we've got a couple of guys named 'Nancy' and

'Annie'. But you won't be as cool as, say, 'Hornet'. The operation is named Teapot, but I guess we'll be calling you 'Apple 2'."

"Figures," I said, with a mock grimace. "Why not 'Superman', eh?"

He laughed and said, "I hear you there."

For the first time, Zebra stepped into my line of sight. Looking me up and down, he muttered, "You sure about those handcuffs?"

Zebra was a different deal. He barely took me in; it was just the slightest flicker of a glance from dark, sunken eyes. Furtive and surly, he was of maybe Italian descent.

Orville was looking at the cuffs and shrugging.

"What's the problem? They worked fine for the others."

"The chief said he was the strongest yet." Zebra was cleverer than Orville but did not emanate the same intensity of power.

The Second Lieutenant peered at me, wrinkling his nose. He didn't enjoy lateral thinking.

"You're not going to give us any trouble now, Major?"

Time to channel my inner Brando…

"Now listen," I said, "I've seen three more centuries than you – hell, I witnessed the signing of your Declaration of Independence! Since that day, I've been a fan of America. Boys, I landed at Gold Beach with the 47 Commando and pushed through Port-en-Bessin to hook up with your brothers coming out of Omaha Beach; in the days that followed, I was honoured to fight beside the best of you…

"Seems to me you fellas have been having all the fun around here. Now, like Mister Churchill said, our countries have a special relationship – and if the Yanks are having fun…" I winked at them. "This Limey wants in."

They blinked. Then Orville laughed and declared, "Now that's what I'm talkin' about – hot-damn, I do love the way you guys talk!"

Zebra shrugged and moved off. After a moment, Clyde crossed over and muttered, "T-minus thirty minutes, sir."

Orville nodded. Once the scientists had finished removing the wires from my temples, he said, "Thank you, gentlemen – we'll take it from here." As the MPs and scientists headed out of the door, he and Zebra effortlessly picked me up in the chair and carried me out to face the dawn.

I died, Bill – sorry. Just didn't see them coming. You have to know: these supercharged psychic soldiers the Invisible Nation are growing, there are fifty-three of them – and counting...

The air was cool and smelt of rain. Moonlight had been replaced by the first hints of morning twilight. Looking up, I caught the last of the stars blinking out and thought, *"This is a place I would have liked to spend more time."* The chance to commune with a night sky free of light pollution – I wondered why I hadn't made more time to do that.

And I thought about her: my wife, mother of my child. After failing her over and over again, I'd finally failed her for the last time.

That rain smell... I remembered reading once that the desert scrub – what was it called, *creosote* – had a sagey fragrance reminiscent of fresh rain. The Native Americans used it as a herb, for medicinal purposes, didn't they? It was an ancient plant. They all grew from one seed, spreading and spreading – one colony could be thousands of years old. It was oddly comforting that they'd be here long after we'd test-detonated ourselves into oblivion.

I wondered where I'd read that. It must have been in conversation with a botanist – Alvan Chapman, perhaps, or Asa Gray... *The people I've met! There are always new incredible people to meet. I wanted to carry on meeting them.*

It had to be approaching T-minus twenty-five minutes. I could hear the helicopter powering up, waiting for a full complement before lifting off. That would give me fifteen minutes at most to get out of the handcuffs and run for cover – back to the reinforced house with the basement shelter...

They walked at a brisk pace for several minutes, planting me down in the sand – and I saw the tower. Apple 2 was in a box, sat upon a surprisingly narrow, skeletal scaffold, all latent menace.

Zebra had already gone. Orville patted me on the shoulder, affectionately.

"Don't worry, Major – 'for Queen and Country', right? Your new Queen will be so proud of you. When you come to, we'll be brothers and – trust me – you're going to be *extraordinary.*"

Then he was gone, sprinting for the chopper.

Coming from one of the houses furthest from ground zero, we'd been walking at a fast pace – six, seven miles per hour. We must have covered half a mile. Nine hundred yards closer and exposed in the open, I was now quarter of a mile from a nuclear bomb at least twice the strength of Little Boy.

At fast running speed, Orville made it back to his helicopter in two minutes. As I heard the helicopter lift from the ground, I was already free of the first pair of handcuffs – this was the easy part, I'd been telekinetically working at them since I'd woken up. My mind was the key.

The handcuffs weren't secured as tightly to the arms of the chair as they were to my wrists, so both pairs remained on my wrists as I pulled free. Then I waited, my heart beating pounding, as I allowed the whirring of the rotors to grow distant. Waited, breathing fast, until I figured they were out of sight.

Hitting the ground running, I was mentally checking my sums: fifteen minutes at the outside, twelve more likely. Two minutes later, the little hamlet of houses was looming large before me – but I suddenly came to a dead halt in my tracks.

Orville Green was standing just beyond them, gazing back at me. He looked disappointed.

"Aw, heck, Major – why'd you have to go and do something like that?"

"You didn't get on the chopper, then, Orville?" I ventured, my mind racing.

He slowly shook his head. "Just kinda had a bad feeling all of a sudden. It's a crying shame, because I don't think we're buddies anymore."

In a split second, he'd lifted his hand and performed a flicking gesture with his fingers. I was knocked back about two hundred yards, landing hard on a rocky outcropping. My shoulders took the impact and I heard something snap.

He landed on the ground a few feet away, breaking no sweat – it had been little more than a hop for him. His eyes were blazing – and I mean actually glowing red – as if his blood was rushing into the whites of them.

"You know what, sir? I'm seriously pissed at you."

Another flick of the outstretched hand. I was spun around and hurled several hundred yards, head over heels, crashing once more – a softer landing this time. Before I could unfurl myself, he was beside me again – picking me up without touching me. Pulling my collar tight, so I couldn't breathe.

His face was darkening and cracks were appearing in his wrinkles and pores.

"I tried to be nice. But now you've made me look stupid. My bosses will think maybe Orville Green is a bit slow."

He raised his shaking hand again. Another long throw. I took the opportunity to get some air in my lungs, but the landing was bad – crippling – as I hit hard steel with my head.

The tower.

We were right beneath the bomb.

Now the world spun from the inside and I retched onto the sand. Struggling to pull through the nausea, I hadn't heard him land but I knew he was close by. I had no choice but to try and reason with him.

"Orville, listen – we're too close. We'll be vaporised."

"I am *Trinity*," I heard him snarl. "T-minus three minutes. We'll stay right here until there's no chance you can run to shelter. Then you'll see how it feels…"

I could barely move, or even get my eyes open. He came into sight, just on the periphery of my vision – shambling, as if his legs were heavy. His nose was bleeding, gushing so much he had to wipe it several times with the back of his hand as he was talking. The cracks in his skin were opening up to reveal an almost luminescent power surging beneath, like vivid red electricity.

"So you'll burn and burn," he continued, rage and excitement mounting in equal measure. "And you'll pray for death, sir, but death she ain't coming – and slowly you *change*. The outside of you is tatters, but the *inside*… It starts as a kind of fury rippling through you, eating you up. The old you, all you cared about, drifts away like ashes on the breeze – all that worrying, all that caring, all that *empathy* cremated…"

He spat these last words as if they disgusted him and his eyes were fixed hungrily, voraciously, upon me – his nosebleed looking like bloodied drooling.

"You come back made of rage," he was saying, "ready to do your master's bidding."

But in those final moments I'd twigged onto something about him: the shaking in his arms when he used the terrifying power inside him, it meant he was struggling to direct it – after all, he was only young. Just as I had nearly four hundred years ago, he needed to use his arms, to stretch them out…

"God bless America," I whispered.

He frowned. "What did you say?"

Coughing, I raised my voice – beckoning him to come closer. "God bless America."

It seemed so absurd that he stopped and began to laugh. I found that I was laughing too, as the hysteria set in. We were surely long past T-minus two minutes now. It was over.

Although… *Something* had changed…

"Help me up," I said, the laughter taking over – and I reached out for his hands. We were like two drunks, giggling uncontrollably.

Was that *chanting* I could hear? For a second, I swore I'd fleetingly caught music on the wind…

He took hold of my hands and just for a moment I felt the vibrations within. It was as if I was touching that first bomb. Looking into his eyes, it felt like the man had gone long ago and that the spirit of a virgin destroyer of worlds had crept in to permeate his vacated soul.

What was that Oppenheimer quote? "Now I am become Death, the destroyer of worlds…"

As Robert Oppenheimer had witnessed the birth of the nuclear age, on the 16th July 1945, it had brought to his mind words from the Hindu scripture, the two thousand-year-old 'Bhagavad Gita' – part of the epic spiritual masterpiece, the 'Mahabharata'. On the eve of a great battle, a warrior prince realises that his warmongering will jeopardise the lives of his own relatives and friends – and recognises the enemy as fellow man. Awash with doubt and despairing, he seeks the counsel of the God Krishna, who tells the prince has a duty to reestablish *dharma* – the natural order of things. Its allegorical battlefield is man's battle for his soul in the face of ethics and morality, the ongoing struggle to resist doing evil.

I gazed into Orville's eyes and Trinity blinked darkly back.

"Can you feel it?" I whispered.

"What?" He frowned, the rage dissipating to be replaced by childlike curiosity – as six miles away, T-minus one minute passed by and the observers were raising their goggles...

"The bomb, it's talking to us. Here, it's in the steel..." Then, as I guided his eager, trusting hands to the scaffold – thinking that really Orville Green was the tragic victim of this whole affair – I quietly said, "I'm so sorry, Orville."

It was the greatest sleight of hand of my life. A true Houdini moment. In an instant, the handcuffs were off my wrists and around his and he was chained to the tower. Then I was running, running, running for my life – and Second Lieutenant Orville Green was bellowing in fury.

There *was* chanting out there, somewhere – like a sort of ritual rhythmic wailing. Wait... Was it in my mind?

"You'll never be able to run fast enough, sir!"

Trinity, I knew, had the power to rip free from those restraints in seconds, but he didn't *have* seconds. And neither did I. I was barreling in desperation towards the nearest building, three hundred yards away, knowing full well that even if I made it, I didn't have a hope in hell.

"Breathe in the light, sir," he roared. "And say goodbye!"

Chanting. And drumming. Intensifying...

There was the briefest of white-outs and I heard Trinity scream. Or maybe it was my own screaming I heard. Around me, the air and sand were drawn backwards like the sea being sucked out before a tidal wave. There followed a rapid release of energy equivalent to thirty thousand tons of TNT – and heat greater than the surface of the Sun...

To be continued...

Printed in Great Britain
by Amazon

55145047R00129